THE RUNAWAY
SORCERER

ASH FITZSIMMONS

THE RUNAWAY SORCERER

FORTUNE'S CHILD, BOOK THREE

THE RUNAWAY SORCERER. Copyright © 2024 by Ash Fitzsimmons.

Print Edition ISBN: 978-1-949861-67-9

Cover design by MiblArt.

www.ashfitzsimmons.com

CHAPTER 1

I should have made an early night of it. Every responsible fiber of my being told me to revert to my collegiate pre-exam routine: a decent dinner, a warm shower, and something soothing on TV before bed. After all, this was the evening before what could potentially be the biggest day of my life—the day on which I made my bid for Pactlands citizenship—and I didn't want to stumble through my interview. I hoped to seem eloquent, poised, mature…more like the sort of person to whom one would entrust the secrets of a magical pocket universe than, say, like a half-drunk raccoon crawling blearily out of a dumpster two days after a party.

But it was Valentine's Day, and Connor took the night off.

This news had come as a pleasant surprise to me over the weekend. We'd only been a couple for about two months, and I had yet to pin down his schedule. Though he was the police chief of Whitford, the next town over, and policing there was more likely to involve scaring bears away from rental cabins than actually arresting anyone, he pulled his share of bad shifts, and free nights were never a guarantee. I'd assumed that Valentine's Day might be a no-go because of the elevated risk of inebriated lovebirds out for a drive. But no—on Saturday afternoon, he'd called to ask whether I wanted to do anything Monday night, or should he just deliver chocolate-dipped Prozac and check on me later in the week.

I'd been a nervous wreck for days, ever since the

counselor at the Division of Laws handling my case had given me the date. Despite our slightly rocky initial meeting, Daffodil venGiep had been nothing but professional, and she'd sounded upbeat the previous Wednesday when she called with the news. "Next Tuesday morning at ten," she'd said. "You're in. We've got all three of the sorcerer reps booked, so you'll only need to interview once. I set it for midmorning so you'll have plenty of time to make the drive, and I'll be waiting for you at the Forum." She'd paused then as a thought had occurred to her. *"Portal creds.* I'll have temporary permission put in the system for you. Do you know how to call the attendants, or will you want an escort? I suspect that Liogh wouldn't mind."

Of all of DOL's detectives, Liogh Birrid surely knew the way to my house, but the trip from Beukal to Ragged Gap and back was more than two hours because the nearest portal to the north Georgia mountains was in western South Carolina. The nymph was a friend of my father's, and I knew they'd come if I needed them, but I'd been pleased to tell my counselor that I had a ride already lined up. "Dad's going to drive me. He should know how to work the portals, right?"

"I would hope so," she'd replied, chuckling. "Try not to be late, hmm?"

And that was that. I wasn't going to forget the date—it was my twenty-eighth birthday, after all—so I put the interview on my calendar, took a brief moment to appreciate that the last month's planning had come to fruition, then sat down at the kitchen table and tried not to panic.

This was going to work. It *had* to work.

Liogh was confident. In the previous six months, I'd called in a murdered faun in my backyard and helped uncover his killer, busted a ring of illegal producers who'd preyed upon the would-be witches in my hometown, and united one of the three Forum reps I needed to impress with the daughter he'd never known he had. As far as DOL was concerned, I was a demonstrated asset, and if my existence was proof that my dad had *technically* broken the law...well, some mistakes could be overlooked.

Daff had been more tempered in her prognostication than had her colleague. Cases like mine had been rare over the Pactlands' nearly five-hundred-year existence, and with good reason: sentient nonhumans had fled into their homemade hiding place as a matter of survival, and few ever emerged to sleep with the enemy. Pact law provided that if one of their citizens decided they couldn't live without a human, the only choice was the so-called death draught, a potion that would leave them powerless and kill them within a few decades.

When my sorcerer mother decided she loved my human father more than her life in the Pactlands, her boss should have given her the draught. Instead, he'd let her go...and then I was born, a half human with a wild talent for pyromancy. My father had died, my mother had split, and her boss, who couldn't bear to give his underling the potion that would kill her, had raised me as his own, safely tucked away in a mountain town no one in the Pactlands cared about. Maybe I wasn't the greatest sorcerer in the world, and Dad admitted there were gaps in my homeschooled magical education, but I could hold my own. I obviously had talent, and I'd been useful, so surely the sorcerers who controlled my fate would overlook the tiny matter of my paternity...right?

If they didn't, the alternative was a life spent passing for human, hiding my abilities and trying to blend...which might not be so bad unless it turned out that I'd inherited my mother's natural longevity. I was too young to really show how quickly I was aging, but since sorcerers could live three centuries, I was facing a potential life spent reinventing myself every few decades to keep off the normies' radar. And there would be no chance for me to learn better techniques in the Pactlands. No way for me to visit the cousin who'd quickly become a confidante. No opportunity for me to do more than call Sage, my one-time charge who sounded better every time we spoke and couldn't wait to see me again. Like Liogh, Sage was sure that I was getting in—and since I was hard-pressed to imagine her father voting against me, I took comfort in the fact that I almost certainly had one representative in the bag.

Still, I'd been antsy ever since Daff delivered the news, and I hadn't tried to hide my nerves from Connor. He was perceptive, a useful if sometimes annoying trait, and he hadn't asked much of me that week while I fretted and stewed. So, when Connor asked whether I wanted to celebrate Valentine's Day, he offered to take me out somewhere low-key—the Mexican restaurant we both liked, or Mama Hen's in downtown Ragged Gap, which was running a special couples' dinner menu. Honestly, I told him, I wanted to stay in, and I offered to make dinner. I bought a pair of T-bones, he brought wine and a heart-shaped cheesecake from the grocery store, and I tried not to think about the morning as we ate and chatted about everything but the Pactlands.

I'd fallen *so* hard for him.

It wasn't just his pretty brown eyes, though those had certainly drawn my notice. Connor was kind, especially for a guy who ran around with a badge and cuffs. He'd easily scared off a handsy drunk guy the one night he took me to Eight Ball's to play pool, but he was never possessive, never overtly jealous. Maybe that was the result of his own self-confidence, or maybe he just knew better than to act the fool around a woman who could set his SUV on fire with a word and a touch of will. He was a hard worker, the first to come running when one of his officers needed backup; he'd even babysat Sam, Whitford's lone K-9 and a very good boy, when the German shepherd's handler went out of town.

But what I appreciated most was that Connor didn't

look at me like I was a freak. Most folks in Ragged Gap who had any inkling of my abilities gave me a wide berth and whispered when they didn't think I could hear them. Connor, who had talent as well—"the touch," they called it out at East Branch, his extended family's commune— accepted it as routine that I could alter my appearance with a spell and create flames from thin air, that my dad brewed potions professionally and I had long chats with my cousin in a language he couldn't understand, that I'd considered adopting a child who was half centaur and had a naga for a lawyer. He was intrigued, sure, and I'd seen those pretty eyes of his go wide quite a few times, but he rolled with all of my inherent weirdness. In the few months since he'd come by to interrogate me about an arson—officially an act of God after our chat—he'd fit his way into my life like a key sliding into a lock, a friend, cheerleader, and partner.

I'd never had someone like him. While I'd had friends and a few flings in college, nothing had lasted, and I had yet to coax anyone up to Ragged Gap to hang out. Most of the locals who knew me avoided me—all but Tabitha Bradley, the pharmacist and Wiccan who exchanged desserts for my magical home renovations. And now I had this guy coming around, calling me with stories about bizarre tourists he'd stopped or picking up Chinese on a random Tuesday night or carefully mimicking me as he tried to improve his own brand of casting.

Strange, yes…but in a good way.

I wanted to make him a special dinner, just to prove to myself that I could do a decent steak without resorting to magic to save me from my mediocre culinary skills, and though my meal wasn't in the same league as the spreads I'd devoured in Tabitha's kitchen, Connor ate every bite and went back for seconds. We made short work of the cheesecake and drank the whole bottle of wine, and then, deploying my best awkward flirting, I invited him to follow me to my bedroom.

I'm not positive about the precise order of events that

followed, but soon, I found myself sprawled across the mattress, and Connor...hell, I lost track of where his fingers and tongue went, but oh, *God*, he knew how to touch me.

When my back arched and a noise like a yodeling banshee's cry erupted from my throat, I was ever so grateful that I didn't have close neighbors. As I drifted back into my body, sighing and spent and throbbing, I sent a silent word of thanks into the universe for the unknown soul who'd come before me and impressed upon Connor the truth that women generally weren't in love with the jackhammer technique. He was, by far, the most conscientious lover I'd ever had.

Pulling myself together and out of the puddle into which I'd tried to melt, I felt the mattress dip and realized that Connor was sliding into the space next to me. He straightened out the blankets, then gently nudged me onto my side and spooned behind me, holding me close as he sighed.

"What are you doing?" I mumbled.

"Cuddling?"

"It's your turn—"

He softly shushed me, cutting my protestation short. "We can fool around another time. That was to help you sleep."

"But it's Valentine's Day." I rolled over to face him and found myself pressed against his entirely unobjectionable pecs. "Here, I can—"

"Don't worry, Firebug. You get some rest, okay?" he murmured. "I like this, too."

"You *cannot* be serious," I mumbled into his chest.

"I mean...there are other activities I'd enjoy with you, but not tonight. Sleep," he said, and kissed me.

And to my surprise, I did.

I woke with a start in the darkness, my mind churning with the already fading details of half-formed dreams.

Home. This was home, I recalled, grounding myself. My bed, the sheets faintly scented with my lavender linen spray. The warm presence behind me was Connor, who seemed to be sleeping deeply, lucky boy.

I eased myself out of the hollow we'd made in the middle of the bed and checked my phone. Twenty minutes past midnight, and I was *wide* awake.

Fantastic.

I wanted to go back to sleep, *needed* to doze off for a few more hours so I could be at my best in the morning, but with my thoughts circling and my heart still slowing after the running dream my jerk of a brain had cooked up, sleep didn't seem to be an immediate possibility. Instead, I lay there with the blankets tucked to my chin and closed my eyes, trying to pick apart the knot of anxiety in my gut.

This might be the day. By the time I left the Forum building, I might finally have the question of my citizenship settled and the freedom to explore the part of my heritage that I'd largely been denied. I'd be able to visit Canna on my own terms, maybe become a sort of "fun aunt" to her four kids. While I didn't know how the rest of the family would feel about me, surely someone in the extended Nerin clan would be curious enough to get to know the weird little cousin from the outside. My mother had been one of five daughters, and Canna said my aunts and both grandparents were still alive—even Canna and my mother's grandparents still lived, both of them shy of two hundred. Canna's mother and my grandfather were two of another brood of five siblings, and I had yet to count how many cousins and second cousins I had out of that family. Maybe a few of them would want to meet me, at least for the novelty.

I loved my dad—I couldn't have asked for a better parent—but the prospect of forging bonds with my blood kin, of belonging to a family bigger than the two of us, thrilled me for reasons I couldn't quite explain. I didn't know these people beyond Canna's stories and the odd picture she'd shown me via phone, and I shouldn't have cared what they thought of me, but I couldn't release the dream of meeting people who would make the rest of *me* make sense.

My father had been murdered when I was two weeks old. My mother had walked out of my life about two weeks later. I desperately wanted that anchor of kinship, something to connect me to a line of people who wouldn't recoil in horror if I levitated a teacup across the room.

In fairness, they might recoil for other reasons—the impression I'd gotten from Dad was that a human in the family was a deep, dark, way-back-of-the-closet secret for most families in the Pactlands—but maybe they'd be willing to tell me about my missing mother before they shunned me.

But then there was the matter of Connor.

For Pactlands natives, hooking up with humans was forbidden, which was what had gotten me into this mess in the first place. While I knew Connor wasn't human—not entirely, at least, not with talent like his—precisely *what* he was remained a mystery, and he didn't appear to be in any great hurry to sort it out. I suspected he was waiting to see how my experience went, because once it became known that Connor was something other, the rest of East Branch would be in the crosshairs.

He seemed both embarrassed by and protective of the commune. East Branch had been around for a couple centuries or so, but the community had remained closely knit and resistant to outsiders for all that time, to the point that the sheriff's department had a policy of venturing there only if someone within the fence called for help. They lived off the grid, using a few generators and well water, and on the rare day that one or two visited town for supplies, they seldom wandered beyond the hardware store. East Branchers had a healthy distrust of the rest of us in the area, and for good reason: a significant number of them were born with what they'd dubbed "the touch," a bit of magical ability. Connor's parents hadn't had the touch, and they'd moved into Whitford once they married, looking for a better life outside the community. When their only child had shown the touch, they'd brought him back for occasional instruction, but they'd chosen to raise Connor with more modern comforts and a better education. Having been homeschooled myself, I had no personal experience of adolescent savagery in a school setting, but Connor told me he'd been teased mercilessly about his roots until he caught a growth spurt and beat the snot out of the worst of his bullies.

It wasn't just the fact that the East Branchers lived a more primitive life that fueled the taunts—it was the rumored inbreeding. Yes, Connor admitted, the families who'd settled East Branch had intermarried a bit too often, and he was likely kin to most of the residents, but it wasn't *Deliverance* back in there. Aside from a high number of miscarriages and the odd magically gifted baby, he said they were fairly normal, if suspicious of strangers. For that reason, he had yet to take me to visit. Assuming our relationship continued, I wanted to meet his family—and since his parents' deaths, the East Branchers were his only family—but I decided that was a matter Connor would resolve in his own time.

And if we stayed together, Connor would eventually need to look into his ancestry. I suspected that one or more of the original East Branchers had been a sorcerer, which could explain the talent that had trickled down through the generations. Considering how much the East Branch families had intermarried, it was possible that Connor was genetically more of a sorcerer than I was. But we wouldn't know until he was prepared to investigate, and until that time, as far as Pact law was concerned, he was human. While this fact didn't keep *him* up at night, I worried. Regardless of what happened in the morning, I wasn't about to break up with him, but assuming I gained citizenship, I knew we'd have to be cautious.

He *would* pursue citizenship. Wouldn't he?

What if he didn't? What if Connor swore off the Pactlands as a bizarre enclave and decided not to threaten the status quo for his kin? If he and I got serious—and I strongly suspected we were heading in that direction—then how far was I prepared to go? My mother had abandoned her family and friends to be with my father. Would I do the same, if it came to that? Fake my death, change my name, and go on the run? Would Connor be willing to leave Whitford and the commune to live on the lam with me?

What if Pact agents caught me and gave me the ultimatum, a one-way trip back to the Pactlands or the death draught? Was Connor worth a couple hundred years of my life?

Maybe it was too soon to answer all of the questions that circled my mind like turkey vultures on a warm morning, but this right here—*this*, lying there with Connor snuggled up behind me—felt right.

Still, as I suspected sleep would elude me for the rest of the night, I eased my way out of bed and whispered a golf ball–sized flame into being, a homemade will-o'-the-wisp that floated ahead of me as I threw on a bathrobe and lit my way to the kitchen. There was no sense in both of us being up all night.

I filled the kettle and began readying a mug for tea as the water heated, opting for chamomile and hoping it would calm my thoughts.

In a few hours, I'd need to impress three people, only one of whom I'd ever met. Mirrik Voln was the surest bet of the trio, a relatively young man of about one hundred twenty who, per Daff, served on the Tribunal Committee. He was fair, she reported, generally even-tempered and polite. And since I'd purchased his daughter's freedom back in November, I doubted that he'd screw me over. Mirrik had told me that he was in my debt, and this seemed as good a time as any for him to balance the ledger.

Older than Mirrik but newer to the Forum was Elm Carinar, of whom I knew only two things: she was pretty, and she was almost always in lockstep with her patron, the third sorcerer, Gerem Aniap, who had financed her campaign and in so doing virtually bought himself a second vote. The Aniaps were an old, wealthy family. Gerem's grandfather had been a Pact signatory, and both he and Gerem's father had served as representatives. Gerem had been a rep since 1900, Canna told me, having run for his father's seat before it was decently cold. Though he was a political fixture, he was, according to my cousin, an asshole of the first order, prone to making dramatic speeches about his enemies and throwing his money around.

Daff, who took a more moderate position concerning the representative, counseled that I show deference and do my best not to antagonize him, just in case. She also suggested a more charitable reason for Gerem's general unpleasantness. The poor man had lost most of his family. His one sibling, a sister, had died young, and his father had died when Gerem was but forty-four. Gerem had married and had several children, but all had died underage, and then his grief-stricken wife had killed herself. He'd been remarried to a much younger woman and had another three children, but two of them had also died, leaving Gerem a middle-aged man with only a teenage daughter to carry on his legacy. Even some of the Aniap cousins had lost their lives in their twenties and thirties, Daff relayed. Small wonder, then, that Gerem was crotchety; grief could do terrible things to a person. I pitied him, but as mercenary as it sounded, his personal tragedies did give me a modicum of hope. I'd lost my father, and my mother was nowhere to be found—perhaps Gerem would see something familiar in my situation and approve my citizenship petition.

I was ruminating and absently bobbing my teabag in the mug when Connor shuffled into the kitchen and croaked, "Janie?"

"Hey," I said, turning to find him by the table, shirtless, squinting at the sink light, and bed mussed. "Just making tea. Go back to sleep."

"It's too early for tea."

"Chamomile."

He grunted, then halfheartedly covered a yawn with his fist. "Got enough water for two?"

I tried to convince Connor that I was fine sitting up alone, but he wouldn't hear it. Soon, I found myself propped against him on the couch, covered in a blanket and watching one of the true-crime docs in my queue.

"Happy birthday," he murmured as I closed my eyes, lying to myself that I'd just listen to the TV for a while.

"Thanks. I think we're kicking this off too early."

Chuckling, he said, "I'll wake you for breakfast," and with that promise, I drifted to sleep to the sounds of witness interviews.

CHAPTER 2

Like me, Connor wasn't a great cook, but he had mastered the fine art of adding eggs and oil to muffin mix. I awoke to winter sunlight, the warmth of the blanket cocoon I'd created, and the smell of double chocolate muffins cooling on the counter. When I unwrapped myself and carried our long-cold mugs of midnight tea into the kitchen, I found him prepping my place setting at the table: a bowl of the grocery store pre-cut melon mix I kept on hand, a properly caffeinated brew, and a pair of muffins on a salad plate, topped with a squirt of canned whipped cream and mismatched birthday candles.

"You don't want me to sing at this hour," he warned, his morning voice almost a bass, "but you should still blow something out."

Smiling, I took a seat, lit my candles with a fingertip, then daintily extinguished them. Connor gave me a golf clap and kissed the top of my head as he passed, heading back to the muffins to fix up his own plate. "Made a wish, right?"

"*Maybe.* I—"

"Don't tell me! The magic won't work if you do," he said with mock solemnity, but his grin slipped through to dispel the illusion.

We settled into comfortable silence as we ate, but after a moment, Connor sighed. "I wish I were going with you today."

"I'll be fine."

"Yeah, I know, but still…"

I reached over and took his hand. "You're sweet, but it'll be okay. Dad will be there, and Canna, and my lawyer…it's going to be all right. I'll give you a call as soon as we have a decision."

"And you'll be home tonight?"

"Yeah, absolutely. Come by after your shift, eh? I'll order birthday pizza."

"Ooh. I haven't been to a good birthday pizza party since…fifth grade? Sixth?"

"Play your cards right, and I'll make it a slumber party."

His eyebrows waggled. "Coed?"

"With movies *and* beer."

"Well, that's my RSVP, then," he replied, and finished his breakfast.

By the time Dad rolled up—driving his gray Altima, I noted, not one of the trucks he used for deliveries of iron pieces or his homemade booze—Connor and I were ready to face the day, him in his uniform and me in a conservative blue dress, something that I hoped looked professional and wouldn't turn heads. I'd taken care with my hair, eschewing the usual blonde ponytail, and I'd even left out my earrings, as the only group in the Pactlands who wore such with any regularity were male fauns. My triple piercings were simple enough to hide with the slightest of masks, and Connor declared the illusion perfect. He nodded to Dad and shook his hand, then hugged me and whispered, "You're going to be great. See you tonight."

I locked up, leaving the spare key under the mat in case Connor came by before I returned, and slid into the car with Dad. Odd, I thought, to see him dressed so formally. Catching Dad in clothes both unstained and unsinged was relatively rare, but he'd pulled together dark trousers and a plain white button-down for the occasion, and he appeared to have polished his shoes.

"Ready, girlie?" he asked, his smile only somewhat disguising his nerves.

"Ready," I said, tucking my purse by my feet. I'd opted for a wrap instead of my usual winter coat, as the Pactlands' artificial climate was more temperate than that of the world outside. Between that and the seldom-used car's heater, I was comfortable for the trip, though nothing could soothe the ball of nerves in the pit of my stomach. Dad wasn't in a particularly chatty mood that morning, either, and the radio kept us company over the border into South Carolina and up toward Clemson. The portal was hidden in an undeveloped area near a lake a bit west of the town of Central. If one knew what one was looking for, one could turn onto an unmarked dirt road and head into the pines toward the place where it seemed to dead-end, and a crumbling, abandoned house would appear. Whoever had built the spells that hid the house had added another layer to keep the place upright, as it seemed liable to collapse with the next stiff breeze. The front of the house leaned badly, its gray boards rotten and devoid of anything resembling paint, but the back was worse: the rear wall was missing, exposing the interior to the ravages of the weather and the encroaching weeds. The jumble of junk inside the house looked like the start of a quick trip to the doctor for a tetanus shot.

Dad parked the car behind the house, leaving it idling, and pulled what appeared to be a garage door opener from the glovebox. It had a single button, one marked with a pair of concentric circles, which Dad pressed for three seconds.

A moment later, a male voice filtered through the car's stereo system, asking in Pactish, "Name and location?"

"Yacovi Hewt," Dad replied. "With a passenger. Central."

"Passenger is?"

"Jane Fortune. She should have temporary credentials from Director Erenani."

The attendant on the other side disappeared briefly—checking for me, I guessed—then said, "You're both clear.

First in the queue. Prepare for opening."

"No wait today," Dad murmured as he tucked the call button back into its hiding place. "Guess we're doing something right, eh?"

"Guess so," I replied, watching as the portal opened, a hole in space bordered by flickering lights in a rainbow of hues. It was only about six feet in diameter, but Dad had been navigating portals for decades, and he passed through like a pro.

We emerged into the external portal building on the outskirts of Beukal, the lone point of entry to the Pactlands, and Dad drove to the attendant's booth. A sorcerer waved at us from the stool within and raised the barrier arm, and off we drove into the morning.

While I'd seen cities—Atlanta, certainly, had been a fixture of my childhood—I'd lived in my small town long enough to be impressed when the glass skyscrapers of Beukal appeared ahead of us. With no trees to obstruct the view, the city seemed to rise from the winter-brown fields like a living thing, sprawling outward and reaching toward the sun. The tallest of the glass spires belonged to DOL, where Daff, Liogh, and Canna worked, and a shorter one housed the Division of Plants and Potions, where Dad had once been an agent. As he navigated through the city, I tried to recall what I'd learned when Canna and her husband, Pars, had taken me on driving trips the previous fall, and I was pleased that I recognized the Forum building before Dad pointed it out.

The Pact Forum was the Pactlands' governing body, a group comprised of representatives from each member species who served nine-year terms. Exactly how said representatives were chosen varied; sorcerers voted for their three, for instance, while the heads of the elven Halls took turns on a rotating basis. They met in a large limestone building in District 1, a structure with a low dome atop roughly hundred-foot walls and ringed by a covered colonnade. Like most of the Pactlands, its landscaping was devoid of trees, though someone had worked enough magic to support the well-tended flowerbeds dotting the putting green lawn, which sat full of blooms even in February. Clearly, the edifice was built to impress.

Dad pulled into the visitors' parking lot and cut the engine, but he stayed me before I could open my door. "Do me a favor, honey, okay?"

"What's that?"

"Don't tell them you're a pyromancer." Before I could object, he explained, "It's nothing to be ashamed of, but it's the kind of wild talent that gives people pause, *especially* when you haven't had formal training. Just keep that under your hat for now, eh?"

"Uh…sure," I replied. I didn't really see the issue—my pyromancy was no secret to my contacts at DOL—but since Dad had spent much of his career in agency work, I figured he knew best.

He smiled tightly and patted my shoulder. "I'm proud of you, Janie. This is going to be the start of something great for you."

"Assuming my petition is approved," I reminded him.

Dad scoffed, flicking one hand as if waving away my anxiety. "With the backing you've got, they'd have to be nuts to reject you. Don't be afraid, now." He paused, studying my face, then murmured, "What's really on your mind? You're not still concerned about me, are you?"

After years of worrying that one wrong move would land him in prison, Dad had a guarantee from DOL that they wouldn't bring charges against him for failing to give my mother the draught. That was certainly a load off my mind, but my early-morning insomnia had brought more problems to the fore.

"It's…Connor," I said. "If this goes well and I get citizenship, what if they try to tell me to break up with him?"

"First," said Dad, leaning toward me, "we're not going

to mention Connor. No one who gives a damn about you would bring him up in front of the representatives, so put that from your mind. Second, today is about *you*, Janie. Connor's a problem for later."

I grinned at that. "A problem, you say?"

"I'm still not sure how I feel about him—"

"*Daddy*. He hasn't turned you in for moonshining yet, has he?"

"Please," Dad scoffed, "the Ragged Gap cops are on my customer list, and the sheriff besides. I'd like to see him try."

With that, he slipped out of the car and opened the rear door to retrieve a garment bag I hadn't even noticed stretched across the back seat. From within, he extracted a dark purple formal robe, sleeveless and made of thin wool, with delicate silver embroidery at the collar and down the front. I laughed as I joined him, and Dad gave me a little twirl. "Still fits, doesn't it?" he protested.

"I didn't know you *owned* a robe."

"Keep a few in mothballs, just in case."

"Well, you could have shared," I said, gesturing to my dress. "Some of us haven't gone shopping for formalwear over here, you know?"

He raised my chin with his knuckle and smiled. "Sweetheart, after today, you and I will go shopping, and I'll buy you whatever robes you want. Promise. But you look lovely, so don't worry."

Trying not to gawk, I followed Dad up the stairs, across the covered walkway, and through the bronze double doors into the lobby. A security guard waved us through, and automatically, my neck bent back to take in the high ceiling, painted to mimic a summer sky dotted with puffy clouds.

"You're early," said a familiar female voice, and I snapped back to attention to find Daff waiting to one side, a folder tucked under her arm. She sported her customary black counselor's robe, though hers only fell to where her hips would have been, had she legs. Below the belt, she was built like the sort of snake that might star in a low-budget monster movie, thick and patterned in brown and black bands of scales. She kept her tail coiled beneath her as she sat. I'd read that nagas were constrictors and could unhinge their jaws to swallow large prey, and having seen my attorney, I believed it.

"Morning," I said, heading over.

She smiled and dipped her hairless head toward Dad. "Agent Hewt, I trust?"

"Yacovi," he replied, and shook her hand. "Nice to finally meet you, Ms. venGiep."

"Daff, please. Glad we're finally getting this one sorted," she added, patting me on the back. "Good choice on wardrobe, Jane. How was the trip?"

"Uneventful, fortunately," I said, and waved as I noticed Liogh approaching. "Hey, stranger!"

"Youngling," they called back, and grinned. "Nice to see you without adding a case to my files. Let's try to make this a habit. Yacovi, how old is that robe?"

"It's a classic," Dad protested, and briefly hugged the detective. "Glad to see you. Thanks for coming."

They straightened their robe, a simple number in dark blue that nicely complimented their lighter blue braid and pale green complexion. "Wouldn't miss it. We're expecting a few more, and they should be arriving soon...*ah*," they said as two people were quickly shepherded past the security line. "Seniority has perks."

One of them I recognized: Kabno Erenani, the director of the Division of Laws, a white-haired gnome in a delicately detailed, albeit preschooler-sized, rose-colored robe that put Dad's and Liogh's to shame. Scaling her up to human proportions, she'd have seemed perhaps my age or a few years older, but I knew from Dad that she'd seen more than three centuries. Though not magically talented beyond their camouflaging abilities, gnomes were fast and tremendously strong, and I suspected that one discounted

Kabno in a fight at one's peril.

The other was a stranger to me, a slender, youthful man about twice Kabno's size with long brown hair, dark eyes, and a forest green robe at least as expensive as his companion's. He was an elf, that much was clear—the ears and high cheekbones were a giveaway, even if you couldn't see the sharp teeth—but I hadn't met him in my admittedly brief trips to DOL.

Dad, however, beamed and headed toward them. "*Teme*. I'll be damned. How are you?"

The other man chuckled and hugged Dad. "It's been an age, hasn't it? You're looking well, Yacovi."

He snorted. "I'm getting *old*. Avoid arthritis—it's no fun."

"Noted. Have you met my counterpart from Laws?" he asked, gesturing toward Kabno. "This is—"

"Director Erenani, yes," Dad interrupted, and stooped slightly to shake her hand. "I don't believe I've had the pleasure."

"I've heard all about *you*, though," she replied with an impish smile. "Mostly good."

"And for overlooking the rest…thank you."

"The law is a useful tool, but no one ever said it was perfect." Lowering her voice, she said, "As I'm rather familiar with the antics of forty-something trainees, I can't fault you for being unwilling to kill a child. Ah, Jane," she continued, looking past him. "Nice choice on the dress."

"Thank you, ma'am—" I began.

"And where are my manners?" said Dad, motioning me closer. "Teme, have you met my daughter?"

"Not yet," he said, and took my hand as he gave me a quick once-over. "Pateme ti"Tam. Your father and I endured *far* too many meetings together when he was with DPP. Speaking of which, say the word, and I'll bring you back," he added, turning to Dad. "The current head of the greenhouse is entirely competent, but he's not you."

"Appreciated, but I'm content in my retirement," Dad

replied.

"If you stick around here," Pateme said to me in an exaggerated stage whisper, "then perhaps he'll change his mind."

Daff cleared her throat. "Director...uh, *Directors*," she amended, nodding to both, "we should probably head up."

"Of course," said Pateme. "Yacovi, you'll allow me to buy lunch when this is finished, yes? I'm pretty sure I still owe you a few meals."

"Drinks, more like."

"Yes, but it's *midmorning*. Incidentally, I hear you're still brewing?"

As they walked on, Kabno drew closer to me and quietly said, "Considering what you did for DPP last fall, Pateme thought it only proper to come in support of your petition, as did I. Just in case."

Some of the weight of my anxiety lifted at that. I had two agency heads in my corner—that had to count for something, right?

We were only halfway across the lobby when a woman behind us called, "Wait for me!" I spun around to find Canna hurrying in our direction, purple healer's coat flapping in her wake. "Sorry, *sorry*," she said as our little pack paused. "Been a bit of a morning already."

Kabno looked her up and down. "Everything all right?"

"It will be, ma'am, once the trainees learn not to drink potions on a dare."

The director groaned and closed her eyes. "I'm almost afraid to ask what they took."

"Invisibility."

Dad, Liogh, and Pateme grimaced in unison, and even Daff winced. I understood the cause: the invisibility potion worked beautifully in a pinch, but it was short-acting and left the drinker puking. Much preferred, per Dad, was invisibility jewelry, but it was expensive, and agency loaners were carefully protected.

"*Why?*" said Kabno shaking her head. "And who am I reprimanding for this?"

"One of my assistants is compiling the incident report for you. Anyway, sorry I'm late. It was an 'all available healers' situation for a minute, there."

"That's...understandable," said Daff with a look of distaste. "Better you than me. Shall we?"

The seven of us crowded into an elevator, and Canna gave my hand a squeeze as the doors closed. "I broke the news to the family last night," she murmured.

My nerves, which had been behaving for a moment, flared again. "Oh?"

"They're *thrilled*." She pulled a folded piece of paper from her pocket and showed me a list of names in her handwriting. "All four of your aunts, a bunch of cousins, my mother...see? In case the representatives have concerns, you have family here eager to meet and support you."

Blinking back sudden tears, I took the paper from her and scanned the neat Pactish characters. "Is that..."

"Your grandfather," she said, tapping one of the names. "My uncle Yonth. That's your grandmother, Chara, right below him. And down here, those are your great-grandparents—Jalien Nerin, Teka Merefon. They *cried* when I told them," she added as the elevator slid to a stop. "And they're very grateful to you for saving Essa," she added, glancing at Dad. "Aunt Chara especially wanted to convey that."

"You tell her I'm just sorry I don't know where Essa's gone," he said, and held the door open as we disembarked.

The hallway continued the building's theme of slightly understated opulence: a thick green runner on the floor, carved wooden doors with brass knobs, and an assortment of art pieces. Daff, who'd taken the lead, finally paused beside a door marked MEETING ROOM 6 and smiled at me. "Ready, Jane?"

"Let's do it," I said, willing the butterflies in my

stomach to settle down as I put on my most professional smile and followed her into the room.

The meeting space was dominated by a round mahogany table that could have accommodated twenty, but a handful of security personnel and what I took to be aides loitered along the wall, and only the three representatives were seated when we arrived. Mirrik I recognized on sight, a handsome man who wore his black hair in a ponytail that fell over his gray robe. Sage had inherited her mother's eyes and quasi-equine build, but I saw many of her features in her father's face—particularly her smile, which he flashed as he rose. "And there's the lady of the hour!" he said, his brown eyes crinkling. "Come in, come in. Do we need more chairs?"

Daff directed me to the seat directly opposite the trio, and I quickly considered the other two. The platinum blonde in the peach-colored robe had to be Elm, while the man in the middle was the notoriously prickly Gerem Aniap. His hair was lighter than Mirrik's and fell loose to his shoulders, barely covering the rich gold embroidery of his crimson robe. His eyes, blue and deeply hooded, regarded me steadily. Though he and Dad were almost of an age, Dad seemed considerably younger.

As the rest of my entourage filed in and found chairs, Mirrik's smile never faltered. He greeted the directors and Liogh, then turned back to me and said, "Sage sends her greetings. She wanted to be here today, but, you know, *school.*"

Having never been given a formal education, Sage appreciated the bevy of tutors who were trying to prepare her to integrate into a class of kids, but she'd griped to me about how her head swam after a barrage of lessons. "Poor baby," I replied. "Tell her hello for me, won't you?"

"Naturally. Are we all present?" he asked, scanning our side of the room, then nodded and returned to his chair. Opening the folder in front of him, he said, "All right, Gerem, would you like to do the honors? Any questions for Jane?"

"Let's start with the scofflaw," Gerem snapped, glaring across the table. His gaze flicked to Kabno and Pateme as he pointed to Dad. "Why is that man still allowed to live outside the Pactlands? He's a *criminal*."

Pateme appeared unfazed by the demand. "As Laws has declined to prosecute, I have no reason to pull Mr. Hewt's permission. His inspections have been flawless for nearly thirty years."

"Then *you* explain yourself," he said to Kabno. "Why is that man being given preferential treatment?"

Like her colleague, Kabno didn't flinch. "Since Mr. Hewt is one of your constituents, I don't see why you're so upset," she replied. "But to answer your question, this is a matter of prosecutorial discretion. If his only crime after a meritorious career was not giving the draught to an agency employee little more than a child…" She shrugged. "I'm inclined to overlook it."

"That's your final decision?"

"It is."

"Then you leave me with no choice," said Gerem, and nodded to the guards.

Before I knew what was happening, one had pressed Dad into his chair by the shoulders, while the other had jabbed a syringe into his arm. "What the hell?" I cried, jumping out of my seat, but Gerem ignored me.

"I am initiating a Forum prosecution against Yacovi Hewt for crimes against the Pact," he said. "You will be held until trial as a flight risk."

"*What?*" Mirrik yelled. "No! I…you can't unilaterally—"

"What are you doing?" Kabno interrupted. "You have no right, not without two-thirds of the Forum! And what did you inject him with?"

"The same potion DOL uses for all of its inmates," he said, smirking back at her. "That'll keep his talent nice and dampened until we decide what to do with him. I'm surprised you would ask."

"Again," she said through gritted teeth, "you have no right to hold him. Call off your guards."

"As I said, Hewt is a flight risk, and since it's obvious I lack agency cooperation, I'll be holding him here until such time as the Forum can vote as to how we would like to proceed. And I *will* have the votes," he added, lowering his voice as he turned to Mirrik. "His crime is evident."

I fought the panic in my chest, barely conscious that Daff had gripped my wrist to keep me from bolting around the table to my father.

Dad didn't resist, but he didn't show fear. "I don't deny what I did concerning Essa Nerin," he said, and Gerem wheeled back on him with a smug look of triumph. "As far as I'm concerned, I committed the lesser evil by not condemning her to an early grave over young love. So, tell me," he said, holding Gerem's stare, "what would Lonvi say if she were here?"

Gerem's mood shifted in an instant, and his eyes narrowed as he glared at Dad. "How dare you?"

"*I* know what she'd say. Is this how you honor her memory, Gerem?" He shrugged beneath the guard's hands. "No matter. You and I can talk of her another day. The important thing is that whatever I may have done wrong, the result is Jane, and she's an incredibly talented sorcerer—"

"Why didn't you give her the draught?"

Dad jerked as if the representative had slapped him. "Who, *Jane?*"

"You had her in your custody, did you not?"

"I *raised* her," he protested. "That's my daughter, and I would never do anything to hurt her. Do what you want to me, but she's innocent in this. She didn't create herself, and she's done nothing wrong."

"If I may, sir," Liogh ventured, "Ms. Fortune has been very helpful to Laws and DPP in the last months. Despite her youth, she's put herself in harm's way to assist us."

"And she could do great things with a full education," Canna cut in. "That's my cousin's daughter. Our family is ready to help her. With a little training, she would be a credit to us—to the community. Think of Rose ti'Dana."

"They're absolutely right," Mirrik began, but Gerem cut him off with a snort.

"What the elves do with their half-breeds is their business," he said. "As for that little freak—"

"Watch your tongue," Pateme snapped.

"I speak the truth—she *is* a freak of nature. And she's a one-in-a-million freak of a farseer, is she not?"

"Rose…is unique," he grudgingly allowed. "Or so says Diriem."

"All right, so maybe that's enough for you people to overlook her human ancestry. Or *some* of you people, at least. I'm sure I couldn't say." Turning then to me, he asked, "What can *you* do that's so special, hmm?"

I stared across the table at the trio—sneering Gerem, stricken Mirrik, and silent Elm—and though I wanted nothing more than to throw a few fireballs, I minded Dad. "Nothing," I said, balling my fists at my side. "I'm just myself."

"Then what would our community gain in compensation for sullying itself with the likes of you?"

"I agree," Elm murmured, perhaps recognizing her cue from her handler. "We have no need for humans here."

"Did you two *look* at her petition?" Mirrik asked, flabbergasted. "Do you see the support she has here? By the heavens, she rescued my daughter!"

Gerem softly grunted. "While you seem to have a soft spot for all manner of freaks—"

"Mirrik, *no*," Kabno ordered as the younger sorcerer pulled back his fist. "Do *not* make me haul you in on assault charges today."

"But—"

"*Sit.*" Climbing out of her chair, she stepped onto the table, giving herself a momentary height advantage.

"Gerem, if you intend to hold Mr. Hewt, then we need to discuss logistics, as I sincerely doubt anyone in this building knows how to properly manage inmates. If we could all stop with the insults for a few minutes and act like adults—"

"So, that's it?" I interrupted, shaking off Daff's hand. "Petition denied? What am I supposed to do, just go home and hope to see my dad again someday?"

Gerem rose to his feet and folded his arms. "No. As I said, Hewt should have given you the draught years ago. I intend to rectify that error."

"You can't!" Canna shouted, jumping out of her chair so hard that it flew back into the wall. "She's committed no crime!"

"And a memory potion," he continued, disregarding her outburst. "Once you've forgotten about this place and magic in general, you'll no longer be a risk to us." He nodded to his aides, who reached into the pockets of their robes—

And suddenly, the aides and the representatives alike were flying across the room. As they hit the back wall with meaty thuds, I saw Pateme standing a few seats down with one arm outstretched, red-faced and furious. "I can't hold them long," he said. "Jane, *run*."

CHAPTER 3

I've never been an athlete. I didn't play team sports as a kid, and while I tried to stay in reasonably decent shape, I would never be mistaken for a gym rat.

But as I dashed down the hallway, fleeing the raised voices and the sorcerers armed with potions that would steal my memories and condemn me to an early grave, I might have qualified for the Olympics.

At least I'd worn flats.

Panic pushed me, manifesting as speed instead of fire for once. I raced past the uniform doors and occasional potted palm, looking for a way out. The elevator was no good—if Gerem's security guards were smart, they'd lock that down immediately, trapping me—but I had to shake my pursuers while I had a head start. I could hide...but no, surely a troll could find me. Even if Gerem had nothing in particular with my scent on it, I had to be stinking of sweat and fear.

I saw a sign for the staircase and ran down a level, hoping to throw Gerem's goons off my trail. Surely they'd assume that I'd head for the ground floor and the exit, right? If I could hide long enough, maybe lock myself in a storage closet until DOL could restore order...

White lights mounted in the ceiling began to strobe as a far too calm female voice echoed from the embedded speakers: "Unauthorized personnel in the building. Please inform security if you see the following..."

The voice paused, and a male voice filled the gap: "Human female. Blonde. Brown eyes. Blue dress."

Fuck.

As the security alert replayed and my heart pounded, I rounded a corner and spotted a tall, brown-haired man in a charcoal robe about twenty yards away. He was walking in the opposite direction, and I wasn't a hundred percent certain, but his rack of antlers marked him as one of the Wild Hunt.

"*Wylan!*" I screamed, sprinting toward him. "Help me!"

The man turned, and I realized as I closed on him that it wasn't Wylan after all—similar dark ponytail, same amber eyes and slightly pointed ears, but a different face. Still, I was out of good ideas, and at that moment, throwing myself on the Huntsman seemed like a better option than waiting to be captured.

"Where's Wylan?" I begged, panting for breath. "Please, I need help, is he here? Or Annie? Please?"

The man pointed to the ceiling. "That's you, is it?"

I grabbed his arm. "*Please.* They're going to kill me—"

His arm twisted, and he gripped me in turn. "Hold on," he said, and the world went black as the ground fell away.

I stumbled as gravity returned and found myself in a vastly different building. Gone were the green carpet, tasteful paintings, and strobing lights, replaced by a flagstone floor, dark wooden walls, and the muffled sound of men laughing in the distance. A window behind me spilled morning light into the apparent hallway, and I turned to see a tall forest beyond the glass, thick conifers and the skeletal forms of winter-denuded hardwoods.

"Here, sit down," the Huntsman told me, ushering me to a beautifully carved wooden bench along the wall. "I'll speak with him. Wait here."

I collapsed onto the cushion, my legs quivering and my heart hammering, and tried to catch my breath.

He walked a few feet away to the door at the end of the hall and knocked twice before poking his head inside. "Wylan? Someone to see you. Are you available?"

"Who is it?" came a baritone voice I recognized.

"I don't know, but Forum security has an alert out for her, and she asked to speak with you. I brought her here…"

"Thanks, Derat. I'll handle it. You've got that committee meeting at lunch, yes? Why don't you head back?"

"Thank you. She's, uh…" He glanced over his shoulder and saw me hyperventilating where he'd left me. "She's out here."

A moment later, Wylan stepped from his office. With him standing next to Derat, I could see the difference—Wylan was taller and broader than his brother, sporting a short beard and wearing a lace-up shirt and leggings instead of a formal robe—but the family resemblance was unmistakable. I didn't have long to study them, however, as Wylan's expression shifted from curiosity to concern when he spotted me.

"*Jane*? What's going on?" he asked, striding down the hall. "Derat, return to Beukal. You know nothing of this."

"Understood," Derat replied, and vanished.

By the time Wylan reached me, my legs weren't the only thing shaking. I trembled from the chemical cocktail in my bloodstream, and as I looked up at him, I started to sob.

"What's happened?" he murmured—in English, I distantly noted. "Come on, this way."

He helped me into his office, locked the door, and plucked a crystal decanter from a side table as I tried ineffectively to pull myself together. Pouring a generous double into a matching tumbler, Wylan led me to a leather couch and pressed the drink into my hand. "Sip that. Breathe."

I smelled a familiar bouquet—he'd poured me booze, not a potion—and realized it was Dad's aged moonshine when it hit my tongue. That sent me into a fresh fit of tears, and I clung to the glass, mentally berating myself as I fell to pieces.

After a moment, Wylan said, "Tell me what happened."

He was still standing, I realized, and blinked my eyes clear to find that my skin had erupted in flames. "Oh, shit," I mumbled, and hiccupped as I concentrated, withdrawing the fire into myself. "Sorry, did I singe your couch?"

"If you did, it can be repaired." Taking a seat beside me, he offered me a box of tissues and waited while I swiped at my face. "Are you hurt?"

I shook my head. "You were right. Gerem arrested my dad…"

Wylan groaned. "I'm so sorry. Just now?"

"Uh-huh. Dad…he brought me over this morning. The reps were considering my…my citizenship petition…" I drank in an effort to stop the tears. "Mirrik was nice about it, but Gerem had, like, *planned* this whole thing. He argued with Director Erenani and…and the guy from DPP, Pateme something—"

"Ti'Tam. Good support for your petition."

"I thought so," I said, and set the glass on the floor while I blew my nose. "And when they wouldn't do anything to Dad, Gerem said he was arresting him, and the guards sneaked up on him with a potion…I think it dampened his power…"

"I know of it. Laws uses it to keep the magically gifted from fighting their way out of custody. The effect is temporary," he assured me. "He'll be fine. But Gerem can't have legally arrested him—we haven't voted for that."

"Well, I guess no one told him that," I muttered. "He and the other rep, Elm what's-her-face, rejected my petition, and then he said he was going to do what Dad should have done and give me the draught and a memory potion—"

"*What?*"

I'd met Wylan before. I knew his wife, and he'd never been anything but polite to me. But in that moment, seeing the anger in his eyes, I recalled that there was a good reason why most people never sought out the freaking *Hunter* for help. The guy was a massive source of power whose primal purpose was to occasionally go out and kill things. The look he was giving me set off sirens in the ancient part of my brain that feared creatures with teeth and claws.

"I...he didn't get me. Pateme threw everyone across the room and told me to run—"

Wylan rose and stalked away, and I took another sip of 'shine to calm my nerves. After a moment, he said, "The man's a cretin. That's the potion he tried to give Annie, the one to erase her memory..." When he turned back to me, he seemed controlled, but his anger hadn't dimmed. "He almost took her from me, you know? He was furious, but he couldn't touch Annie after she joined the Hunt. Pateme and Kabno were there, and they didn't try to stop me, so this may very well be some sick attempt at revenge, or at least a display of power."

"What do I do?" I asked, clutching the tumbler. "He's got Dad, and—"

"Your father will be unharmed. I'll see to it personally," he promised. "Even if we can't have him freed before the vote, I'll ensure that he's provisioned. But we need to worry about you first."

"Could you take me home, please? Annie knows the way..."

He grimaced. "It's not a matter of ability. I don't think you're safe. Let's get Annie's input," he said, and plucked his phone from his desk. A few seconds later, he said, "Hi, gorgeous. Situation back at the house. Can you come? I'm in my office—"

Annie appeared before he could finish the call, wearing a black T-shirt with the DOL logo on the breast pocket and loose black pants. "What's up—oh, hell, Jane? Hon, what's going on?" she asked, slipping into English. Her southern accent wasn't as thick as mine, but it seemed to deepen with every word. "Are you okay? Are you hurt? How did you get here? Wait, isn't this your petition day? Pars said—"

"Gerem arrested her father and tried to come after her with the draught and a memory potion," Wylan explained. "Derat brought her here."

"I thought he was you from behind," I said. "Started yelling, and he gave me a lift."

"*Jane*," said Annie, slipping beside me on the couch, and wrapped me in a tight hug. "I'm so sorry. We'll figure this out, don't worry."

"I was just asking Wylan if y'all could take me home."

"And I don't think that's wise," he said, shaking his head. "Her father's address is surely on file."

"I moved out—"

"Yeah, but you're in the same town," said Annie. "Tracking you could be difficult without your blood or a close relative's, but maybe Canna's would do. I don't know."

Wylan grimaced. "I'd be more concerned about trolls. Unless there's nothing of Jane's at her father's house…"

"I was there last week," I mumbled. "Still have some stuff in my old bathroom, just in case…"

"That settles it. You're absolutely not staying in Ragged Gap," Annie declared. "But you're safe here. No one but a Huntsman can reach this place."

"And that puts y'all in a bind," I said. "I don't want Gerem trying to bring charges against either of you for…I don't know, treason or whatever. Interference with Forum business? Hell, ask Daff," I muttered as I drank.

Annie and Wylan looked at each other, and he drummed his fingers on his arm as he thought. "What about your parents?" he asked her. "I hate to impose, but under the circumstances…"

"I think they'll understand," she said, pulling her phone from her pocket.

Two minutes and one quick explanation later, Annie

flashed me a thumbs-up. "They're happy to host. Do you want to pack? What sort of a lead time do we have?"

"It's a little more than an hour from Central…"

"Then let's get to it. Here, I'll take you home," she said, reaching for my hand.

"Let me come as well," Wylan cut in. "Just in case."

I had no complaint there, and so Annie popped the three of us out of the Pactlands.

She landed in my kitchen, and I had time enough upon opening my eyes only to register Connor, wearing khakis and a sweater instead of his uniform, standing on a chair by the window with the corner of a HAPPY BIRTHDAY! banner in one hand and a thumbtack in the other. He whipped around, dropped everything, and reached for his hip as he shouted, "Holy *shit*, what the—"

"It's okay!" I said, rushing between him and Annie and Wylan, and grateful that he'd left his service weapon elsewhere. "They're with me! Don't freak out!"

I understood his fear. From a distance, and especially if Annie's dark hair was fluffed enough to cover her ears, she still passed for human, but Wylan was clearly anything but. He lifted his hands in placation and took a step back, and Connor clutched his chest and quickly climbed off his perch.

The banner was, I saw, the second of its kind. The first, CONGRATULATIONS! spelled out in shiny, multicolored letters, had already been strung across the window. Helium balloons bobbed in the corners, and a trio had been tied to the back of my usual chair. A bouquet of pink roses and baby's breath sat in the middle of the table in a pebbled glass vase.

"Con, what's all this?" I asked. "Why aren't you at work?"

"Your dad said you wouldn't be home until later, so Tabitha and I were in charge of setting up for the, uh…surprise party. Which is no longer a surprise." He rubbed the back of his neck and shrugged. "Sorry, Janie.

Tabitha's making dinner, so she won't be over until later..." He paused briefly, considering my escorts, then frowned and hurried toward me. "Honey, your makeup's all smeared. What happened? Where's Yacovi? And who are...uh..."

"Hi," said Annie, extending her hand. "Remember me? Annie Humphries, I'm with DPP."

"She helped me burn down that cabin last fall," I mumbled, too dazed to manage a better introduction. "And ferried Sage and me back and forth."

Connor shook her hand reflexively, then squinted at her. "*Right*, I remember you. You disappeared on me...and wait, *you're* with—"

"I'm originally from Virginia. Which is where we're taking Jane once she packs. Jane, *scoot*."

I ducked into my bedroom and dug my suitcase from my closet, only to hear Connor's voice rise from down the hall: "The *fuck*?" Rapid footsteps followed that, and he came to a halt by my bed. "You're not going anywhere without me. Let me throw my things together and make arrangements, and I'll come with you."

"Connor—"

"*No*. If there's any chance of a band of fucking sorcerers coming here to hunt you down, then you're getting the hell out of town, and I'm going with you. Someone needs to have your back."

"Connor," I said more gently, rubbing his tense shoulders, "I'll be okay. You've got a job to consider."

"And I've got weeks of vacation time banked. No, *ma'am*. Look," he said, "I may be scraping the bottom of the barrel when it comes to magic, but I can put a bullet in anyone who tries to kill you. Because that's exactly what that death draught shit is—that's death in a bottle. Now, I realize we haven't been together all that long, but if you think I'm the kind of guy who stays at home and goes on about his life while his girlfriend's on the run from, and I cannot stress this enough, *sorcerers*, then I've done something wrong."

My eyes began to well again, and Connor folded me into his arms. "I've got you, Firebug," he whispered. "Let me help you."

"Okay," I mumbled, resting my cheek against his sweater. "If you're sure…"

"Of course I am." He moved back just far enough to kiss me, then said, "I'm going to run home and grab my stuff. Could you call Tabitha and let her know what's up? I'll be back as soon as I can."

He hurried out, and I heard the engine of his Explorer start. Connor often used his Whitford PD vehicle in his jaunts around town, and no one seemed to particularly care. If anything, it cut down on speeding tourists.

I was shoving toiletries into their travel bag when I heard my microwave beep, and a couple minutes later, Annie ventured into my room, mug in hand. "Thought you might want this," she said, offering it to me. "Just tea. I know Wylan tried the booze method, but sometimes this hits the spot."

"Thank you," I said, and sipped. A true southerner, Annie had properly sweetened the brew. "I'm sorry to mess up your day—"

"You're not. I've spoken with my boss, and everything's okay. Well, not everything," she amended, nodding at my open suitcase, "but I've got myself under control. I checked with my mom, and they're fine with you and Connor coming. He's *pissed*," she said. "Probably a good thing for Gerem that Connor can't get to him."

"Connor's not ready to tangle with a full-grown sorcerer yet. Maybe never. I've only taught him a little—"

She chuckled to herself. "You remember Yven, right? Rose's fiancé? Pars says he's awful with defensive magic, so when this siren tried to kill Rose, Yven just up and shot the bastard. The only person I know who's pretty much immune to bullets is Wylan, and Gerem has to sleep eventually. Did you pack a hairdryer? I'm sure Mom and

Dad have an extra, but it's probably twenty years old."

I stepped into the bathroom to grab it, Annie on my heels. "Did Wylan go home?"

"Nah. He's lurking at the door in case our timing is off."

"*Ah*. And, uh, he and Connor..."

"I didn't explain everything, but Connor's more concerned about you right now. Ooh, did you make those?"

I glanced at the glass cannister of bath bombs. "Yup, and could you do me a favor? If you go out to the shed, you'll find some prepackaged bags of them on the workbench to the right. Bring me one, would you?"

"Planning on a relaxing soak?"

"I hate to show up at your parents' house emptyhanded."

"Jane," she protested, "this is an emergency situation—"

"And I'm literally still packing. If there's anything else out there you think they'd like, chuck it in, eh?"

She returned a few minutes later with a bag of bath bombs and a lavender-scented candle, which she nestled atop my robe as I called Tabitha's cell.

Apparently, business at the pharmacy wasn't pressing, as Tabitha picked up on the second ring. "Hey, birthday girl! Finished already?"

"Yeah, and it went south pretty horribly," I replied, pacing by my bed. "Long story short, Dad's in custody, one of the representatives tried to give me the death draught—"

"*Jane!*"

"I know. So, I'm going on the run. Connor's coming along."

"Where are you going?"

"I don't want to tell you. You're safer not knowing," I replied, thinking of the damage truth serum could do. "But could you do something for me?"

"Name it," she said.

"If you get the time, could you drive past Dad's house every so often? It's the one place they know to look for me, so if it stays quiet, I might be able to come home sooner."

"You've got it. Not a problem. I'll keep an ear to the ground, too, just in case we get weird tourists." Tabitha paused, then said, "You *call* me, okay? Let me know you're alive and safe. Is there anything I can do for Coby?"

"I wish," I mumbled. "Got some folks who're looking out for him, but as of right now, he's stuck in the Pactlands. You take care of yourself, yeah? If you think you see Pact agents, don't engage."

"I don't know nothin' about nothing'," she agreed. "Just your friendly neighborhood pill-pusher. But if something changes and you need my help, you let me know."

I smiled to myself. "You're the best, Tabitha."

"Oh, I wouldn't go that far. So, uh…is it too late to wish you a happy birthday?"

"Connor told me you were making dinner. I'm sorry to miss it."

"Me, too. Tell you what, once this blows over, we'll have a redo. Cake and everything."

"That's sweet of you, but don't go buying ingredients yet. I don't know when I'll be able to come home again."

Tabitha hesitated before answering me. "I know you think my version of magic is bullshit—"

"I never said—"

"You didn't have to. But I've got a couple spells for protection and such in my book, and if it's all right, I'll try to cast them for y'all."

That was, I mused, Tabitha's version of putting us on her prayer list, and I appreciated the thought. "Only if it's no trouble."

"I can make time. Y'all be careful out there," she said, and let me go.

About forty-five minutes after my return to Ragged Gap, Connor roared up the road in his personal vehicle, a black Santa Fe Sport. He jumped out of the SUV, then threw open the trunk and jogged to the door, where Wylan, who'd finally masked, was waiting like the bouncer from hell. "Schedule's clear, I'm packed and gassed up, and I've got a small arsenal in there," he announced. "Ready, Jane?"

I stowed my gear in the back, then locked up and hid my key. "I should put a hold on my mail," I said, thinking aloud. "And I've got to get word to my customers—"

"Which you can do from Richmond," Annie interrupted. "Okay, y'all get in there. We'll do the heavy lifting."

Connor and I climbed into the front and closed the doors. "Do you think we should buckle up?" he asked. "What are they doing, exactly?"

"Give me your hand," I said, then gripped the door and closed my eyes. "You might want to hold your breath…"

Teleportation Huntsman-style wasn't nearly as awkward if you were sitting, I decided, though Connor yelped on landing and tried to fall out of his seat. "You're okay," I said, squeezing his hand before I released him. "And I think we're here."

The world outside the vehicle had shifted from the familiar tree-covered mountains and gravel driveway of home to a flat suburban backyard—tidy but dormant with the season—and the side of a two-story white brick house. Peering through the garage door windows, I could just make out the shape of a car within, and I hoped my old F-150 would still have enough juice to start once I made it home.

If I made it home.

Annie, now masked herself, rapped on my window, and I opened the door and slid out. "This is the place?" I asked.

"Yup. Welcome to Chez Humphries," she said, and pointed to a cement walkway leading around to the rear. "Mom's out buying more groceries, but Dad's waiting for us."

Leaving my luggage, I followed her and Wylan to the back door, which opened to an organized mudroom. "Dad?" Annie called. "It's me!"

A moment later, a middle-aged man with thinning gray hair, gold-rimmed glasses, and a green cable-knit sweater and jeans appeared in the doorway. "Anniebell! Come in, it's just me here." He hugged her as she passed, then gripped Wylan's arm and smiled tensely. "You two all right?"

"We're fine, Dave," Wylan replied. "I'm sorry for the short notice—"

"Hey, not the first time we've had houseguests. Speaking of whom..." He turned away from Wylan and nodded to Connor and me. "Welcome, y'all. Right this way." As we neared, he asked, "No bags?"

"They're in the car, sir," I said. "We're in the driveway..."

"Oh, that's fine. And aren't your legs cold, honey? It's freezing out there."

The weather wasn't terrible for mid-February, about thirty-five degrees and overcast, but the wind did make me wish I'd thrown on tights that morning...which by then felt like several days ago. "Didn't bother changing clothes before I came," I explained.

"Well, you look very nice, but if you want to put on something more casual, you won't hurt anyone's feelings. Watch your step, there, don't trip on the threshold."

The kitchen was warm and smelled like coffee, and I zeroed in on the half-full pot sitting by the sink. Annie sniffed the air, then smiled at her father. "Finally gave in and ground up the Kona, did we?"

"It's smooth," he allowed. "Not bad, kid. Got to be

honest, I can't really smell the difference…"

"Oh, trust me, it's there." Wylan emphatically nodded, and Annie kissed Dave on the cheek. "I'd love to stay and chat, but I've got to get back to the office, and this one has committee reports he should be reading."

"Not until after I see to Yacovi," said Wylan. "But Dave, if you're uncomfortable—"

"We'll be fine," he insisted. "Y'all be careful out there, and your mom's going to want you for dinner before too much longer," he added to Annie. "She's offering meatloaf."

"Meatloaf?" Wylan asked, perking.

Dave nodded. "It's a beef, pork, and venison blend. Whole thing's wrapped in bacon and covered in barbeque sauce."

He nodded thoughtfully. "The offer still stands if you two ever want to retire closer to Annie…"

"I don't even want to think about how many meatloaves it would take to feed the pack of y'all," Dave replied, grinning. "But you two pick a date, and you know Maggie would love to feed you. Now go on, we've got this in hand," he continued, shooing them toward the door.

"Thanks, Daddy," said Annie, and looked at Wylan. "See you tonight, babe."

She vanished, but Wylan lingered for a moment longer. "Seriously," he said to Dave, "if *anything* seems amiss, call us. I don't want you dealing with sorcerers or worse on your doorstep."

"They'd have to find us first," he said, and patted Wylan's arm. "You leave this to Maggie and me."

"I mean it," Wylan insisted, gripping Dave's shoulder. "Vehicles you don't know, strangers on the street, anyone who looks suspicious—"

"It's under control—"

"*David.*"

The two stared each other down for a second, and Dave blinked first. "I'll call. Don't worry."

"And thank you," I said to Wylan. "I mean it. If you could thank Derat for me…"

"Of course. We'll be in touch," he said, and disappeared without another word.

CHAPTER 4

Dave chuckled and shook his head. "Oh, he's in a *mood*."

"I did kind of interrupt his morning," I said. "And Annie's…"

"Hmm? Oh, no, I don't think Wylan's upset with you—he's peeved, but he's in protective mode. Don't see it too often, but when it pops through…" Noting our bemusement, Dave explained, "Those two have only been married about eight months, and he's normally deferential to a fault around us. Took until deer season last year for him to finally tell me he's old enough to be my father. *That* was an awkward conversation to have up a tree stand."

"He is?" Connor murmured, glancing at me for confirmation.

Dave nodded. "He'll be ninety-one in April. I mean, when you throw immortals into the mix, I guess age really is just a number, but still…anyway," he said with a shrug, "Wylan minds his manners around here, and he doesn't seem offended when Maggie starts mothering, but I see that other side of him peek out every so often. When we went out one night and some guys started catcalling Annie…" He whistled. "He didn't throw a punch. Didn't *need* to. Those punks left with wet pants. Now, if he's worried enough to act like he just did," said Dave, folding his arms over his slight paunch, "I'm going to go out on a limb and suggest that Maggie didn't give me the full story before she ran out for breakfast food. So, uh…who *are* y'all, and what's going on?"

"Sorry, Jane Fortune," I said. "This is my boyfriend,

Connor Willow. I, um…shit, it's been a day," I muttered. "I'm from Ragged Gap, up in north Georgia—"

"Wait, are you the sorcerer?" he interrupted, squinting. "The…what's it called, the pyro?"

"Pyromancer, and yes, sir. Annie mentioned me?"

"Oh, sure. Told us you were in a weird situation, but you were tough. She said she and her friend Rose were just excited to meet someone else who straddles the line, you know?"

"Annie's been wonderful," I said, and was pleased to see him smile. "The weird situation is that my mother was a sorcerer, but my father was human, and the man who raised me was just *arrested* for not giving my mother this potion when she ran off with her beau—"

"It's called the freaking 'death draught,'" Connor interjected.

Dave stiffened in surprise. "Say what?"

I nodded. "Yeah. Hook up with a human, and you're turning your back on the Pactlands. It kills your talent, and it's supposed to give you a more human lifespan, but it'll do you in within thirty years. Dad didn't want to be responsible for doing that to my mother, and now that the secret's out, he's in custody."

He rubbed his chin. "I see. And you're in trouble, too?"

"You could say that. The Forum rep who had Dad arrested tried to come after me with the draught *and* a memory potion, and if his people had injected me, there's no telling what he'd have made me forget. Dad, my home, my own name…"

"Putting aside, of course, the issue of the *draught*," Connor added.

"Shit." Dave leaned back against the kitchen island, his brow furrowed. "This rep who tried to mind-wipe you, he's not a sorcerer by any chance, is he? Because one of those assholes was going to do it to Annie—"

"Same guy," I replied. "Gerem Aniap. Wylan thinks this might partly be revenge for how things shook out with her. Anyway, one of the other Huntsmen got me out of there, and Wylan and Annie took me home, and Connor was setting up my birthday party…" I laughed weakly. "Sorry, it's…a *lot*."

"But why was he going to erase your memory?" Dave pressed. "If he'd stuck you with the draught—"

"I'm a liability. Legally, I'm still human, and I not only know about the Pactlands, but I've been there. Been through the portals, been in government buildings…I've got intel, for whatever it's worth. I'm sure he'd want to stick y'all, too, if he knew you'd been clued in—I take it Annie didn't get approval for whatever she told you, right?"

He smirked. "Don't think so, no. She and Wylan said that Rose's…grandfather? Great-grandfather?"

"Great, I think. The farseer?"

"Yeah, him. He told them to tell us the truth. Maybe this is why," he said, cocking his head. "But I know what that memory potion can do. Has Annie mentioned Maya?"

"I don't think so," I said, racking my brain. "Who's Maya?"

"Friend of hers. She's got a restaurant over in Carytown. Maya and Annie got dosed with that Roulette shit at the same time, and they were roommates in the Pactlands until DPP found an antidote. She opted to come home, so she got the memory potion."

I winced. "She doesn't remember anything about it?"

"She wouldn't," he replied, "had she not still been dealing with Roulette in her system. She knows the cover story they implanted, but she's still got all her memories. Annie introduced us a while back—nice to talk to someone who knows the crowd my kid's running with."

"Question," Connor interrupted. "Carytown?"

"It's a Richmond neighborhood," Dave explained. "Shops and restaurants, mostly."

"And we are…"

"You're in Henrico County. We're part of the

Richmond area, but the city's actually independent...doesn't really make much difference for y'all, but that's how it works. We used to live in town, but we moved north after Annie fledged. But y'all can get your bearings later," he said, and pointed toward a hallway. "Let's go upstairs and figure out the rooming situation."

The Humphrieses had two guest rooms with a jack-and-jill bathroom in between, one set up with a four-poster canopy bed that had to have been a hand-me-down from an ailing aunt and the other with a more standard model probably purchased to fill the space. I took the four-poster, saving Connor from a night beneath several layers of lace and crocheted blankets, and Dave cleared his throat as we awkwardly stood in the doorways. "Y'all make yourselves comfortable. I know that one's a little fusty," he added, cocking his thumb toward my room, "so do what you need to do. I'm working from home today, and I'll be in the basement, but come get me if you need anything. Fridge is open, and Maggie should be home soon. Hope y'all brought appetites—she loves feeding people."

We thanked him, and as Dave headed downstairs, I sat atop the bed and stared at the wall, waiting for my mind to stop spinning.

This wasn't right. I was supposed to be out with Dad and Canna right now, maybe eating lunch or looking for a robe. Heck, in another timeline, maybe I'd be meeting my grandparents at that moment. Connor would be finishing party preparations, and I'd be blissfully ignorant of the surprise until Dad brought me home. Instead, I was somewhere in central Virginia, camping in Annie's parents' house and on the run from a sorcerer who'd attacked me.

Gerem Aniap tried to *kill* me.

No matter what I'd made of myself, no matter what I'd done, I was just a problem to be eliminated.

That fact finally began to sink in as I sat there, contemplating a faded antique sampler, but I was too numb in the moment to do more than replay the end of that meeting in my mind's eye: Gerem's smirk, the advancing aides, Pateme's attack on that whole side of the room. I hoped Mirrik was okay, and I absently wondered how much trouble the director was in for assaulting the representatives.

Sage. I wanted to text her to reassure her that I was all right, but on the off chance that someone in Beukal had the means to track me via cell phone—

"Janie?"

I snapped out of it and found Connor at the door, his eyes soft and worried. "Honey?" he asked. "You okay?"

I shook my head, and he joined me on the bed, holding me. While I seemed to have run out of tears that morning, I felt a little less broken with him there, as if his arms were keeping me intact.

"I've got you," he murmured, rubbing my back. "Whatever you need, wherever we have to go, I've got you, okay? You're not alone."

The sound that escaped me lay somewhere between laughter and a sob. "I don't know what to do."

"We'll figure it out."

"This is my fault. They got Dad, and if I hadn't—"

"Stop. He knew this was a possibility, right? But he wanted the best for you, and he took that risk."

"If I'd just sucked it up and been content—"

Connor pulled back enough to look me in the eye. "It is *not* your fault. The fucked-up Pactlands is to blame, and if those idiots can't see how great you are, then they're blind. It's their loss, Firebug. And honestly, I'm proud of you for not barbequing anyone on your way out."

Chuckling, I fit myself back against his chest, and Connor wrapped me up again. "At least this answers the question of what I was going to do about you."

"What do you mean?" he asked.

"If I had citizenship and you didn't…"

He grunted. "I'm perfectly fine with the status quo for now. Those assholes don't need to know about me, especially if *this* is what I'd have to look forward to. Can you imagine what that Gerem clown would do if he knew about East Branch?"

"I don't want to think about it, and something tells me the few who have any idea of its existence are keeping their mouths shut."

"*Good*," he said, and sighed. "Thanks for not breaking up with me. Might be the silver lining to this whole mess."

Before I knew the words were escaping me, I replied, "If it came down to the Pactlands or you, I know which I'd pick. This is the safest I've felt all day."

"Hell, I'm just some guy. You're the freaking pyro wizard."

"Don't care."

Connor didn't argue with me, and we remained there together on the bed until the back door opened and Maggie swept in with grocery bags.

Her love language was evidently food, as she sent Connor and me to the kitchen table and told us to stay there while she made the best grilled cheese sandwiches I'd ever put in my mouth: thick, gooey layers of cheddar and brie with clumps of goat cheese smooshed between buttered slices of fresh French bread and served with a grape-balsamic reduction she whipped up on the fly. Too bad I had no appetite, as it felt criminal to let her work go to waste.

"I got the skinny from Annie," she told us as we ate, "and here's how this is going to go. Y'all are welcome here for as long as you need. The only people who know you're in town are Annie and Wylan, and Lord knows *they* won't say a peep."

"I should mention there's a non-zero chance that a farseer knows I'm here," I mumbled, breaking my crust into pieces.

Maggie frowned. "Who, that Diriem fellow?"

"You've met him?" I asked, surprised.

"No, I just know of him. Annie said he's been good to

her, so that's all right by me. You don't think he'd come after you, do you? Isn't Rose partly human, too?"

"Yes, ma'am," I allowed, "but...it's not paranoia if someone's actually out to get you, right?"

Unsure of my next step, I lingered over my half-eaten sandwich as if I'd find answers in the crumbs, but Connor came to the rescue. With a little coaxing, he lured me back into his SUV, and then he set off for a drive around the area—whether to get the lay of the land or to distract me, I couldn't say, but at least the ride gave me something to stare at besides the walls. He found an oldies station low on the FM dial and left it there, and I let the familiar songs wash over me as I watched the houses and lawns turn to commercial districts, then to the city proper. Occasionally, I felt pressure on my hand and saw that Connor had taken it, anchoring me.

The Humphrieses couldn't have been kinder, and they oohed and aahed over my impromptu hostess gift, but I crashed shortly after dinner, too drained to fake polite conversation. Despite my exhaustion, however, I remembered to plug in my phone—a good thing, as Tabitha woke me around five-thirty Wednesday morning with a call.

"Sorry," she said as I croaked a greeting. "Rough time zone?"

"No, I'm just sleeping in. What's up?"

"So, I just made a sweep. Your house looks untouched. Lights are off, door's closed, and the only vehicle on the property is your truck."

"That's good..."

"Yeah, but your dad's place is a different story. Lights on in the house, and I saw a handful of dark-colored SUVs parked in the driveway. Couldn't get an accurate count with the trees and the lack of daylight, but it's more than two. If you want, I can make another pass tonight—"

"Don't take any chances."

"Assuming I go by at roughly the same times every day, they'll have no reason to suspect me," she replied. "In any case, it's definitely not safe for you to come home yet...I mean, unless you know someone who'd be camping at Yacovi's house."

"I'm the only other person with a key, so no. Be careful."

"You, too. Are you and Connor somewhere safe?"

"Pretty much."

"Okay," said Tabitha, though she didn't sound wholly convinced. "Keep me posted, hon."

Having been awakened, I knew I wasn't going back to sleep, and so I tiptoed downstairs, assuming our hosts wouldn't begrudge me a cup of tea. I found the teabags and sweetener packets, then poured in tap water and simply willed the brew to heat in the mug—not my preferred method, but I didn't want to wake anyone else with a whistling kettle or beeping microwave.

And that's how Connor found me: sitting alone in the dark at the kitchen table with my hot mug. "Couldn't sleep?" he murmured, taking the chair beside me.

"Not after Tabitha called. She says there's activity at Dad's house."

"Then I'm sure as hell glad you're not in Ragged Gap. Is there enough water for two?"

"I warmed it manually. Just a minute..."

He watched bemusedly as I repeated the process with a second mug, then touched the ceramic and hissed as he withdrew his fingers. "*Hot.*"

"Yeah, that's why I don't usually make tea that way," I said, carefully lifting mine by the handle.

"Fair." He considered his mug for a moment, then asked, "Going to teach me to do that?"

"Eventually. Let me wake up first."

Connor sat with me while I drank and put my thoughts in order. An idea had come to me in my sleep, and my brain had gnawed on it until I almost had a plan…well, the skeleton of one, anyway. "Been thinking," I said.

"Yeah?"

"All of this mess comes back to my mother. I want to find her, get some damn answers once and for all. It's been almost twenty-eight years since she walked away, and I think she owes me a conversation, don't you?"

"Long overdue," Connor concurred. "But how do you plan to track her down? Hire a PI, tell him to look for a sorcerer?"

"Not exactly." I sipped again, then sent a burst of heat into the mug to counteract the cool kitchen. "Do you remember back in December when Sage's aunt showed up one night? Enne Tumari, the portal attendant?"

He laughed incredulously. "Yes, I remember the freaking *centaur* in your den."

"Okay, so do you recall how she found us?" When his brow furrowed, I explained, "She had a tracker. It's an ensorcelled compass, more or less. You set it up and use the target's blood, and the compass points in that direction. Glows when you get close. I've never used a tracker, but I think I can make one."

"How?"

"Well, if Enne could use Remari's blood to get to her daughter, then surely I could use mine to find my mom. I remember seeing instructions in one of Dad's grimoires, and there's a potion you dip the compass into…I *think* I remember the ingredient list, but I'd feel better with a book."

Not to mention supervision. Dad had only been teaching me to brew for a few months, and beginner potions were the ones least likely to explode if brewed improperly. I didn't have any sense of how complex the tracker potion would be, though I knew some of the ingredients would be next to impossible to acquire without finding a greenhouse. Dad's being out of the question, I needed to locate another master grower willing to help me, but the only other greenhouse I knew of was the DPP facility. It was relatively close, hidden near a small town somewhere west of Richmond, but since I was now a wanted woman, rolling up to a Pact installation and asking for plants was out of the cards.

Again, I had the skeleton of a plan, but I couldn't *quite* flesh it out.

I had yet to come up with a solution by the time Maggie caught us and asked how we liked our eggs. Truthfully, if this was mothering, I didn't mind it in the slightest, though not even bacon could solve my problems that morning.

Around ten, while Dave worked in his basement office and Maggie drove off to buy more yarn—she was knitting Wylan a cardigan, she explained, and swore us to secrecy—I'd showered and knocked on Connor's open door. "Hey," I said as he looked up from his laptop, "I was thinking about a walk around the block, if you're interested—"

My trilling phone cut me off, and I dashed back to my room with Connor right behind me. When I saw the screen, however, my hopes came crashing down—an unknown number, probably a telemarketer—but still, I tapped the button. "Hello?"

"Thank the heavens," came a familiar voice in Pactish on the other end.

I clung to the phone like a lifeline. "*Liogh?*"

"It's me," said the detective. "This is a burner, so don't bother saving the number. I've got a stash of cards, and I'll be rotating."

"Are you okay?" I asked, then saw Connor cup his ear and put the phone on speaker. "I'm here with Connor," I said, switching back to English.

They followed my lead. "Good, good. I was hoping you weren't alone. *Don't* tell me where you are," they hastily added. "Ignorance is best for all of us right now."

"What's going on?"

They groaned. "You're familiar with the concept of a shitstorm?"

"Is Dad safe?" I asked, my heart racing.

"He's fine, relatively speaking. Still in custody, but Director Erenani convinced Forum security that DOL is much better equipped to look after him. All they have is a holding cell—it's not meant for more than a few hours' use. So, he's been transferred to the tower, and he's in minimal custody."

"What does *that* entail?" Connor asked.

"More than you're used to, Chief. He has a private cell, a television, access to books, time in the inmate gymnasium, though he's being kept segregated from the other minimum custody inmates on hand for his own safety."

"I'm pretty sure Yacovi can take care of himself..."

"Undoubtedly, were he not being dosed with dampening potion. He can't cast at the moment, and I think we'd all prefer if he didn't wind up in a fistfight with a troll."

"Is the Forum going to prosecute him?" I asked. "Don't they have to take a vote?"

"Oh, we've heard *all* about that," said Liogh. "Mirrik's been quite vocal, and the Hunter's joined him. Can't imagine why," he added dryly. "This is all secondhand, of course, but I've spoken with Fell ti'Mal here, who's in contact with Annie over at DPP, and it sounds like Gerem is calling in his favors. Mirrik and Wylan are leading the opposition, and the directors are lobbying."

"Did Director ti'Tam get in trouble?"

"What, for that little show of force? No. Gerem started squawking, but Director Erenani pointed out that he's unauthorized to administer the draught *or* a memory potion, so Director ti'Tam was defending you against assault and, frankly, attempted murder. I think he got the message."

"*I* don't."

"Why not?" Liogh asked.

"Because I've got eyes on the ground in Ragged Gap, and there are strangers camped at Dad's house right now."

What followed from Liogh's end of the phone was unintelligible to me, but I assumed it was profane in Nymphic. "Any idea who? How many?"

"No good details. My source is trying not to be spotted."

"That's probably for the best. I'll pass this to the director. Not sure if she wants to send our people out there for a potential fight on top of everything else, but she needs to know. And as for you, youngling, I shouldn't have to tell you to stay away."

"No worries there," I muttered. "But how long is Dad going to be locked up? When will the Forum vote?"

Liogh hissed through their teeth. "I wish I had a date for you, but I can't say. This is the first potential Forum prosecution in years, and as I mentioned, there's quite a bit going on behind the scenes. If my gut feeling is accurate, the vote to prosecute will be a decent proxy vote for guilt, so no one is rushing this. It could be a couple weeks."

"*Shit.*"

"I know. And even if we could arrange for Yacovi to be released before the vote, Director ti'Tam has been forced to withdraw his portal credentials. He's stuck here for now, incarcerated or not." With a sigh, they said, "I'm so sorry, Jane. I never expected this to happen, but then Canna reminded me of how Gerem was embarrassed with Annie, so…damn it. I'll keep you apprised as well as I can. I've asked Canna not to contact you until things settle, but of course, I can't stop you from reaching out on your end." They paused, then asked, "Do you need help? Is there something I can do? I shouldn't slip out right now, but if there's anything else…"

"Maybe," I replied, leaning closer to the phone. "I want to find my mother."

"Wish I knew where to point you—"

"I can make a tracker. Dad taught me," I fibbed. "But I need a grower and brewing equipment to make the potion. Since the DPP greenhouse is out of the question, do you know of another source?"

"I...know of many growers and brewers," they replied. "I *have* been liaising with DPP for a while. Without going into specifics, any particular geographical region I should consider?"

"Who's closest to DPP's facility?"

Their answer was immediate. "Liliol ti'Cren. She's got a place in the Blue Ridge in Virginia. Master grower with a brewer's license, just like Yacovi."

When I glanced up, Connor nodded. "Do you think she'd be willing to help me?" I asked Liogh.

They chuckled softly. "She's Rose ti'Dana's great-aunt, but she's more like a grandmother to that girl. You tell me."

I smiled to myself as my admittedly amorphous plan began to solidify. Sure, trusting strangers was inherently risky, and I couldn't discount the possibility that Rose was tracking us with farsight at that moment, but if I had an in with a grower, then maybe...

"Could you send me her address?"

We packed while Maggie was out shopping, and when she returned, we explained that we were moving on. "I can't thank y'all enough," I said, squeezing her hands, "but this will keep you safer, too."

"Honey, I'm not worried about safety," Maggie replied. "I've got about four dozen burly men on speed dial, including my virtually indestructible son-in-law. You're welcome to stay."

"And I appreciate that, but...this is something I need to do. Dad saved my mom's life, and then she dumped me with him and walked away. I want to know why."

"You might not like what you find," she said gently.

"I know. But if I don't get at least *some* sort of answer from her...plus, this whole mess started with her, and she needs to know what's going on."

"I understand, but...well." Maggie hugged me, then broke away to hug Connor. "Can I at least make y'all lunch before you hit the road?"

"*Would* you?" Connor asked.

"Oh, sure, hon," she replied, and patted his cheek. "And I'll send you with some snacks, too."

The message in the look Connor shot me when Maggie turned to the stove was unmistakable: *Do we really have to leave?*

"Sorry," I whispered, and kissed him before offering to set the table.

CHAPTER 5

The address Liogh texted me was in a place called Briardale, which a quick search revealed was the sort of mountain hamlet I knew well, though perhaps with fewer tourist cabins. I looked at the street view of our destination: an open metal gate, a sloping driveway, and at the top, a cluster of low buildings comprising a garden nursery, all tucked against a mountainside. Eden's Bounty, the place was called, and local reviewers had left glowing notes about the plants and the pricing.

I saw no indication of a greenhouse from the limited street pictures, but that didn't surprise me. Dad's was accessible through a basic garden shed, which, when properly triggered, revealed a massive greenhouse that partially existed in a pocket connected to the Pactlands—a good thing, as the facility, about the length of a football field, wouldn't have fit on Dad's property otherwise. His brew room was hidden within the house through a door both concealed from prying eyes and magically protected. Liliol ti'Cren's surname marked her as elven, and I'd have been shocked were her facility not as disguised as Dad's.

We left the Humphries house around noon, our stomachs full and a freezer bag of cookies thawing in the back seat, and picked up I-64 west toward the Appalachians. The drive shouldn't have been much more than an hour and a half, but snow had blanketed the area in recent days, and though the main roads were mostly clear, Connor slowed considerably once we turned off the Interstate and hit the delightful obstacle course of half-plowed mountain streets. He crept through the little downtown area, noting the tiny police station as we passed, then turned up the winding mountain road as my phone barked directions and managed not to skid into a ditch before we reached the nursery.

The driveway was open—a welcome development, as the temperature had dropped about ten degrees since we left Richmond, and I had no desire to get out and wrangle with the gate—and Connor drove up the steep path and came to rest in a leveled gravel parking lot. The long rows of wood and cinderblock benches straight ahead would be laden with flats come spring, I mused, but they offered only a smattering of cold-hardy potted evergreens that day. To our left, past the barren nursery shelves, squatted a little shop. While we appeared to be the only customers there that afternoon, the lights were on inside the building, and so Connor and I hurried in out of the chill.

A bell jangled as I pushed the door open into a blissfully warm room that was far better stocked than the outdoor portion of the nursery was. Tables, shelves, and mismatched antique hutches offered small tools and knickknacks, while the windows were lined with houseplants for sale, everything from delicate orchids to tiny cacti. A small table on the far side of the shop offered a coffeepot and a stack of paper cups, and the familiar aroma made the space even more inviting. To the right, separating the shop from what I suspected was the office space, stretched a checkout desk outfitted with a roll of brown paper, a receipt pad, and a mug from a local bank half filled with pens.

As I took in the place, a door in the rear of the building creaked open, and a little old woman appeared from the back. She was petite, probably only an inch or two above five feet tall, and sported a denim work shirt and a green canvas apron over khaki slacks. Her hair, solid white and thicker than I'd have expected for a woman of her apparent years, fell behind her in a long braid, and her dark eyes crinkled when she spotted us. "Good afternoon," she drawled. "Help y'all find something?"

Connor glanced at me and raised his eyebrows, and I cleared my throat. "Um...sorry to bother you, ma'am. I'm looking for a lady named Liliol..."

She chuckled, and her accent shifted in an instant as she switched to Pactish. "It's Lily around here, dear. You must be Jane. Don't look so surprised," she said as I stiffened. "Got a call from Rose about an hour ago. She said a detective was sending you my way."

"Liogh Birrid. They said—"

"Oh, I know *them*. Snores like a jet engine. And you are..." she hinted, looking past me.

"This is Connor, ma'am," I replied, "and he doesn't speak Pactish."

"That so?" Slipping back into English, she said, "I was told you weren't coming alone...but running around with a human, are we?"

"Eh?" said Connor, shaking one hand back and forth.

"We're not sure *what* he is, precisely," I explained, "but he's with me. If that's a problem—"

"No, no. I've met my share—my little brother notoriously married one. And from what Rosie told me, you know how that goes."

I spread my arms. "Half-blooded. Now one of the Forum reps is trying to give me the draught—"

"Yes," Lily muttered, "so I heard. The Aniap boy's gone too far this time."

Considering that Gerem, like Dad, had more than a century and a half behind him, I had to wonder just how old Lily might be. Surely she was masked—elven aging slowed almost to a stop in the mid-twenties, and one naturally as wrinkled as she appeared to be would have seen millennia.

"Well, since I'm not exactly swarmed by customers today," she continued, leaning on the counter, "what can I do for you?"

"Rose didn't tell you what I'm after?"

She shook her head. "My Rosie is training with farseers now, and they're a tight-lipped bunch. Selective with information. Want to fill in the blanks?"

"Sure," I said, shoving my hands in my pockets. "Uh...I'm trying to find my mother. She walked out on me when I was a baby, and I want to know why. And because she's the reason my dad is in custody, seems as good a time as any," I muttered.

Frowning, Lily replied, "I thought your mother was a sorcerer. If your father's in the Pactlands—"

"Adopted. Bio-dad was human. Actual dad was Mom's boss back in the day, and now he's in trouble because it's come to light that he didn't give her the draught—"

"Wait, *wait*," she cut in, squinting, "don't tell me your father is..."

"Yacovi Hewt."

A satisfied smile broke across her face. "I'll be damned. The story I heard was that he retired from DPP after he had to give a trainee the draught—that it broke him. But this, now..."

"Dad helped them run off together and faked the rest, and then he retired to Georgia," I explained. "Mom found him after she had me and my bio-dad was murdered."

"I'm so sorry," she murmured, her brown eyes softening. "But I *am* glad to hear the truth about Yacovi. My brother spoke well of him, and I hated to think he'd killed that poor girl." She paused briefly, her lips tight as she stared into space, then sighed and smiled. "So, how did you plan to find your mother?"

"A tracker. I know I've seen the recipe for the potion in one of Dad's grimoires, but that's...back in Georgia, and the house is being watched," I said in a rush, "so is there any chance you'd be willing to sell me the ingredients and loan me the instructions?"

Lily's white eyebrows rose. "Not a chance, dear."

"No?" I asked, my heart sinking.

"Trackers—well, *legal* trackers—are regulated, and you need authorization to brew the potion that makes them. Since you don't know that, I'm going to hazard a guess that you haven't done much brewing."

"No, ma'am," I mumbled. "Dad was teaching me…"

"This isn't a beginner potion. It's volatile, and if you don't brew it properly, it can be highly explosive."

"Oh." As a flush rose up my neck, I said, "Sorry to waste your time. We'll get out of your hair—"

"I won't sell you the ingredients," she said gently. "That doesn't mean I'm unwilling to make it for you."

My deflated spirits rose at the offer. "Really? You'd do that?"

"I'll need authorization first. My license is my livelihood, you understand. But assuming I can secure permission…yes. It'll take two days to brew up, but I can do it. Follow me," she said, and started for the door.

Lily turned the wooden OPEN sign to CLOSED, then led us along the gravel paths across the nursery toward a pair of outbuildings on the edge of the woods. One appeared to be an ordinary shed, though having grown up around Dad's, I knew appearances could be deceiving. The other was half buried—a storm shelter, I realized, wondering whether tornadoes were as big a problem in Virginia as they were in my end of the country.

She descended the short cement staircase and popped the padlock on the storm shelter's door, and the door opened to darkness. Rather than step inside, she stood in place and spoke in Pactish, following a formula I'd heard Dad employ on many an occasion: "I am Liliol ti'Cren, owner of this greenhouse, licensed and approved. Open."

The storm shelter seemed to waver, and as the image cleared, a second door appeared atop the open one, white-painted wood with cutout glass panels about five feet off the ground. The door opened on its own, and what lay behind it was a greenhouse every bit as large and verdant as Dad's.

"Holy shit," Connor muttered.

I turned and grinned at him. "Greenhouses like this one exist partly in this world and partly in the Pactlands. They're kept hidden."

"Obviously." He ventured a step closer and whistled as he took in the long benches of bushes and flowers. "Wow. Mind if we come in, or do we wait out here?"

"I don't see the harm," Lily replied, and addressed the greenhouse in English that time. "Let them pass. They're with me."

She strode into the greenhouse, and I followed her. That the greenhouse was warded, I had no doubt, but it didn't surprise me that its owner could turn the protective spells on and off with a command.

As Connor closed the door against the February chill and I examined a blue-flowering rosebush, Lily said, "Behave yourself, Sally, we've got company."

I turned, expecting to be introduced to Lily's apprentice. Instead, a green vine the size of my forearm was rapidly snaking across the floor. The tip rose until it was perhaps five feet high, then bent toward Lily in a strange approximation of a head. Though it had no visible eyes or ears, I could swear that the vine was studying us as its "head" swiveled back and forth between us and Lily.

Amazonian slithertrap. It had to be.

There are few truly sentient plants, and most stay small, or at least sedentary. Slithertrap is the great exception, a rare jungle species that, while rooted, has highly motile vines. Should a slithertrap grow in poor soil, it would simply fix the problem by killing animals and bringing them back to its base to decompose, naturally fertilizing itself. Dad never tried to grow them because he didn't see the need—seedlings were expensive, and they had few uses for the average sorcerer.

Apparently, he'd overlooked the possibility of planting one as floral security. And given the size of this one's vines, I assumed that Lily was feeding it *very* well.

"Uh…hi?" I ventured, giving the vine a tentative wave, then elbowed my boyfriend. "Connor, say hello to the nice plant."

"I'm…sorry?" he mumbled behind me.

"Connor. *Say hello*."

I heard him swallow hard. "Hi, um…Sally?"

The head dipped under Lily's hand like an expectant dog, and she gave it a fond pat. "Rosie named it. Got stumbling drunk here with Yven in my absence, and that was the result."

I chuckled. "Didn't really think of them as the 'blackout drunk' kind…"

"Oh, they're not, but that's what you get when you drink things you shouldn't around a brewer's house. I make an augmented beer that's about ninety proof, and they didn't realize what they'd helped themselves to. Don't tell them I told you, eh? But yes, this is Sally," she said, gently scratching the vine's head as it butted against her, "and while slithertrap is, strictly speaking, hermaphroditic, Sally doesn't mind female pronouns. Or so it seems. It's difficult to have a conversation about the nuances of gender with a plant."

"She's, uh…a big girl," I said.

"Raised her from a sprout," Lily replied with pride. "I've had her about fifty years, and this is a good environment for her, but…you know, floramancer," she said, and shrugged. "Yacovi is, too, is he not?"

I nodded. "And half of his cover business is moonshine—"

She laughed aloud. "Not at all uncommon in our line of work. Most of us have hobby brewing or distilling operations. But we can talk about that later. What I need to do first is secure permission. Come with me, and don't touch *anything*," she said, staring at Connor. "Don't even brush against it. Nasty rashes are on the low end of unpleasant side effects from standing too close to the wrong plants in here."

We followed her single file down the center aisle of the greenhouse, flanked by exotic plants and Sally's tendrils, which she'd tucked away neatly below the benches. At the rear of the greenhouse was Lily's workstation, a long wooden table stocked with a roll of butcher paper for packing and a pair of plastic bins I recognized from Dad's greenhouse as a mailbox to the Pactlands. "I've got a phone I use purely for this business," said Lily, plucking an ordinary-looking cell phone from the table. "Makes the necessary parties more likely to take my calls when they don't think I'm just being social." With that, she gestured in front of her face, and her mask dissolved in a blink, leaving her looking about my age and blonde. "Hope he's not in a meeting," she muttered, her voice having lost its years as easily as her face did, and put the phone on speaker as she placed a call.

The other party picked up on the second ring. "Liliol?"

"Hello, Uncle," she said—in English, to my surprise. "I need a favor."

After a pause, the man on the other end answered her in kind, though he sounded bemused. "What sort of favor?"

"Authorization to make a tracker."

"May I ask *why*? Or for whom?"

Lily smirked to herself. "My customer is listening in right now, and she came with a friend. Who do you suppose she might be?"

Again, the man paused before answering her. "I don't need to know, do I?"

"If you're desperate, Rosie can tell you, but—"

"No, *no*, this conversation did not happen, and should I be put under oath, you did not inform me of your customer's identity." He sighed. "But should your customer be concerned about Yacovi Hewt, I can tell you that he's safe and unharmed. Not *thrilled*, naturally, but Kabno has put people she trusts in charge of him, so he has no reason to fear bodily harm."

I released a slow breath and bit back the urge to thank him.

"I'll pass that along, should my customer be interested," Lily replied. "But you'll update my permissions?"

"Before the end of the day."

"Thank you. And might I ask another favor, Uncle?"

"Ask whatever you like, my dear—whether I can give you what you want is another matter entirely."

She rolled her eyes; the joke, apparently, was an old one. "If Rosie isn't too busy, ask her to keep an eye on my place through Friday, will you? I'd rather not be caught unawares if someone has followed my customer here."

"I'll make it her priority," he promised, then said something unintelligible to me. Lily followed suit, and the call soon ended.

She smiled at me as she put the phone in her apron pocket. "Have you met my uncle? Pateme ti'Tam?"

My eyes widened. "The DPP director?"

"Precisely."

"Yeah, he came to my citizenship meeting…he may have saved my life," I murmured, rubbing my arm. "Gave me time to run away, at least."

"Good. I still haven't quite forgiven him for how he treated Rosie, but…that's good."

Lily didn't elaborate, and before I could ask, she'd pulled a thick leather-bound book from the shelves behind her table and carefully opened it. "Now," she said, leafing through the yellowed pages, "let's see what I need…"

The potion was fairly complex, requiring eleven ingredients added in specific fashions at several points, but Lily preferred the "mise en place" approach to brewing and assembled the components ahead of time. While Connor stood well out of the way, she and I walked around the greenhouse with old tomato baskets from the farmers market, picking leaves, flowers, and berries from a variety of plants that had no business being in flower and in fruit simultaneously. I knew Lily had given me the easier half of the list, and I caught her sneaking glances at me as I made my selections, but when she reviewed my basket, she nodded in satisfaction. "Very good, dear. You help Yacovi?"

"A little. He's particular about letting me mess around in the greenhouse, but he's taught me what not to touch."

"An excellent first lesson...oh, well done," she called as one of Sally's distant vines shot out and grabbed a mouse, wrapping it up and dragging it back under a bench almost before I noticed it. "Snack time, eh?"

Seeing Connor grimace behind Lily, I grinned briefly before turning back to her. "What can we do to help?"

"Not much, I'm afraid." Planting her hands on her hips, she leaned back to crack her spine and groaned. "I'll set up the brew in here. Now, it'll be Friday before I finish. You two can stay in my guest room, if you'd like. It's cozy, but it's free."

"That would be lovely," I replied. "Thank you. We could go buy dinner while you work..."

"Or we could look after the nursery," Connor offered. "I'm no expert, but if you need muscle and someone to run the cash register, I'm happy to help."

Lily's face lit up when she smiled. "You've got a deal. Business is slow right now, but just in case someone comes by, I'd like to keep the place open. Tomorrow? You're sure you don't mind?" she asked, looking between Connor and me.

"Not at all," he told her. "I spent my teenage summers moving stock around at the hardware store. This'll be fun."

With our plans settled, Lily told us to bring our luggage up to her cottage, which squatted on the hill just above the nursery. The guest room lay off the den to the left—and she was correct, it wasn't large—but the bed looked comfortable, and it came with its own bathroom. Connor and I settled in, and then I popped back into the greenhouse to check on things with Lily, who'd already set up a small pot and portable heater. "We're going to go down toward town and look for travel provisions," I said. "Thought we'd bring dinner back, if that's okay."

"Sure. You'll want the Walmart by the Interstate—it's a bit of a drive, but they should have what you need," she told me. "The shopping around here isn't great. As for dinner, the options in Briardale are limited, but I'd suggest getting takeout from Mabel's Place. Typical home cooking, nothing unique, but it'll hold body and soul together."

"Sounds good," I said, pulling out my phone. "Is takeout through their website directly, or do I need to use—"

"You'll need to stop in," she interrupted with a chuckle. "Mabel is a fine woman, but I wouldn't be shocked if she still uses dial-up."

Connor and I spent the afternoon prepping for a road trip of uncertain duration. My mother might be in the next county, or she might be states away...or, my oh-so-helpful doubts reminded me, she could have fled the country. Canna was sure she hadn't returned to the Pactlands, but that still left a *very* wide search area.

Still, I picked up a basic compass from the sporting goods section, added it to the cart of road snacks, and hoped for the best.

Mabel's was everything Lily had promised, an old diner outfitted with wood-paneled walls, vinyl booths, and yellowed flooring. The eponymous Mabel was on duty at the register, a woman somewhere north of sixty with a wide smile and artificially dark brown hair, and she pegged us immediately as visitors to town. I told her we were staying up at the nursery for a few days, and her face brightened with recognition. "Oh, are you helping Miz Lily? Bless you. She's spry for a woman her age, but winter ain't kind on the joints." Peering at us more closely, she asked, "Are y'all Rosie's friends?"

"From college," I fibbed, but Mabel bought my story.

"Well, isn't that nice," she said, and pressed a pair of slightly sticky menus into our hands.

We made it back up the hill about half an hour later, laden with takeout bags. Lily had left the gate unlocked, but as we pulled in, we found the nursery quiet and dark. There was no sign of the greenhouse, and the only light on the property came from a security lamp and the glow from the cottage windows.

Connor cut the engine and frowned. "Do we go in and wait, or…"

"I'll get her," I offered, and slipped out, following the gravel path to the storm shelter. At the top of the staircase, I said in Pactish, "Hi, I'm Jane. Back again. Just wanted to tell Liliol that dinner's ready."

The door appeared in front of me, and as I cracked it open, one of Sally's vines poked out from its hiding place to investigate. "Hey, girl," I murmured, patting the thick green tendril, which began to vibrate as it rubbed against my arm. "Um, Lily?" I called into the greenhouse. "We brought food—Mabel sent your usual. And, uh, is something wrong with Sally?"

"What do you mean? I'm coming," Lily said, and hastened up the aisle toward me, still unmasked. "Show me."

"Feel her." As the tip of the vine had snaked around my wrist like a bracelet by then, I lifted my arm and extended it toward Lily.

She touched the vine, then patted it, and Sally released me. "I call it her purr. She must like you. Dinner, you said?"

Only slightly disturbed by the friendly slithertrap, I followed Lily up to the cottage, where Connor had set the table and laid out the offerings. Lily tucked in appreciatively, and though she offered us beer and wine, she didn't touch it herself. "It's going to be a long night with the brew," she explained. "Please tell me one of you knows how to make coffee, because I'm going to be dead on my feet by about sunrise."

While Connor and I weren't qualified to brew potions, we were both adept with a drip coffeemaker, and we woke early to keep Lily fed and caffeinated. She moved into the greenhouse for the rest of the week, instructing us to call her business phone if there was an emergency with customers, but the only people to make the drive were a woman in need of cactus soil for her new succulents, a young couple who stopped in to buy a housewarming plant, and an old man who showed up bright and early Thursday in his ancient green Cadillac, nearly took out a cement birdbath in parking, and left just as quickly when I told him that Lily had gone on a jaunt out of town.

"That would be Jack Carpenter," she explained over dinner, which she ate standing at her table in the back of the greenhouse. "Widower. Sweet but nearly blind. He keeps hinting that he'd like to take me out, and I keep playing dumb. Suppose he has nothing better to do this time of year than try to flirt, but you'd think he'd turn his attention to one of the nice church ladies by now."

I could see the twofold problem. One, Lily had an identity and business to keep hidden, not to mention her true face. Two, while I didn't know Lily's age, I suspected that for her, dating a mere octogenarian would be tantamount to cradle robbing.

Finally, as I set the table for dinner Friday night, Lily entered the cottage with a weary but triumphant smile, carrying a vial of translucent, pale blue liquid. "Finished," she announced, "and without fireballs. I'll call this a win. Where's Connor?"

"Gone back to Mabel's," I said. "He wanted more of that chicken-fried steak, and I can't really blame him."

"Ah. Well, we can make the tracker while he's out. You've got a compass?"

I broke it free of its clamshell, and Lily turned it over in her hand, giving it a quick inspection. "This'll do. Now, the last ingredient is the bodily fluid of the person you're trying to track. Saliva *can* work, but blood is much more reliable."

"Mine's close enough, right? I know of a tracker that found a woman's daughter using her blood…"

"Oh, sure. It's how these things usually work—difficult to take samples from a missing person, yes? A parent or child will do the trick. Any further removed than that, though, and the efficacy drops off dramatically." Fishing through her cutlery drawer, she extracted a paring knife, then pulled a small bottle of rubbing alcohol and a box of band-aids from beneath the sink. "We don't need much blood, so don't worry," she said as she sanitized the blade. "You're right-handed?"

"Yes, ma'am…"

"Then give me your left."

I held out my hand, bracing myself for the cut. Instead, Lily gripped my wrist and pushed up my sleeve, then made a quick, superficial incision in the bend of my elbow. "Ever had an infusion?" she asked as blood welled up along the cut. "This is usually where the IV goes in. It'll heal up without much fuss."

Standing still, I watched while she gently squeezed my arm over the open mouth of the vial, dripping blood into the potion, which turned purple where the fluids met. "I thought you'd prick my finger or something."

"Ah, yes," she said dryly, "let's cut open one of the most highly enervated parts of your body. And only fools who think it looks dramatic slice their palms."

As I bandaged my arm, Lily recapped the vial and shook the potion to mix it, then held the compass over the sink and poured a small amount onto its face. She rubbed it until the purple disappeared, and then the compass began to glow bright blue. The needle, which had been pointing north, spun sharply toward me, and Lily nodded. "That works. Good." She gave the compass a quick wipe with a damp paper towel and handed it to me.

I held it closer, then farther away, then put the compass on the counter and moved around the room, but whatever I did, the needle followed. "Sorry, but it's stuck on me."

"Exactly," she said, putting the paring knife in the dishwasher. "It's keyed to your blood, after all."

"So, how do I use it to find my mom?"

"You need to tell it to look for the maternal component."

"Um...how?"

"How...*oh*," she said, and extended her hand. "Here, I'll show you."

Holding the compass, Lily made a few rapid gestures over the top, and the glow faded almost to nothing as the needle spun away from me. "Sometimes," she said, looking mildly sheepish as she passed it back, "I forget what it was like to be your age. Not a complicated piece of magic, but not something Yacovi would have had any need to teach you."

"Thanks," I replied. "Which way is north?"

Once Lily had oriented me, I checked the compass and found the needle pointing west. "Looks like we have a direction. Any idea how *far* west of here she is?"

Lily shook her head. "No, but I can tell you she's not close. The compass will glow brighter the closer you get— you know what it looks like at maximum proximity. More than that, I can't say."

"Hey, it's a start. And what do I owe you?" I asked. "I don't have much cash on me, but I'm happy to run to town in the morning—"

"This one's on the house," she interrupted, and squeezed my shoulder. "I got the full story from my uncle. Take the compass, find Essa, and see if she'll help you. If she testifies before the Forum, she can explain the circumstances with your father and why Yacovi did what he did."

"If I drag her back to the Pactlands, they might force

the draught on her," I countered.

"Doubtful, assuming she's not in a relationship with another human. If she's on her own and her only romantic entanglement was with your father, then where's the harm in allowing her to come home? Maybe she'd face a few years' incarceration, but I can't imagine a tribunal being too hard on her, considering her youth. My brother was...gosh, past two hundred fifty when he took the draught. He was old enough to really understand the consequences. Essa was barely more than forty, though, right?"

"That's what Dad said."

"There is still a degree of leniency for youthful indiscretion. And if Essa were to return, it might help Yacovi's case."

My gut clenched. "Have you heard anything more about it? Gerem's not going to have the votes, is he?"

Lily spread her hands. "I'm a floramancer, dear, not a farseer. But..." She hesitated, then softly said, "I find it never hurts to expect the worst."

CHAPTER 6

Connor and I were off at the crack of dawn Saturday morning, eager to be on our way. I'd offered to rent a car and continue searching on my own—after all, I had no idea how far away my mother might be—but Connor insisted on chauffeuring, for which I was quietly grateful. If nothing else, I appreciated his company.

We'd stopped at a McDonald's near the I-64 junction, and I ate my breakfast sandwich as Connor steered us toward West Virginia. The Interstate would take us west for a bit, then curve north to Charleston before turning onto a southwesterly course into Lexington. From there, I-64 cut across Kentucky, the tip of Indiana, and southern Illinois before joining I-70 around St. Louis. The compass sat in a shaded compartment on the console, its blue glow almost invisible, but I hoped that would change before long.

As I started on my hashbrown, Connor cleared his throat. "So."

"So?"

"Lily...is an elf," he said slowly.

"Yep."

"You don't seem surprised."

I shrugged. "I mean, it's not like I've met many, but I've always known they exist. And I've met her great-niece."

"That's this Rose person I keep hearing about?"

"Bingo. She came out with Annie and the others to help with the Oil of Life mess."

"I see." He mulled that over for a moment, then said, "I don't mean to sound like an asshole, but it's...a lot. All of this."

"Hey," I said, rubbing his shoulder, "it's okay. You're doing great, Con. I've been told about this stuff my whole life. You've had, like, three months. Freaking sorcerers," I began, grinning, "centaurs, Liogh—"

"I still haven't seen him unmasked.

"Them, not him, and they're green."

"*Seriously?*"

"Water nymph. Blue hair, too. *Really* long ears."

"If you say so. And then your buddy with the antlers materialized, and I mean, I'm *trying*, but—"

"It's fine. They expect you to freak out, trust me."

His mouth moved into a tight smile. "Don't think much of humans, do they?"

"Probably not," I admitted, "but the ones who've been around here know humans aren't all terrible." I paused to finish my hashbrown, then licked my fingers clean. "They could test you, you know? If you're ever interested."

"And get a target on my back from your friends on the Forum?" he retorted.

"Someday, then. Assuming Gerem calls off his dogs," I allowed. "Even if I can't legally get in there, Annie and Wylan can take passengers. All we would need to do would be to get you into the DOL building—"

"Oh, yes, let me just sneak into the *law enforcement* office—"

"Let me finish. If we could get you to Canna, she could take a blood sample and run it. You wouldn't even have to stay for the results—she could do it by phone. Easy-peasy."

"Unless I got caught."

"Well...yes."

He chuckled to himself and sped around a tanker. "You know, for now, I'm perfectly happy with being a mystery. Less chance of ending up in magical jail that way.

We bought gum, didn't we?"

I dug a pack out of the shopping bags and handed him a piece. "If you want me to drive, say the word."

"I'm awake, but thanks." Connor chewed in silence for a moment, then said, "So…this Rose person, she's a farseer? Like that guy last fall who looked back at Sage's parents?"

"Ganti ti'Van. He's at DOI."

"Which is…"

"The Division of Intelligence. They've got a group made up of farseers, and their director is future-oriented, so…"

He frowned. "Oriented?"

"They only see in one direction. Ganti is backward-oriented—give him a focus, and he can look at the past. The future-oriented folks apparently see probable outcomes, but I sure as hell don't know the details. And then there's Rose, who sees what's currently going on. Present orientation. That's why Lily wanted her assigned to check on the nursery, to make sure none of Gerem's people were lurking."

"You think Rose is tracking us." It wasn't a question.

"Probably," I admitted, "though I can't imagine that she'd lead Gerem to us. She's at DPP, anyway, so I suppose Pateme could shelter her somewhat if the Forum came calling. What concerns me is her great-grandfather."

"Oh?"

"Yeah, the aforementioned DOI director. I *know* he's aware of me because he told the director of DOL not to prosecute Dad."

"Do you think he knows how this'll play out?"

I shrugged. "Can't say. I've never spoken to him, anyway, and the impression I get is that it's not wise to cold-call farseers and ask for hints about your future."

Connor snorted. "Well, now, *that's* convenient."

"What's the point in being a seer if you can't make enigmatic pronouncements on your own terms?" I teased.

"True, I guess." He waited while a pack of early-morning motorcyclists sped past, then slipped behind them to get around a loaded U-Haul. "Since there's a chance that people are looking in on you, is there any way to stop them? Tinfoil hat?"

"I wish," I said, crumpling up the breakfast bag and tucking it down at my feet. "There's a potion—"

"We couldn't have bought it from Lily?"

"No, and it wouldn't have done us any good. Blinding potion is expensive, and once you've got your hands on it, you need a sorcerer and an elf working in tandem to make it take effect. Allegedly, it hides you from farsight until it wears off in a few months, but I've never tried it. And before you ask," I continued as his mouth started to open, "I don't know the spells required to put the potion to work. That's higher-level stuff. Look, I'm great at setting things on fire, but I'm not the most *technical* sorcerer, if you catch my drift."

"I see. So, other than this potion, is there any way to hide? What's plan B?"

"We cross our fingers and hope we're boring."

The land continued to rise toward the peaks of the Allegheny Mountains, higher than the near-foothills of my hometown but still somewhat familiar. As the SUV chugged along up and down the Interstate, the West Virginia state line sign came into view, and Connor glanced over to grin at me. "I feel a little John Denver coming on."

Before I could tell him it was too early for a singalong, even one so thematically synchronized, my phone rang. "It's Tabitha," I said, and tapped the screen to put her on speaker. "Hey, there. What's up?"

"Oh, just another day in paradise," she replied. "Are y'all okay?"

"We're fine. How are things in town?"

She huffed a sigh. "Your dad still has company."

"*Shit.*"

"Yeah. I've been driving by morning and night, and those vehicles haven't budged."

"Do they really think I'm stupid enough to go by the house?" I griped.

"Don't know, but I *can* tell you it's not safe to come home yet. Wherever you are, I hope there's a heated pool and a swim-up bar."

"Ooh," Connor interjected, "that *would* be nice…"

"No such luck," I told her. "You don't think they've noticed you?"

"I mean, I'm no psychic, but since I've been driving by at the same times every day this week, they have no reason to suspect me."

Leaning toward the phone, I said, "You're the best. Just promise me you'll be careful."

"Will do. Tell you the truth, I'm kind of enjoying this espionage gig," said Tabitha. "Since I hear traffic, happy trails, wherever you are."

Once we'd signed off, I leaned back into my seat and stared out at the mountains, the sun casting long shadows ahead of us. "Just curious," said Connor, "but any change on the compass?"

I pulled it from its nook and checked the needle. "Negative."

"In that case, mind if I turn on the radio?"

"You drive," I said, reaching for the dial. "I'll find something that isn't conspiracy theories or gospel."

We stopped for the night outside St. Louis, having covered more than seven hundred miles. The compass was only slightly brighter, and though Connor didn't complain, I could tell he was flagging. He pulled off at an exit with several motels, and I rented a room for the night—one with two queen beds. Though I hadn't minded bunking with him at Lily's, I didn't want to presume, especially as I had a bad habit of waking in a cocoon of blankets I'd tugged around myself overnight.

I slept surprisingly deeply, and when I came to on Sunday morning, it was to the gurgling of the single-serving coffeemaker in the bathroom. Connor padded out a moment later, wearing a T-shirt and boxers, and lifted his mug in salute as I sleepily waved. "She's alive," he whispered.

"She's comfy," I mumbled.

He sat at the foot of my bed while I untangled myself and held out the compass, the blue glow of which was visible in the dark room. "Still pointing west. We've got to figure out where to go from here."

I grunted my agreement, and the two of us unpacked our computers. Ignoring the notifications of new messages on my business account, I opened the browser to a map and considered the collection of thicker and thinner lines running across the continent. "Any preference?" I asked.

Connor, who'd set up camp at the room's lone desk, said, "Zoom out to the multistate view with me. We've got options. I assume the compass needle will move eventually, but let's pretend we need to head due west for now. That puts us aiming roughly at San Francisco, yeah? A little north of that. So, plugging that in…" He bounced one leg as he studied the results. "Okay, we could take I-70 all the way to Denver, then pick up I-25 to I-80 through Wyoming, Utah, Nevada, and down into California. It'll make a more northerly arc once we hit Denver, but there's no better western route from there—either we stay on 70 and still end up going through Salt Lake City, or else we're stuck with I-15 all the way to the coast, and that'll take us to LA. Wrong end of the state."

"I-70 to I-80 sounds reasonable," I said, tracking the route on my screen.

"Yeah, but it concerns me a little. That leg from Denver to Salt Lake City goes right through the Rockies.

My Santa Fe is all-wheel drive, and the tires are only six months old, so I think we're okay...but if there's major icing, I'm not sure. I've driven in winter weather in the Blue Ridge, of course, but the *Rockies*..."

A quick search revealed a host of cautionary tales and travel restrictions on that corridor. "Do you even have chains?"

"Actually, yes—they're in the back with the jump box and the bungees—and we've got enough food and such if we got stuck. If it came down to it, I trust that you could start a fire," he added with a half-smile. "But there's another option: I-70 to Kansas City, then we pick up I-80 in Lincoln. It avoids Denver, arcs north through Wyoming, and then hits Salt Lake City, as before."

Again, I searched for hazards and came up with plenty. "It says here that stretch through Wyoming sometimes closes due to wind *alone*, not to mention the snow. And no matter where we pick up I-80, we'll have to go through Donner Summit in California if we do end up all the way on the coast, and that place looks like it gets gnarly. It's got its own tire and chain requirements, too."

Connor sighed. "So, it's risk cannibalism or drive to LA?"

"Donner *Summit*, not Pass...oh, never mind, they're close," I muttered. "What do you think?"

"How about the forecast? Are we due for snow along the route?"

I quickly switched sites to check. "Not for the next five days. Maybe next weekend."

He was quiet for a moment as he considered that, then leaned back in his chair and folded his hands behind his neck. "I'm thinking I-80. It's the most northerly, but it'll avoid Denver."

"You're sure?"

"No, but if conditions deteriorate, I'm not too proud to turn back." He stood and pushed his messy hair from his face. "I've got you, Firebug. Don't worry. And hey, for all we know, your mom could be hanging out in, like, Nebraska."

"Maybe," I said, trying to think positively, but my pessimistic gut insisted she was probably halfway to Japan.

The compass brightened incrementally, but the needle remained stuck on the west all day. Even when we stopped and aligned ourselves with the sun to check, it pointed stubbornly in the same direction, insisting that we still had a ways to go.

Connor pushed himself hard, trying to take advantage of the decent weather while it held, but he called a halt while we were in western Nebraska after a grueling twelve hours on the road. I-80 remained passable, but it wasn't exactly *clear*, and neither of us wanted to risk hitting black ice after sunset and spinning into a ditch.

"I'm sorry," he said, picking at his chow mein. I'd suggested Chinese for our late dinner, and Connor had finally relinquished the wheel to me for the quick drive into town. "I'd hoped to make Cheyenne, but—"

"You do *not* owe me an apology," I insisted, reaching across the booth to take his free hand. "At all. I'm the one who's dragged you halfway across the damn country on a wild goose chase."

He held my gaze. "We're going to find her. Promise. Even if we have to camp with the freaking Donner Party, we'll find your mom." Rummaging through his noodles for a piece of chicken, he said, "We're going to track her down, maybe chew her out for *making* us track her down—"

"I feel that."

"Right? And then...what? Take her out for coffee, have a little mother-daughter time? Go bonding?"

I laughed to myself. "Uh, *no*. My plan is to tell her about Dad and drag her sorry ass back to the Pactlands. Lily thinks it might help his chances, especially if she hasn't married another human. If I can get her home, and the only resulting problem is me, then—"

"Janie, you are not a problem."

"Current circumstances would suggest otherwise, but thanks. Anyway, that's as far as I've gotten. Any suggestions?"

He ate in silence for a moment, mulling it over. "What if she refuses to go?"

"Yeah," I mumbled, "that's the big issue."

"You don't think you could take her?"

"She's a well-educated sorcerer with agency training. Probably not. And while I'm not suggesting you shoot her in the leg or anything…"

"Now, that would be a terrible way to meet my girlfriend's mother."

"Some mother," I said, and bit into my eggroll. "Honestly, I just want to know *why*. She must have loved Aaron—my bio-dad," I clarified when his brow furrowed—"and I'm a piece of him, right? Maybe she needed to get her head on straight or get a job or something, but she just…walked away. Poof, no more kid. And I *love* Dad, don't get me wrong, but—"

"It's okay."

I sighed and reached for my grassy green tea, the handle-less ceramic cup almost too hot to touch. "I shouldn't give her this much mental real estate. She doesn't deserve it. But—"

"I get it," Connor said gently. "However you want to justify it, she abandoned you. And you can rationalize that, but between your mother and those assholes in the Pactlands, I wouldn't be surprised if there's some part of you stuck wondering why you're not good enough."

My eyes pricked, and I sipped the scalding brew to buy time.

"I'm here to tell you that you *are* good enough," he continued. "Okay? You don't have to believe me, but I wish you would. Because I am…*grateful* to have you in my life," he said, his grip firm on my hand. "I mean that with all sincerity, Janie. And if it comes down to it and I need to punch a fucking wizard for you, I'll do it."

I smiled despite my watery eyes. "Sorcerer."

"Whatever. That includes your mom if she gives you any trouble. I'll slap the bracelets on her and haul her all the way to that portal thingy in South Carolina if I have to."

"Pretty sure that'd be illegal, babe," I whispered.

"Well, since I can't tell the local cops that I need to arrest a *sorcerer*, we'll play this by ear."

I squeezed his hand and released him. "Let's get you to bed first, cowboy. We can scheme again once you've slept."

With no movement in the compass overnight, we pushed on Monday morning for the trek across Wyoming.

The drive, which should have taken about eight hours, wound up as ten between a jackknifed semi and a few ice-driven slowdowns. The Laramie Mountains were less treacherous than I'd feared, but deep drifts of windblown snow on both sides of the road past the town of Laramie served as a reminder of the conditions we could face. I'd been watching the weather, and while the early part of the week seemed fair, the forecast called for a wet system moving in from the Pacific and snow up and down the Rockies come Friday. Wherever we were going, I wanted to get out of the mountains as quickly—and safely—as we could, as the Rockies made their far older eastern cousins look like hills by comparison.

I received a text from Tabitha that morning—no change at Dad's house—but the surprise of the day came after a brief stop for lunch around Rawlins: a call from an unknown number with a 762 area code.

"Who's that?" Connor asked, rooting through the chewing gum cup for a fresh piece.

"Don't know. Probably a telemarketer," I said, but took the call anyway. "Hello?"

"Jane?" asked a female voice on the other end. "Jane, is that you?"

It took me a beat to recognize the speaker: Stephanie Love, the proprietor of Mystic Mountains and a large part of the reason why much of the witchy side of Ragged Gap loathed me. "Uh...Stephanie?" I replied, unable to keep the confusion from my voice. "Everything okay?"

"I don't think so. You've got stalkers."

Shit. "What do you mean?"

"I'm not sure—they didn't leave business cards," she replied—"but these three guys came in a few minutes ago and asked about you."

Playing dumb seemed like the best idea. "*Me?*"

"Yeah. Wanted to know if I could tell them where to find a witch named Jane. I said I had no idea."

People around Ragged Gap had come to me with their major problems ever since I moved home after college—it wasn't that odd for someone to seek me out, and something told me that Stephanie had gritted her teeth more than once when a desperate soul came to her shop, looking for me. "You didn't send them to my house?"

"No. Not this crew," she said. "They're not from around here, for one. *Weird* accents. I couldn't place them if I tried."

Pars had told me that the agencies kept linguists on staff to assist agents who'd acquired languages from potions. Learning English might be as simple as downing a drink, but learning to sound like a native took time and practice. I suspected that the Forum didn't offer the same resource to its people.

"Didn't see the vehicles or anything?"

"No. Just three men in long-sleeved polo shirts and khakis. It almost looked like a uniform, and I could tell they were freezing—definitely underdressed for the mountains. Uh...let me think, one white, one black, one who might have been Middle Eastern? No facial hair, but two of them had ponytails. Sorry, I can't do any better than that. But you might want to be careful," she continued. "If someone mentions your business…is your address on your website?"

"No," I said—fortunately, I'd invested in a P.O. box. "And thanks. But why didn't you send them to me?"

Stephanie sighed quietly. "Look, Jane, I know I've been a bitch to you. I've…had time to dwell with what happened last fall. With, um, Oil of Life. You know?"

What I wanted to say was, *You mean the time I saved you and your followers from being an unlicensed sorcerer's drugged drones, and you let everyone think I stole magic from them?* Instead, I replied, "Yeah, I remember."

"What I did was shitty. Things could have ended *really* fucking badly, and I was embarrassed, and—"

"It's okay," I heard myself say. "It's over."

"It's not okay," Stephanie insisted. "You've never done me wrong, and I've treated you poorly. Because…well, let's be honest," she mumbled, "I'm jealous, but you also kind of scare me. But that doesn't matter—I should have been a better neighbor to you. To a fellow practitioner."

I didn't mention that Stephanie's idea of magic was so far from mine that the two had virtually nothing in common. The fact that she was extending an olive branch was almost miraculous.

"Thank you," I told her.

"Yeah, sure. Anyway, I just didn't like the look of those guys today. They gave me a weird vibe. That's not the sort of group that wanders in here, and something told me they don't need to know where you are. So…is there some reason why you'd have stalkers?"

I hesitated, formulating my response, then said, "I can't tell you what's going on right now, but I'm not in Ragged Gap at the moment, and you need to avoid those men. Pass the word. Your people will be safer if they don't know me, got it?"

"I...okay. Yeah, I'll do that," said Stephanie. "Are you all right?"

"Just fine."

"Well, um...be careful," she blurted. "If they come back, do you want me to call you?"

"Please. And thanks, Stephanie. I mean it."

When I hung up, I stared at the phone for a moment, not quite believing that Stephanie, of all people, would give me a heads-up. But that quickly gave way to my concern about the fresh development.

"Who was *that*?" Connor asked.

"Stephanie Love from Mystic Mountains," I replied.

He frowned. "I thought you two avoided each other."

"She feels bad, and it sounds like she just got a visit from Gerem's posse, so..."

"Shit," he grunted. "You sure?"

"Three strange men with weird accents, hanging out together in polos and khakis and no coats in *February*, wandering into the crystal and incense shop on a random Monday afternoon?"

"They sound underdressed, for starters."

"Because the Pactlands is much more temperate. These guys may never have experienced true winter. Anyway, Stephanie's internal alarms went off, and she didn't tell them where I live, but that still means they're looking for me."

"But they haven't found you," Connor pointed out. "Guess they don't have a tracker if they're poking around Ragged Gap."

"True...unless they split up."

He reached over the cupholders and gripped my hand. "*If* they're following us, then they'll have to navigate the Rockies, won't they? You think these sorcerers or whatever who don't even have sense enough to pack a coat can manage chains?"

"Probably not," I allowed.

"Then we've still got a solid head start," said Connor,

and turned his attention back to the traffic.

But as we trekked westward toward the Utah line, I kept a potential problem to myself.

I didn't know where the portals were out there. If my pursuers got a lead on me, they might be able to lie in wait.

Trying not to catastrophize, I leaned my head against the cold window and watched as the snow-covered wilderness rolled past.

CHAPTER 7

By Tuesday morning, the compass was unmistakably brighter, but it continued to be stuck on west—not northwest or southwest, nothing to show that we were close enough for finer directions to be an option. I found it disheartening, but I felt for Connor, who was faced with the Utah leg of I-80.

At least the skiers who flocked to Park City were getting their money's worth. Snow blanketed the mountains along the route, and between the sensible drivers taking it slowly along the route and the tourists searching for scenic pull-offs, what my phone calculated as a three-hour trip turned into five. We stopped for lunch just over the Nevada border, and while the map warned of more mountains once we left the Great Salt Lake Desert, I had hopes for a less white-knuckled drive.

Even in Nevada, the compass remained fixed on the west, though I spun in circles outside our car to try to dislodge the needle. With no better lead, Connor and I pushed on.

As he slowed to give room to a pair of barreling semis, Connor said, "I still can't believe that Essa would leave without any explanation. I'm not doubting you," he quickly insisted, glancing my way, "but...you know, I was fortunate to have great parents, and the thought of my mom up and disappearing like that is pretty much unfathomable."

"Lucky you," I said with a little smile.

"That's insensitive, and I'm sorry—"

"No, it's okay. And I'm glad you had them. I mean, it sucks now that they're gone, but at least you knew them well enough to miss them. Dad's got a photo of Mom, and he says he kept her goodbye note, but I can't bring myself to go digging through her things."

"She left stuff for you?"

"She left stuff—whether it was for me or she was just using Dad's place as storage is up for debate. But yeah, Dad put it all in a closet for me whenever I want it. I...I'm not there yet," I said, "because this irrational part of me insists that if I don't read her note, she really isn't gone, and she could come back for me at any moment. Stupid, I know, but I've kept hoping all this time. And instead," I muttered, "since she obviously had no intention of coming back for me, now I'm hunting *her*. Thanks for nothing, Mom."

Connor reached over and briefly squeezed my shoulder. "What about your dad's people?"

"Yacovi's or Aaron's?"

"Fair," he replied, chuckling. "Okay, start with Yacovi's."

"No immediately family left. Dad's parents started pretty late, so they've passed on. He's the youngest of three, but his brother died in a brewing explosion when he was forty-two, I think, and his sister died in childbirth. No nieces or nephews, never married. He probably has cousins, but he doesn't talk about them. I always got the sense that Dad was married to his job when he was at DPP, and after he retired, he got saddled with me. So, it's not like I have some big adopted family waiting for me in the Pactlands. My cousin told me..." I paused to count back the days. "God, was that a *week* ago? Anyway, Canna said she'd broken the news of my existence to my maternal family, and some of them were excited to meet me, but the only part of that family I've met is Canna's."

Conor nodded. "What's the story on Aaron's family, then?"

"Hell if I know," I said, and shrugged. "Essa never told Dad about Aaron's people—he was just this kid bartending near the greenhouse. I don't know if he had folks living around there or was estranged, a foster, adopted…it's a blank. There could be a whole town full of Fortunes, and I wouldn't know." Rooting through the gum pack, I said, "I suppose I could go to Virginia and try to look up his birth certificate. Maybe I'd find cousins or something—maybe even grandparents. Online DNA is out of the question."

"Understandable."

"I've just never had the urge to go digging," I continued. "If I found his family, how would I explain myself? 'Hi, I'm Aaron's kid. No, I won't take a blood test. And oh, did you know Aaron's dead? You didn't? *Yikes.*'" I shook my head. "If he wasn't close enough to them to have them in his life when he was with Essa, then I suspect they'd have little use for me. He may have gone no contact, for all I know." I chewed for a bit, letting the mint flavor exhaust itself, then said, "I do wish I had a picture of him. There may be one buried in Mom's things at Dad's house."

"Or maybe she can give you one when we find—oh, shit, sorry," muttered Connor, pulling out of a skid on a patch of black ice. "Surely she has pictures of him."

"I hope. She owes me that much, right? I'm grown, I don't need a mommy, but she owes me the truth. And she owes Dad *big* time."

We sat in silence for a few minutes, listening to the rock station, and then Connor asked, "Have you thought about what you're going to say?"

"Say?"

"To your mother. Do you have a speech prepared? 'Hello, my name is Jane Fortune, you dumped me with my father, prepare to talk'?"

"Not exactly," I replied, cracking a smile. "Guess it all depends on what she's done with herself. Like, did she move out into a cabin in the woods? Hippie commune? Cult? Or did she marry again and have another family? I...I don't think it'd be as bad if she's living alone, but if she started over and had more kids, but she never came back for *me*..."

"We'll play it by ear, then," said Connor. "And maybe she'll surprise you. Maybe she's got a damn good reason for not coming back. Like...I don't know, is there a magical version of the plague or something?"

"No. We don't tend to get as sick as humans, either. Well, I say *we*," I muttered. "Legally, we know where I shake out."

"That's bullshit. You literally throw fireballs—how the hell would anyone classify you as human?"

"The vote of confidence is appreciated. But, uh...I'm still close enough for you, right?"

"You listen to me, ma'am," he murmured, cutting his pretty eyes to me for a second before returning his focus to the messy stretch of road. "I don't give a damn *what* you are. *Who* you are is much more important."

"What did I do to deserve you, huh?"

"Are you kidding? I'm the one with the scarily talented girlfriend who more or less overlooks the 'kissing cousin' situation in my extended family. I got *lucky*."

"Seriously."

"*And* she's hot."

"Connor Willow, I have never been hot in my life."

"Solid dime."

"Six on a good day," I countered, but grinned at him. "Thanks for trying."

He smiled back at me. "Hey, if it keeps you hanging out, I'd say it works."

We overnighted west of Reno, just on the Nevada side of the California border. While we'd only covered about six hundred miles that day, the drive had been long and slow, and Connor didn't complain when I suggested pulling off for dinner and calling it a night.

I hadn't looked at the compass for a few hours, and as we settled in at the diner attached to our motel, I pulled it from my purse and examined it under the table. The glow was definitely brighter—at least we were on the right track, I mused. "Con, which way is north?" I whispered once the waiter had taken our drink order.

He pulled out his phone and opened the compass app he'd downloaded, then pointed straight at me.

"Thanks." I aligned the compass and squinted at the reading. "Holy shit."

"It's moved?" he asked.

I nodded. "Northwest. We're too far south."

"But we're *close*." He beamed as I packed the compass away. "Eat quickly. We've got homework tonight."

Back in our room, we forwent unpacking in favor of pulling out our computers to check the potential routes. "Okay," said Connor, taking a pull from his to-go Coke, "the good news is that we're avoiding Donner Summit. The bad is that we're leaving the Interstate, and we'll need to backtrack." He turned his computer toward me and began pointing to the secondary roads. "If we want to go northwest, the quickest route's going to be U.S. 395. We double back to Reno, pick that up, and follow it into California…and then we have to make a choice. We can stay with 395, which runs a bit to the north before we take Route 44, or we can pick up Route 70. Either one will get us roughly to the northwest of here, but I don't have any clear idea of which would be better."

I pursed my lips and studied the screen. "Using 395 would probably be faster. Might be a wider road, anyway."

He nodded. "What's the weather like tomorrow?"

"The models say it's deteriorating. Rain at least, maybe snow at elevation."

Connor considered the map again, then grunted. "I think you're right about 395. Time is *not* our friend if we have to drive back through a snowstorm."

I tried to imagine how that would work: Connor and me in the front, my mother perhaps handcuffed in the back, making a slow, slippery haul through the Rockies with an angry sorcerer...

"Maybe she's nearer than we think," I said, though with the profusion of national forests in our path, I suspected we still had a long ways to go.

Neither of us slept well, and so we hit the road shortly after five Wednesday morning, heading to Reno before making the turn back into California. Once we found 395, I kept the compass close, watching the needle jiggle and periodically comparing it to Connor's compass app. By the time we hit Route 44, the compass had shifted to west-northwest, only for the road to veer away from our desired direction. We didn't have many options, however, so Connor pressed on until Route 44 entered Redding, the largest town we'd seen since leaving Reno. Bypassing I-5, a north-south route, we drove on, the compass steadily brightening and the needle coaxing us ever so slightly north of due west. Connor pulled off for a snack and gas, but I couldn't bring myself to eat—my stomach was in knots as I imagined the end of our westward journey. Would we find Essa at home? At work? Maybe chaperoning a school fieldtrip for a half sibling I'd never met?

What *would* I say to her?

And would she even recognize me? Surely not—I'd been a month old when she left—but all the same, part of me pictured my mother locking eyes with me and *knowing* who I was.

An hour later, the promised rain had begun to fall, a light but steady drizzle from a leaden sky, when my phone rang—not Tabitha, as I'd anticipated, but Stephanie again. Putting the compass aside, I took the call, staring out the window at the rolling hills, scrubby pines, and winter-brown underbrush. "This is Jane."

"It's Stephanie. Bad news, I'm afraid."

She sounded genuinely distressed, which boded nothing good. "What do you mean?"

"So...you know Ernie Flores, right? Works in my café?"

I didn't know him to have a friendly chat, but I'd cured him of the potion controlling his mind and left him puking in a blender, which was close enough. "Sure..."

"Well, uh..." She huffed a sigh. "Ernie still hasn't forgiven you for the Oil of Life thing," she said, picking up speed, "and before I could tell him not to say anything about you to anyone we don't know, he...um..."

"Just tell me."

"He went to Junior's, apparently, and had too much to drink, and when someone starting talking to him at the bar—might have been one of those guys who came to the store, but Ernie sure as hell can't say—he ran his mouth. All he remembers is that the guy on the next stool asked where to find you, and he pulled your address out of his phone."

"Why the heck does Ernie have *my* address?" I demanded.

Stephanie hesitated. "Last fall, when tempers were still high, there was talk about going to confront you en masse. I shot it down," she quickly added. "Told folks it was a bad idea, dangerous. They got the hint. But I suppose Ernie never deleted your information, and he gave it to the guy."

"Shit," I muttered, rubbing my head. "And he remembers nothing else?"

"No. But if I were you, I might stay out of town for a few more days. Friendly warning."

On one level, that wasn't so bad—once we grabbed Essa, we could skip right past home and make for the Central portal. On the other, Gerem's people now knew where I lived, which meant I couldn't show my face in Ragged Gap without a guarantee that they wouldn't come after me.

Great.

"Thanks," I told Stephanie. "Tell Ernie…it's okay," I forced myself to say. "Just don't talk to strangers for now."

She apologized again before hanging up, and I stuck the phone in the empty drink holder with a sigh. "Ernie Flores needs to learn to shut his trap," I muttered. "He told them where my house is."

Connor swore under his breath, then tightened his grip on the wheel. "Guy's a blabbermouth, but there's nothing we can do about it right now. If need be, you can stay with me—you know I've got room. How's the compass?"

I pulled it out of its resting place and gasped. "Stop the car."

He swerved onto the gravel shoulder and slammed on his flashers. "What's wrong?"

"Look," I said, shoving it into his hand. "Check that, but I think it's changed direction."

He consulted his phone and the bright compass, then laughed deep in his throat. "Southeast. We've overshot the runway."

There wasn't an easy turnaround on the two-lane road—not with a mountain on one side and a river on the other—but Connor managed it and drove in the other direction. "Keep an eye on the compass and tell me when it starts to drift," he instructed.

The compass reacted once we were past the turnoff for a town called Leighfield, and we turned once again, narrowing our sweep. Connor slowed as he drove through the wet, quiet roads, looking for movement from the compass in my hand. We passed rafting outfitters, an RV park, a motel, and a volunteer fire department, and then he turned again, trying to box in the signal to which the compass was tuned.

My heart raced as we drove by small houses and

modest businesses. Could my mother be living in one of those homes? Working at the diner by the motel? Maybe she was a clerk at the gas station.

But as Connor's circles tightened on their target, I noticed that we seemed to be driving past a fenced-off plot of brown grass—a cemetery, I realized, spotting the low gravestones beneath the leafless trees.

No, I insisted to my rising panic. No, there was no way my mother was in *there*.

Or maybe she was a groundskeeper, I reasoned. She wasn't a floramancer like Dad, but with her résumé, surely she had the skills to keep the place looking tidy...

Connor circled the cemetery twice, and the needle spun to follow it. Pulling over by the gate, he softly said, "Janie..."

"*No*," I rasped, my voice cracking, and jumped out of the SUV.

The cold rain soaked my hair and the fleece jacket I'd worn in the car—warm, but hardly waterproof—while I followed the compass through the rows of graves, irrationally hoping I'd find my mother napping behind one. But no, the needle turned again, and I zeroed in on a simple gray stone marker, arched at the top but otherwise utilitarian.

JANE DOE, it read. 3-7-1995.

I was just shy of thirteen months old then.

As I stared down at the grave, the compass brilliant blue in my hand, I gradually sensed a presence at my right shoulder and turned to find Connor standing there, holding a golf umbrella above us both. "Aw, Janie, I'm sorry," he murmured. "I'm *so* sorry..."

My eyes blurred, and the rain in my face had nothing to do with it. I pressed myself against his chest, and Connor held me while my shock gave way to grief.

My mother hadn't come for me because she'd remarried and set up a fabulous new life in a seaside mansion, as I'd sometimes imagined. She wasn't a glamorous jetsetter. She hadn't slipped back to the Pactlands under an alias. And she wasn't living alone in a little cottage somewhere, pining for the daughter she'd given up and desperate for a way to make things right.

She was dead. She'd *been* dead for almost twenty-seven years. And she would never come for me.

I cried until I felt empty and Connor's jacket was wet beneath my face.

No Essa. All that way for nothing. I couldn't force her into the Pactlands to speak for Dad. Couldn't ask her the questions I'd been living with since I was old enough to understand that I had a mother, yes, but somewhere not *here*.

And I'd have to tell Canna. She loved her older cousin, and I'd given her hope that Essa might still be alive and well…

Oh, *God*, someone would have to break it to Essa's parents. All I'd brought to their lives was embarrassment and pain…

Pulling myself together, I stepped out of Connor's arms and ineffectively wiped my soggy sleeve over my face. "Sorry."

"No, hon, it's okay," he said, moving closer again to keep the rain off me. "Jesus, Janie, I…I don't know what to say…"

"Do you have your phone? I left mine in the car."

He pulled his from his pocket, and I crouched by my mother's gravestone with the glowing tracker in my hand. "Proof of death," I quietly explained, and snapped a few pictures. Rising, I returned it to him and stuffed the tracker into my jacket. "Well, *fuck*."

"We can stay here for a while, if you'd like," he offered. "Or go find somewhere warmer—"

"Excuse me!" interrupted a voice from the other side of the fence, low-pitched but older and female.

I looked past Connor to see another SUV parked beside ours—one bearing markings from what had to be the local sheriff's department. A woman with salt-and-pepper hair sat in the driver's seat, sporting a tan dress shirt that screamed *law enforcement* even without her ride.

"Is everything all right?" she called.

To my relief, Connor took the lead. "Yes, ma'am!" he called back, and deliberately eased his hand into his pocket to retrieve his wallet, which he opened to show the flash of the badge within. "Sorry, we didn't mean to trespass," he said, and guided me toward her vehicle.

The deputy seemed to relax as we neared. "LEO?"

"Back in Georgia," he said, laying the *aw, shucks, ma'am* accent on a little thickly. "PD."

"*Ah.* You two are a long way from home."

"Taking a road trip before the spring break crazies. We both had time, and we're headed to see the redwoods," he lied. "Kind of a spur-of-the-moment thing. We were in Reno and saw how close we were, relatively speaking, so—"

"Oh, sure. Pick up 101—it's a nice drive. Are you, uh…cemetery buffs?" she asked with an arched brow.

"Not exactly. We've been on the road, and we wanted to stretch our legs, and I was looking for a park but found this place. Sorry, we didn't mean any harm—"

"It's public, you're fine. Just don't get many tourists here for anything but camping and rafting. Well, drive safely," she said with a nod. "Maybe dry off first, huh? Get yourselves a cup of coffee to take off the chill."

"We just might," said Connor, chuckling, but sobered quickly. "Hey, question. I saw your Jane Doe in there. Know anything about her? Homicide?"

The deputy grimaced. "Roadside accident. I remember *that* one. It was dark, and one of the tourists came around a corner too quickly. She was hitchhiking, we think. Didn't have much on her. He was pulling a camper and couldn't stop in time."

I tightened my arms, willing my facial muscles to freeze.

"No ID?" Connor asked.

"Nope. She had a driver's license, but it was a fake—we ran it. Only other personal thing on her was a picture of a man and a baby. No names or anything, and no wedding ring."

That wasn't altogether surprising. Dad had said that wedding rings weren't traditional in the Pactlands, and if my parents were as broke as Dad had suggested, I couldn't see them wasting the money.

"We put her picture in the paper, but no dice. Sheriff at the time wanted to have her cremated, but his wife insisted on a burial, just in case anyone ever came looking for her. It's sad," she said, gazing past us into the cemetery. "She was young, pretty, no drugs in her system. I'm sure someone misses her, but short of exhuming her and trying to pull DNA, we don't have any way to find her family."

If only you knew, I thought dully, while Connor made enough small talk to send her on her way. By the time the deputy drove off, he'd picked up a few suggestions for places to grab a bite, but though the hour was nearing noon, I couldn't imagine eating.

So, Connor sat with me in his SUV with the heater blasting while I shivered in my wet clothes and tried to make sense of my options.

My biological parents had been dead for most of my life. My dad was imprisoned in the Pactlands, and even if he were allowed out of custody, he couldn't return to Georgia. Gerem's men were still camping at Dad's house, and now that they knew where I lived, I *really* couldn't go home.

I had Connor—and God, I was grateful for him—but otherwise, I was on my own.

After a time, as I began to warm, I said, "I need to tell Canna."

Connor couldn't understand Pactish, but he sat there and held my hand while I dialed my cousin and hoped I wasn't interrupting her time with a patient. She answered almost immediately, however, her tone a mixture of excitement and fear. "Jane! Are you all right?"

"I'm safe," I said. "Can't tell you where I am so I can stay that way—"

"I understand, don't worry. Rose says there are men at your dad's house?"

I supposed Lily had given her the scoop. "Yeah, which is why I'm not there. Listen, Canna—"

"If there's something we can do to help, tell me. I know Pars wouldn't mind sneaking out."

"That's sweet of you," I said, touched by the offer, "but don't take any risks. Canna...I found Essa."

"You did?" She perked at the news. "That's wonderful! Where's she been hiding?"

"She hasn't. She...she died when I was little. I found her grave."

Silence echoed through the phone, but only for a shocked second.

"Oh, sweetheart," Canna murmured, falling into full mothering mode. "I'm so sorry. Are you...oh, *Jane*..."

"She got hit by a car," I said, the words somehow easier when rendered into Pactish—stranger, less attached to me. "No real ID, and no one claimed her, so they buried her nearby. I'm sorry, I know you loved her—"

"This is not about me," Canna interrupted. "Heavens know I'd be there if they'd let me out—"

"I'm not alone. And, uh...I'm okay for now," I told her, which wasn't entirely false. Honestly, I felt like someone else was piloting my body. "But the rest of her family needs to know, and I don't have anyone's number, so could you..."

It wasn't fair to ask Canna to deliver the news, but I saw no better option.

"Of course," she said softly. "Take care of yourself. *Call me*. Pars and I have been worried sick about you."

With assurances that I'd be in touch, I hung up and put the phone away. "What now?" I asked Connor, closing my eyes. "I'm out of good ideas."

"In all honesty, I could go for a nap. Been a long morning."

I cracked open one eye and tried to smile at him. "You want some food first?"

"Nah, we've still got snacks in the back. Recline your seat. We're not bothering anyone here."

Once I'd adjusted my position, Connor turned off the engine, then draped his emergency blanket over me. "Get some rest," he said, and kissed my forehead. "I'm not going anywhere."

A car isn't the most comfortable place to nap, but the steady rain and the exhaustion brought on by the combination of restless nights in motel rooms and our fresh discovery worked together to lull me to sleep. But my rest only lasted about an hour before my phone started ringing, and I groaned as I groped for it in the cup holder. Canna again.

"Hey," I croaked. "Sorry, did I forget something?"

"Did I *wake* you?"

"It's been a long week."

"I can imagine. Sorry, dear. But here, I've got someone who wants to speak to you."

I could hear the shuffling noises of the phone changing hands, and then a voice that sounded somewhat older than Canna's but not particularly aged flowed through the speaker. "Jane?"

"Hello?"

A soft sob escaped her, but she kept it together. "Jane, darling, this is your grandmother."

I froze, then started to sit up and remembered the seat wouldn't budge with the power off. "Um...I'm really sorry about Essa," I said, my voice cracking despite my best efforts. "We tried to find her with a tracker, and it...I'm sorry," I repeated lamely. How did you properly convey your condolences to someone who'd just lost a child? "She's been gone for twenty-seven years, so that's why she's never called you—"

"My poor youngling," she said, sounding like she was still on the verge of crying, "I'm so sorry."

That was all it took to send me over the edge, and the spring of tears I thought I'd drained burst forth once more. She joined me, this grandmother who was still just a nameless voice in my ear, and though Connor couldn't understand, he leaned over to hold me.

Once I could speak again, I said, "If it's any consolation, I think she went pretty quickly. May not have known what hit her."

But my grandmother wasn't in the mood to be consoled. "Don't give up," she said, a steel edge creeping into her tone. "Don't you dare give up. We *will* find a way to bring you home."

"It's okay, you don't have to—"

"You are my granddaughter. Your grandfather is sitting right here, nodding along," she added. "We lost our daughter years ago, and we're not losing you as well."

"Damn the Forum," a male voice said in the background. "We're going to make this right. That Aniap—"

"Is dangerous," I interrupted. "He's got people lying in wait in my town, asking how to find me."

"Are you serious?" my grandmother demanded.

"I've got eyes and ears there, and they wouldn't lie to me about this. Listen, don't put yourselves at risk, okay? Please. I'll be fine, I'm all right, I just want my dad free—"

"As do we," she said, surprising me. "Yacovi Hewt is a good man, and I...I'm genuinely sorry for the things I've said about him."

I chuckled wearily. "Sure he'd appreciate that."

"I mean it. He didn't kill my baby, and he raised you, so *we* will be at the Forum to support him at his hearing. *Plenty* of us. They'll need more seating for Nerins and Delials and Merefons and all the cousins, I promise you."

"Aunt Chara's got that look in her eye," Canna called.

"I'd believe her."

"Oh, *you*," she replied, though her reproach sounded fond. "Be strong, Jane. We'll fix this. One way or another, you're coming home."

We said our goodbyes, and when I hung up, Connor asked, "Everything okay?"

"That was my grandmother," I murmured. "Essa's mom. Sounds like they're trying to scheme a way to get me in there, but in the meantime, she said they'd go support Dad." Flopping back against the reclined seat, I mumbled, "What do we do? If we drive like hell, we might get through Utah before this system dumps more snow."

His lip rose into a snarl of distaste. "Unless you're desperate to get back across the country, I could really do with a day or two to rest."

"Whatever you need," I said, and leaned over to kiss him properly. "I owe you, Con."

"Shoot, this is the longest vacation I've had in ages. And hey, we *could* mosey on up to see the redwoods. I mean, we're here," he pointed out.

I glanced through the windshield at the rain. "Tomorrow?"

"Sounds like a plan to me." He turned the vehicle back on, and I raised my seat. "What do you say we find a halfway decent motel and make an early night of it? Get a real nap, eat something, come back and sleep it off?"

"I think that's the best idea you've had all day," I replied, and pulled my damp jacket out of the floorboards. Feeling a hard weight in the pocket, I removed the glowing tracker, which began to dim as Connor drove us away.

CHAPTER 8

From the road, the Mountain Vue Inn appeared to be about a generous half-step up from the sort of establishment in which rooms could be acquired by the hour. The building was a single-story midcentury complex of whitewashed cinderblocks, and all room doors opened onto the weather-cracked parking lot. But the elderly man who handed us a pair of real keys was friendly and welcoming, and the room itself seemed clean, if somewhat dated in its floral décor. The television, a fat CRT model, monopolized most of the dresser, while the bathroom lights buzzed like angry mosquitoes. Though the comforters seemed clean, I knew darn well that a pattern that dark and busy could hide any number of stains.

And I didn't give a damn.

I shouldn't have been so tired, I thought, tumbling into one of the full-sized beds beside Connor. I'd had a nap already, and I certainly wasn't the one who'd driven us across the country. But as I lay there with him spooned behind me, the building weight of the week and the blow of finding my mother's gravesite combined into an all-encompassing weariness. I *craved* sleep.

Had I been a conscientious girlfriend, I'd have taken the other bed and let Connor sprawl, but I needed his touch for reasons I couldn't quite articulate, and he didn't seem to mind sharing. So, there we lay as the gray afternoon faded into an early twilight, wrapped in each other and cuddling beneath the scratchy sheet and thin blanket, the heater clanking on every so often to send another blast of warm, metallic-smelling air into the room.

Around five, I awoke to shadows and rolled over to find Connor smiling sleepily at me. "Hey," I whispered.

"Hey, you. Feeling better?"

"Uh-huh. You?"

"Closer to human." He kissed me, then sat up and stretched, his hair and clothes rumpled from his nap. "Dang, we lost the whole afternoon, didn't we?"

"I'd say it was well spent." Propping myself on my elbow, I watched as he rose and padded across the thin carpet. "Hungry?"

"Starving."

"Yeah, I could eat," I said, and yawned as he closed the bathroom door behind him.

The day had been awful, no doubt about it. But having slept enough to think straight, I recalled my brief conversation with my grandparents, and something in my chest seemed to warm.

Canna hadn't been lying—they *wanted* me. Despite my human father and incomplete education and weird accent, they wanted me to join them. To be one of them.

Maybe Canna was just a really skilled saleswoman, or perhaps they'd decided I was an acceptable substitute for the long-absent Essa. No matter. I'd actually spoken to my *grandparents*, Chara and...

Shit. What was my grandfather's name? Had anyone mentioned it?

I'd have to get that from Canna the next time I called her...

And Canna *had* told me to call, had said that she and her husband were worried about me.

The truth settled around me like a quilt: I had a family beyond Dad. People who didn't know me yet but were willing to welcome me in. Who could tell me about my mother and might see bits of her living on in me.

And if I was half human...well, for the moment, they seemed to be looking past that.

Connor smiled at me when he stepped out of the bathroom and saw me sitting on the edge of the bed with what had to be a stupid grin on my face. "Everything all right, Firebug?"

"Better," I said, rising to take my turn. "Not great, but better."

"Good." After kissing me as I slipped past him, he said, "Put on your fanciest jeans. I'm taking you out tonight."

"Sounds hot," I replied through the thin door.

"Then we can come back here, get comfortable, maybe wash some underwear in the sink…"

"Ooh, dirty boy."

He chuckled. "Yeah, that's the problem."

Once we'd made ourselves reasonably presentable, we hopped into the Santa Fe and cruised around, exploring what little there was to see of Leighfield without a tracker in my hand. Connor noted a couple of eateries that the deputy had mentioned, both of which apparently only served through lunchtime, and we wound up at a place that billed itself as a pub.

Stepping inside, I doubted the restaurant had seen a facelift in the last forty years, down to the lingering scent of tobacco in the ostensibly smoke-free establishment. A long bar dominated one wall, set with a pair of flat-screen televisions—okay, a minor facelift—and the rest of the space was dotted with four-top wooden tables and chairs. Since it was only about five on a damp, cold Tuesday night, the pub was dead but for a bored bartender, who regarded us over his phone as we entered and scoped out the joint. "You can sit wherever," he called, making no move to gather menus or cutlery.

We chose a table more or less in his line of sight so as not to be forgotten, and eventually, he sauntered over with a pair of short food menus and a much longer beer list. Connor and I decided that beer wasn't a terrible idea, and the bartender left us to peruse our dinner options while he fetched a pair of longnecks.

I was debating whether I should risk the fish tacos when I heard the door open behind me, but I didn't pay it any mind. Connor, however, had sat facing the door, and I saw him stiffen and reach for his pocket as footsteps approached on the concrete.

Glancing up, I turned and found two men about our age nearing our table, a blond and a redhead who seemed vaguely familiar, though I couldn't place either of them. I made my quick calculations: they were about Connor's height but slimmer, and their waterproof jackets, jeans, boots, and ponytails suggested they had come to Leighfield for the hiking. No immediate threat, I decided, assuming they'd spotted us sitting alone and were trying to be friendly to fellow waterlogged outdoor enthusiasts.

The blond lifted a hand in greeting as they drew close, and I'd smiled and was about to make a quip about the lovely weather when the redhead quietly said, "Ms. Fortune, we need to talk."

That he knew my name would have been troubling on its own, but the fact that he addressed me in Pactish told me my initial assessment was *very* much mistaken.

I sucked in a quick breath, fighting against the flames that wanted to leap out of my arms, but Connor jumped from his chair and stepped around the table toward the pair. "Back up," he ordered, his voice low and controlled. "Hands where I can see them. *Now.*"

I cut my eyes in his direction and saw he'd opened a large folding knife. *Why* he had brought a knife out to dinner was another matter, but since Connor had left his guns locked and hidden in the SUV, I supposed it made him feel better.

The newcomers traded glances, and as the blond slowly lifted his empty hands, the redhead murmured in English, "We're on her side, Mr. Willow."

"Back. *Up.*"

They acquiesced, giving me room. Before I quite knew what was happening, Connor had yanked me out of my seat and pushed me behind him, and he kept the knife at the ready.

Distantly, I thought that he was being ridiculous. I was the sorcerer here, the one of us with an easy projectile weapon, and there was no telling *what* he'd decided to square off against with a six-inch blade. The bartender was nowhere in sight, and I sincerely doubted he'd leap in to diffuse the situation, but a 911 call was the last thing we needed.

"Okay, let's all just take a breather," I said, slipping an arm in front of Connor to draw him away. "Come on, no assault charges tonight."

He refused to budge an inch, but the redhead, while cautious, didn't seem panicked. "I'm going to pull out my wallet," he said, keeping his eyes on Connor. "*Only* my wallet. Nothing to worry about." Slowly, he reached into his jacket and removed a slim black object, which he flipped open to reveal a badge.

I'd seen Pact agency badges before. Pars had shown me his, an eight-pointed silver star with his name and agency designation engraved in the center. The red circle surrounding the writing showed it was a DPP badge, he'd explained. Canna likewise carried agency credentials, even as a healer, though her star had a violet circle for DOL.

This star was marked with green, which left me stumped.

"You're way outside your jurisdiction," said Connor.

His mouth twitched. "So are you. Now, do you truly suppose that knife is going to do you any good?"

"Guess we'll find out, won't we, buddy?"

To my surprise, the bottles on our table began to rattle.

Breaking the standoff, the blond turned to me. "We haven't met properly, but we spoke late last year. Liogh Birrid wanted help on the Voln girl's case…"

My eyes narrowed. "You're…"

"Ganti ti'Van."

A farseer, yes, but a past-oriented one. "How the hell

did you find us?"

"Rosie *has* been keeping track of you," the redhead replied. "You're wide open. And since your actual route synchronized with the best predictions of when you would reach this town, we drove over this afternoon. There's a portal near Klamath Falls." Seeing our bemusement, he added, "Oregon. It's about three hours away in better weather."

"What do you want?" Connor demanded.

"To help Jane."

"And why the fuck should we believe you?" he asked as the bottles shook more violently.

"Because Gerem Aniap is a monster," said the redhead, "and if we work together, I think we can both clear Yacovi's name and remove the threat. That's not a guarantee," he cautioned. "I'm too close to events to be more certain. But I like our odds."

Red was a future farseer, then…

And the pieces fell into place.

"You're Diriem ti'Dana?" I murmured.

He nodded. "Mr. Willow, my colleague and I are from DOI, not Aniap's office. Could we take this somewhere more private, please? Perhaps without violence?"

"DOI?" Connor echoed.

"Division of Intelligence," I quietly reminded him. "They're farseers. And elves. We are *very* much outgunned right now, so let's hear them, okay?"

Connor looked at me, then back at the two farseers, and sighed. "Well, *shit*."

We put in our dinner order as takeout, and given the speed with which it emerged from the kitchen, I suspected the pub wasn't going for a Michelin star anytime soon. Leaving our beers mostly untouched, we piled into the SUV, and the other two followed us in a black Jeep.

"Okay, fill me in," said Connor, turning out of the

parking lot.

"Blond dude is the guy who helped out on Sage's case. That's Ganti. He sees past events—"

"All right, yeah, I remember you mentioned that..."

"And the other is the agency director. Rose's great-grandfather. Future."

He grunted as he slowed at an empty intersection. "And you trust them?"

"I don't know, but since *that* director told DOL's director not to prosecute Dad..."

"Unless he knew that the Forum would do a better job of it," Connor countered.

"Unlikely. Drive slowly," I said, and called Annie.

She picked up after a couple rings. "Hey, there!" she said, an unmistakable note of concern in her voice. "Mom said y'all left Richmond. Are you okay?"

"We're fine...I think," I replied. "Uh, could you give me Rose's number, please?"

"Yeah, sure. Do you need help? If you can take a picture of your surroundings, I can find you..."

"I'll let you know, but I think everything's cool for now," I said, hoping that sounded convincing.

Annie signed off and shot me a text, and I called Rose. Four rings later, just as I feared it would go to voicemail, she picked up. "Hey, sorry, forgot where my hand was for a moment," she said groggily. "Ugh...use farsight too long, and there's a *hangover* when you come back."

"Are you stalking me?" I snapped.

"Just to make sure Gerem's crack recon team hasn't found you. I haven't seen anyone on your tail yet, so—"

"We literally have Ganti and the director on our tail *right now.*"

"Yeah, I know. Pop said he and Ganti were driving out to intercept you."

"Did he say *why*?"

"Not to me," muttered Rose. "That's par for the course with future farseers—they tell you what they think you need to know as long as it won't prevent the outcome that doesn't result in craters. But I can assure you that Gerem has no clue where you are. I've been watching, and DOI has kept its ears to the ground. He sent people after you, but the best intelligence suggests they're back in Georgia."

"Yeah, one of my friends has been reporting in, and the woman who owns Mystic Mountains."

"Really?" She sounded surprised.

"You didn't know?"

"I'm not watching you around the clock. But I'm glad to hear that your people and ours are in agreement. Listen, Pop's not there to hurt you," she insisted. "He thinks this whole situation with Gerem and your dad is a travesty. Tell your boyfriend to stand down."

"Don't think that's likely," I said, considering the way he gripped the steering wheel. "But I'll try to keep him from stabbing your...pop."

I'd summarized our conversation by the time we pulled into the motel parking lot, and though Connor wasn't happy, he left his pistols in the vehicle. I carried the takeout bag while he unlocked our room, and when our shadows walked up, he admitted them with a curt nod.

Diriem watched as Connor latched the door, then gestured at the curtains until they closed. "Do you mind..." he began, looking at me.

"Go ahead."

With another quick gesture, his mask fell away, as did Ganti's a few seconds later. Connor gawked but held his tongue.

"Eat, if you'd like," Diriem offered, pointing to the room's rickety two-top table. "You must be hungry."

He wasn't wrong, so I sat and opened my takeout box, revealing a passable club sandwich and some ruffled chips. Connor, however, stayed on guard by the door, one hand in the pocket where I knew he'd stowed his knife.

The director regarded him for a brief moment after he and Ganti took up positions along the adjoining wall. "I appreciate that you don't want to see Jane harmed," he murmured, "but we're not your enemy."

"I'll be the judge of that," Connor said simply.

"As you wish." Turning his attention back to me, he said, "We have matters to discuss."

"What I want to know is how to free my dad," I replied. "And bring him back to Ragged Gap, if possible. How do you plan to do that?'

His mouth twitched. "You are a significant part of it."

"*Me*? I'm no one. I can't even get a day pass for the Pactlands," I said, and bit into my sandwich. My stomach, which had been empty for hours, suddenly remembered what food was and demanded more.

"On the contrary." Leaning against the wall, Diriem folded his arms, watching me eat. "I noticed you last fall. Farsight isn't fully controllable, even with centuries of practice, and I get flashes of events, people, places. Deriving meaning from them is another matter," he said, shaking his head, "but when something starts repeating, I pay attention. And you began appearing with some regularity."

I put my sandwich aside. "Why me?"

"I had no idea at first," he admitted. "That's not uncommon. I observed for a time and got a better picture of your situation. Really, a half-human *pyromancer* would be intriguing on its own, but then I saw that you knew Annie Humphries and Canna Nerin, and I pieced together where Rosie and Yven had gone in September. She gave me the full story, or at least the story as she understood it. After that, I knew there was something more to you. Something to do with Gerem."

"Yeah, sure. He's trying to kill me. Did one of the other directors tell you what he did at my petition hearing?"

"Pateme described it...*colorfully*, let's say," he replied, smirking. "But yes, I heard the news. The only reason Gerem isn't in DOL custody at the moment is because of his position on the Forum."

"Oh, so you get elected, and it's an unofficial get-out-of-jail-free card?"

Diriem remained unflustered in the face of my sarcasm. "Don't tell me this is a completely foreign concept here. I wasn't born yesterday, girl."

I raised my hands in surrender, then ate a chip. "Okay, go on. What's the connection?"

"Patience," he murmured. "I've had a strange feeling about Gerem for years. His father and grandfather...well, his grandfather was a friend of mine, and his father and I were certainly civil. I respected them both. Kereb Aniap—that was his grandfather—was a Pact signatory, and he played a significant role in designing the Pactlands. Both men were Forum representatives, and when Ban—that was Kereb's youngest, Ban—when he died, Gerem campaigned for his seat and won. He's been a representative since 1900."

Connor whistled low.

"I'll grant you that, his has been a long tenure. Ban's was as well. But Gerem's rather unlike his predecessors. We've never seen eye to eye, and when we've been forced to serve on committees together...yikes," he muttered. "I've wanted to look into him, see if I can work out what makes him such an unapologetic *ass,*" Diriem continued, glaring at the wall, "but I haven't been able to do so."

"Why not?" I asked.

"Two reasons. First, we have a code of ethics in my unit, and random digging without a good reason or a vision to support the spying, if you will, is forbidden. Second, he's been on blinding potion since he was a young man. I can't see him with farsight. Inconvenient, that," he grumbled. "But when I sensed there was a connection between the two of you, I asked Ganti to see what he could discover," he continued, nodding to the other agent. "He can't see Gerem, either, but he can see *you,* and I was hopeful he'd find the thread."

When Diriem fell silent, Ganti took the floor. "So, a little background," he began. "People have remarked about how unfortunate the Aniap family has been in recent decades. A high number of young deaths."

"Yeah, my counselor at DOL told me he'd lost his kids and his first wife," I said. "And…a sibling, maybe?"

I cringed internally at my naïve belief that Gerem's personal tragedies would make him more favorable toward my position as an orphaned, abandoned child.

"More than those," said Ganti. "The odd thing, if you come at this without considering the politics, is that no one has investigated the family for anything sinister about the deaths. They've all been ruled either natural or accidental. Now, once you factor in the family name, it's far clearer why Laws hasn't gone digging," he allowed. "One doesn't investigate a family with the clout of the Aniaps without a damn good reason."

"But you had one?"

Even without his sharp teeth, his smile seemed predatory.

"Let me put the facts in order. Gerem has been married twice, first to Lonvi Chulb, and more recently to Euvalia Prith. He had five children with Lonvi, and to date, he's had three with Euvalia."

"Big family," remarked Connor.

"Not unusual for sorcerers—or for us, for that matter. If you're not having children every other year, it's far easier to raise a large family. Spread them out, see? Just a moment." Digging in his jacket pocket, he retrieved a small notebook, which he opened to a marked page and scanned briefly. "Right. Gerem and Lonvi married in 1890, and their first child wasn't born for nine years. She didn't last long. Taya died in 1913 when she fell out a window. Her brother Sheshar was born in 1908, and he died in 1925. Fell down the stairs."

"I guess baby gates weren't a thing, huh?" I said.

"Not precisely, but bear with me. Next was Sundir,

born in 1920. He died in 1947 when he choked on his dinner. Fourth was the other daughter, Panalea, born in 1931, died in her sleep in 1964."

Connor frowned as he did the quick math. "At thirty-three? What happened, heart attack?"

"I'll get there."

"And how did the fifth die?"

Ganti glanced at his notes. "The fifth child was Norann, born in 1948, and he was…*misplaced*."

"Huh?"

"They didn't forget the baby on a park bench," said Diriem, and smiled grimly. "It's a truth here and in the Pactlands alike that if one is sufficiently wealthy or powerful, one is seldom deemed 'weird' or labeled a danger to society. One is simply regarded as eccentric and left to one's own devices." He paused, shifting his weight. "I told almost no one that my son took the draught and left until about a year and a half ago. He quit his job, stopped coming to events, stopped being *seen*, and the common explanation was that he'd turned reclusive. Farseers aren't always the most sociable of creatures," he added. "No one insisted on so much as a wellness check because…" He shrugged. "As I said, wealth and power. My son left, married, fathered a daughter, and died, and no one was the wiser."

"Norann Aniap is a known recluse," said Ganti. "No one has seen him socially in years, or so I'm informed. Obviously, he never knew his eldest three siblings, but he lost his sister when he was about sixteen, and then his mother committed suicide five years later."

"Grief?" I guessed.

"And guilt," said Ganti. "While Gerem is protected by potion, neither of his wives nor any of his children have ever been. It took me a week of searching and piecing, but I found Lonvi just prior to her death. The day before, she met with Norann alone and gave him a sealed letter, making him promise not to open it until the morning. He did as she asked, and I read the contents over his shoulder, so to speak."

"Her suicide note," I murmured.

He nodded. "By the time Norann opened it, she had drunk poison and was dead in her bed. The cruelty of doing that to your child, leaving him to live with the knowledge that if he'd acted sooner, he might have saved her..."

"She probably wasn't thinking clearly," said Diriem.

"No, she absolutely was *not*, but that doesn't lessen the blow for him."

I pushed away my dinner, my growling stomach momentarily sidelined. "Why did she kill herself?"

"Because she discovered that Gerem had been brewing and using Oleum Vitae for much of his life," said Ganti.

"What's that?" Connor asked.

"An old and *highly* forbidden potion," Diriem explained. "Think of your drug schedule, yes? Something might be quite dangerous, and you need permissions to acquire it, but it does have potential uses."

"Sure..."

"In the potion context, Oleum Vitae would be a schedule I. Dangerous, addictive, and no legal use. It *works*, but at incredible cost. The name means 'oil of life,'" he added. "Predates the Pactlands. The sorcerer who developed it went with Latin nomenclature, and the name stuck."

"Oh, yeah, I know about that one," said Connor, turning to me. "Those sorcerers last fall—"

"No, that was different," I replied, my stomach churning. "Their 'oil of life' was mostly a binding potion."

Diriem grunted. "Velvet Leash. I've seen the reports. Given those brewers' piecemeal education, I wouldn't be shocked if they'd never heard of Oleum Vitae, so the name is probably just a bad coincidence."

"Dad said the real stuff is horrible."

"He's right. Did he tell you how it's made?"

"Ooh…something about blood? A relative's blood?" I asked, wincing at the unexpected pop quiz.

But Diriem didn't look at me like I was a complete idiot. "Precisely. It's powerful blood magic. But since I'm assuming this is new territory for your friend," he continued, turning to Connor, "I'll give you the brief version. Oleum Vitae is the only known potion that can increase the user's talent for magic. Puts more *oomph* behind whatever he naturally has, let's say. You see the appeal."

Connor nodded. "Yeah, sure."

"Who wouldn't want that, right? The problem is that the extra power doesn't come from midair—it's *siphoned*. The drinker is only stronger because he's draining someone else."

"Shit," he muttered.

"Exactly. Now, you can't pull from just anyone. The potion only works on members of the brewer's family, and it drains them as it's used. All you need is a small blood sample to brew up a substantial batch—a drop will do. Drink it slowly, and your victim will last longer, maybe for as many as three or four batches. Drink it quickly, and the shock may kill him." He paused to let that sink in, then said, "The insidious thing is that once you start using Oleum Vitae, you can't stop. The potion doesn't just affect the blood target, you see—it also pulls a little from the drinker, and it *keeps* pulling. Go too long between doses, and it'll cripple you, if not kill you outright."

As he spoke, a memory surfaced. "Dad said he knew of someone who'd brewed it."

"And that someone would be Gerem," said Ganti. "Has Yacovi ever spoken to you of Lonvi Chulb?"

"No…"

He smiled slightly. "The two of them were childhood friends. Their families were close. From what I've seen, he loved her, but she looked at him more as a brother, and then she married Gerem. An advantageous marriage, certainly, but that did nothing to ease the hurt for Yacovi, especially as he and Gerem had little in common. Lonvi wanted them to get along, but Gerem pushed Yacovi away. A social inferior, you understand," he added, rolling his eyes.

I'd thought it was subtle, but Connor was on alert that night. "Personal experience?" he murmured.

"Would I be mistaken in assuming you don't know the first thing about the Hall system?"

"The what, now?"

"Thought so. To answer your question, *yeah.*"

Diriem, I noticed, kept his mouth shut and his gaze elsewhere.

"Anyway," Ganti continued, "Lonvi finally found Gerem's hidden brew room while he was on a retreat. She put the pieces together and realized he'd killed their children and covered up their deaths."

"And she was next?" Connor guessed.

"Actually, no. Oleum Vitae requires a blood connection—a spouse won't do it unless the couple are cousins. The closer the relationship, the better the potion works, so Gerem's children were easy targets. Maybe he wanted a family at one point, but as far as I'm concerned, he farmed them. As for Lonvi, she couldn't live with the guilt. She destroyed Gerem's supply of potion and all the base ingredients she could find, then wrote her note, gave it to her son, and killed herself the next morning."

"It wasn't just the children, though, yes?" Diriem asked.

Ganti shook his head. "I don't think so. I can't see Gerem clearly, but I looked at some of the other prematurely deceased Aniaps, and I think there's a pattern. His older sister was his first victim. Incredibly talented sorcerer, and her father's likely successor—Gerem's was a middling talent at best. But just as his sister began to make a name for herself as a Forum aide, she began to sicken, and she died in 1898. I think it's likely that Gerem experimented with her. Whether he brewed Oleum Vitae using his own father's blood is unclear, but since Ban died two years later, I wouldn't rule it out. After that, one of his first cousins died…and then he killed his first daughter in 1913. Once brewed, the batches do retain potency, even after the donor is dead, but they degrade with time. He needed a fairly steady source, and between his children and his cousins, Gerem has sustained himself nicely."

"Don't forget that he remarried," said Diriem. "Three children from that relationship…"

Ganti counted them off on his fingers. "A son, Tenelit, born in 1983, fell down the stairs like his brother in 2016. A daughter, Kelir, born in 1996, died in 2020 when she choked—Gerem's not the most creative when it comes to cover stories. That leaves only his youngest daughter, Xila, who's about eighteen. If he's not draining her yet, she's the obvious next target."

"But what about Norann?" I asked. "If he's hiding away, couldn't Gerem still get to him?"

"Well, perhaps," said Ganti, "had Norann not fled the Pactlands."

"He didn't confront his father?" Connor asked, brow furrowing. "Guy kills your siblings, your mother kills herself, you're next on the menu, and he didn't, like, take it to the police?"

"You have to understand that Gerem is *very* powerful. Not necessarily as a sorcerer, but as a politician. He has favors owed him and people in his pockets, and the money to remove impediments. I think Norann knew that if he went public, it'd be suicide. Gerem would have made him disappear. So, he did it on his own. Went to the one person he knew would believe him: Yacovi, who'd help him for love of his mother if for no other reason."

"Wait…seriously?" I said, my heart sinking. Dad's list of crimes was only growing.

"I'm certain—I watched them make *and* execute their plans," said Ganti. "Yacovi sneaked Norann into the DPP greenhouse from the Beukal side, then slipped him into Virginia, and he was free. Helped him forge papers, gave him money to get started, and swore he'd keep the secret to protect him. Norann knew no one, of course, so he didn't go far. He integrated into the local community, but he stayed close enough to the greenhouse to meet up with Yacovi on occasion. And naturally, he adopted a fake name."

My gut churned, but not from hunger. "What was his name?" I distantly heard myself ask.

One side of his mouth quirked. "Aaron Fortune."

CHAPTER 9

I checked out for a minute after that.

I couldn't run—Connor had locked the door, and if I tried to bolt, either he or the two agents would grab me. The sandwich that had seemed so important a short time before was as unappetizing to me as a bucket of sand in the middle of the table would be.

My father was Norann Aniap.

A sorcerer.

He wasn't human.

Ergo, *I* wasn't human.

I wasn't human?

And Dad knew. He'd known all along, but he hadn't said a word—

Wait, if both my parents were sorcerers, then Essa should never have taken the draught. Dad did nothing wrong…

Well, he did sneak Norann out…and lied—

He lied to me. Dad, the person I would trust with my life, had *lied* to me about everything! Who I was, *what* I was…

But he was being held for something that wasn't a crime, so why the fuck hadn't he told me? Was that his plan? Take the fall and go to prison?

Why?

My heart raced, a rushing noise filled my ears, I couldn't catch my breath…

And then I found Connor kneeling in front of me, rubbing my hands as my arms flamed and the wooden chair began to char. "Janie? Janie, honey," he said, staring at me as my eyes tried to focus. "Come on, Firebug, you've got this. Come on back. I'm right here."

His touch gave me a sensation outside my body on which I could ground myself, and I gasped until my head began to clear. I smothered the fire before I could set the chair ablaze—I didn't know how we'd explain the damage, but that wasn't my concern right then—and for what seemed like the tenth time that day, I burst into tears.

"Aw, honey," Connor murmured, pulling me from the chair to hold me. "It's okay. I've got you, it's going to be okay."

The logical part of myself at the back of my brain tried to reason with my overwhelmed emotions. I'd never known my bio-dad. He was just a name, not a presence in my life. I couldn't possibly be *missing* him. This was the result of stress and exhaustion, and maybe anger at Dad, but really, I didn't need to collapse into a weepy mess in front of *company*, for God's sake.

My emotions, which were admittedly not at their most regulated that day, told logic to fuck off, and I soaked Connor's shoulder as he held me.

When I started to calm down, I heard Diriem say, "It takes a brave person or an utter fool to make close contact with an upset, undertrained pyromancer."

Connor ignored him and continued rubbing my back, and eventually, I pulled myself together and dried my eyes. "What was that about pyros?" I muttered, wiping my nose on the paper napkin that had come with my dinner.

"An undertrained pyro is a dangerous thing. You know that," said Diriem. "Your control is excellent, but you're also quite young."

"And that's the Aniap in you," Ganti chimed in. "Gerem's sister was a pyro. He's not, nor have any of his children been pyros, but you got the wild talent."

Well, that was one mystery solved—pyromancy didn't run in Canna's family—but it was hardly the most pressing issue on my mind. "You're sure about my father?" I asked

Ganti.

He nodded, his expression softening. "Absolutely. I'm sorry if this comes as a shock—"

My barked laughter silenced him. "A *shock*? Okay, let's recap: Gerem tried to kill me, he's got people lying in wait for me at home, Con and I just drove across the country in pursuit of my mother, who's fucking *dead*, and now you tell me that basic facts about my family that I've believed my whole life—because Dad *lied* to me, evidently—are bullshit. I don't think 'shock' is the word for this." Stepping away from Connor, I folded my arms and glared at the elves. "All right, someone give it to me straight. How the hell did I get here? What really happened to my parents?"

Diriem gestured to Ganti, who resumed his report.

"Norann lived near the greenhouse for about twenty years, working menial jobs under his alias and masking a bit. He eventually found work as a bartender—"

"At Bobby's Place," I murmured.

"Correct. That was around the time that Essa began working in the greenhouse. A few months thereafter, she went to the bar alone one night and struck up a conversation with Norann. He recognized her cover story as one that the greenhouse workers used, naturally, but he didn't reveal himself." He smirked. "Unfortunately for Norann, Essa was perceptive. They talked long enough that she heard his true accent slip through—he could fake the local drawl well, but not perfectly. She didn't say anything at first, but she kept coming in for several months, they got better acquainted, and when they were alone, she finally asked him who he was. Norann panicked, but Essa swore she'd keep his secret, so he told her everything. She was horrified for him, but she was also savvy enough to know that his best chance of survival was remaining outside until Gerem's death."

"And so they got together?" Connor asked.

"In short order. They fell for each other quickly, and

Essa decided she'd rather have Norann than the life she knew. They met with Yacovi and told him what they wanted, and he helped them assemble their cover story. Essa knew it would hurt her family, and she grieved over her decision, but she couldn't risk telling them the truth about where she was and who she was with." He paused to consult his notebook. "They ran off in August 1992 and worked odd jobs, and then you came along about a year and a half later," he said, glancing at me.

Fearing the worst, I asked, "How did Norann die?"

"What did Yacovi tell you?"

"He was working the night shift at a convenience store, and a robber shot him."

Ganti nodded. "That's correct. What?" he asked as my face scrunched. "You're not *invincible*. He had his back turned to get a pack of cigarettes, evidently not anticipating a problem, and when he faced the man again, he was shot in the head. If it helps, he didn't suffer," Ganti added. "I swear it. He was gone almost as soon as he hit the floor."

"And it was...just a random robber? You're serious?"

"Gerem had nothing to do with it. Wrong place, wrong time. And the authorities did eventually catch his killer—he tried that trick at another convenience store, and an employee who'd been in the back shot the robber in the leg. I followed the case for a couple days. He was stabbed to death in a prison brawl."

"No great loss," Connor muttered.

That answered one question, but not the one that had been plaguing me as long as I could remember. "Why did my mother abandon me?"

"It was never meant to be permanent," said Ganti, and sighed as he flipped to another page in his notes. "Your parents loved you, they wanted you. They were thrilled to have you. Then Norann was murdered, and Essa suddenly found herself an unemployed single mother with no support. They'd kept up with Yacovi, and since she had nowhere else to go, she packed what she could and ran to him. You have to understand that she'd just lost the love of her life," he said softly. "That, plus a touch of postpartum depression, left her lying in the dark for several days while Yacovi tended to you. He tried to give her space to come to terms with her grief, but she...she wasn't in a good place. Like I said, she had no job, no money, no family, and she knew she couldn't go home. If she'd gone back and revealed that she really *hadn't* run off with a human, your paternity would have come out, and she feared that Gerem would find a way to steal you, and eventually kill you. So..." He paused, his face working as he considered his words. "I know how it must look to you, and you have every right to feel abandoned. But Essa left you with someone she trusted to keep you safe because she knew she couldn't be the mother you needed just then."

"Did she ever call Dad?" I asked, trying not to cry again. "Write him? Ask about me?"

"No," Ganti admitted. "But I can tell you that she wandered. Tried to make herself feel better by...let's say unconventional means. Jumped between gurus for a few months. Sold what little she had to feed herself. Around the time of her death, the fog had lifted enough for her to see a path forward. She was trying to hitchhike back across the country to get to you. Unfortunately, that plan ended about two days in, when a vehicle struck her." He paused briefly. "She didn't suffer, either. Never regained consciousness, and she was dead by the time help arrived."

It hit me then that my mother had paid for my life with her own. She could have gone home, admitted the whole thing was a hoax, proven I wasn't human...but she knew what would have happened to me. Would Gerem have gone to court and argued that Essa was an unfit parent? Maybe he would only have secured visitation rights, but little children are so accident-prone, and it would have been a matter of time before he needed to tend to a cut. Would he have drained me then out of spite for Norann, or would he have waited until I was older, more useful? I tried to recall the dates Ganti had rattled off—he was remarried by the time I was born, and didn't he have a kid? Maybe, if he'd been able to use me, he wouldn't have needed to kill his other children so soon…

And he had one left. Xila. She had no idea of the danger she was in…

Pulling myself from my spiral, I asked, "Why did Dad lie to me? Why am I just now hearing this?"

"To protect you," Ganti said simply. "Whether you were orphaned or abandoned, he suspected that you'd jump at the chance to find biological family. His fear was that Gerem would somehow discover you, and if Yacovi told you the truth about him, you wouldn't believe him. You'd chalk it up to jealousy that you'd found your grandfather. He was concerned that your desire to know your larger family would make you easy prey."

Dad…well, he wasn't wrong, I mused, thinking of how I'd felt when I spoke to my other grandparents that afternoon. Connected, *loved*…and I blindly trusted that they meant what they said. If Gerem had come around when I was a friendless teenager…

Oh.

Oh.

"Yacovi wanted to be certain that there was no way you'd ever allow yourself to be close to Gerem," said Ganti. "In retrospect, perhaps he should have mentioned something before now, but as is frequently said in my line of work, the past is fixed."

I thought of Dad in his out-of-date robe at my hearing, lying through his teeth to protect me from the man who'd murdered his own children and driven Dad's old friend to suicide. He'd loved Lonvi, so he'd protected her son and raised her granddaughter.

As if following my thoughts, Diriem said, "The important thing is that Yacovi committed no crime in failing to give Essa the draught. Helping Norann flee was illegal, yes, but given the circumstances, I can't imagine that any tribunal would convict him."

"And as for you, Jane," said Ganti, "legally, you're in the same position as the Voln girl. You're the child of two sorcerers, and a blood test could confirm that. You have no need to petition for citizenship—it's yours as of right."

"Great, but I don't care about that now," I replied. "How do we help Dad?"

Ganti and Diriem looked at each other, and Diriem ceded the floor with a nod.

"Here's our thought," Ganti said, glancing between Connor and me. "Lonvi's suicide note was among Norann's possessions that Essa took with her to Yacovi's house. She left it with him for safekeeping. So, if we could get that note, plus a blood test to show that Jane's not only *not* human, but an Aniap, I could use them with my testimony and whatever Yacovi wants to add. We could exonerate him and take Gerem down. I think that would present a strong enough case to have his blinding protection removed, and after that, I think we'd find *exactly* the evidence we needed."

Connor cleared his throat. "Not to rain on your parade, and I'm not trying to discount whatever abilities you may have, but your story's pretty far-fetched. Essa and Norann are dead, and without more proof—"

"A certified farseer can testify as to his or her findings," said Diriem. "It's perfectly legal."

"Uh-huh," he said, a skeptical look in his eye. "And what's to stop y'all from making shit up? I mean, who's to say that anything we've heard tonight is the truth?"

Ganti muttered something that might have been *detectives* under his breath in Pactish, but Diriem took a more diplomatic approach. "You have doubts. That's fair. There aren't exactly protocols for magically derived evidence out here, right?"

"Nope."

"When we go before a tribunal—when *any* witness goes

before a tribunal, I should say—there's a spell cast. If you say anything other than what you sincerely believe to be true, the spell leaves you in pain, and it's no trivial matter. I've watched witnesses try to lie, and no one yet has withstood the deterrent."

"So...like that stuff Sage's father took?"

Diriem winced. "*No*. That potion does produce truthful answers, but it's too damaging to use outside of very particular circumstances. The spell is enough for tribunals. As for whether we've been truthful with you this evening..." He spread his hands. "This is one of those times you take it on faith. This will mean nothing to you, and I suspect it may not mean much to you, either," he added, glancing at me, "but I swear on my honor and on my Hall that Ganti and I have been honest here."

I could tell that Connor wasn't entirely convinced, but Dad had taught me enough about elves to know what an oath like that meant. "They're legit," I murmured to him, and nodded when he cocked an eyebrow. "I'm pretty sure. So, what's the plan?" I asked the others. "You want to go back, start some sort of court proceeding, drag Gerem in before he can prosecute my dad?"

"Not quite," said Ganti. "Gerem is big enough that any action taken against him needs to be done swiftly, decisively, and in public. Our thought is that we show up on Yacovi's hearing day and...what's the phrase?"

"Crash the party," Diriem offered.

"*Right*, that. We'll sneak you in and make a spectacle of it. Blood test, suicide note, I'll present my findings, and then perhaps Yacovi will drop his charade. Whatever happens, the entire Forum will be there for the vote, so Gerem won't be able to cover up the accusations."

"I...like it," I said, working through the variables, "but for the part about the suicide note. That's probably in a storage closet at Dad's house, and last I heard, Gerem's people are still camped there."

"Oh, we're well aware of that," said Diriem with a little

smile. "Now, how would you like to go about breaking in?"

To that point, our only intel on Dad's place had come from Tabitha. "What about Rose?" I offered between bites of my sandwich. Diriem had suggested that Connor and I might conspire better with food in us, and though my guts felt too knotted to process food, I forced myself to eat.

"Unfortunately, that's not how her talent works," said Diriem. He and Ganti sat on the edge of the unused bed, Ganti having already been out to their vehicle to bring in a half-eaten bag of Cheetos. "Ours either, I should say. We're limited in that we need to focus on individuals—I can't just think of a place and see what happens there. Unless Rose knows who's on the property, she won't be able to remotely view it."

"Does she have to *know* them, or just what they look like?" asked Connor.

"The greater the familiarity, the easier it is, but she could probably manage with a photograph. She did it once with only a name."

Connor's eyes widened as inspiration struck. "Does Yacovi have a security system? Doorbell camera?"

"Uh…he has plenty of security measures," I replied, "but nothing like that."

"What about Mystic Mountains? If those guys who went in the store to ask about you are the same ones who're squatting at your dad's house…"

One quick and awkward call later, Stephanie quashed that plan with an apologetic no. "It's not that I'm tech-averse, necessarily," she said, "but some of my staff and customers have concerns about government surveillance or just the extra electromagnetic radiation, so I keep the expensive pieces under lock and key and hope for the best."

"Okay, so Rose is out," I said as I put my phone aside.

"What if we got someone on the ground? Annie could get in—she's been there. If she popped in, maybe snapped some quick pictures, and then Rose spied until they went to town…"

I let the thought hang, hoping for a nibble, but the agents didn't bite. "Annie *Humphries*?" said Ganti. "DPP?"

"She's a friend."

"And a known asset," said Diriem. "Even if she were quick, if she were spotted, word would get back to Gerem, and we don't want to let him know that we're on to him. Plus, there's the matter of Wylan to consider."

I frowned. "He's got beef with Gerem—"

"Oh, absolutely, but I think he would not take kindly to a request that his wife throw herself into danger like that. Annie's a tenacious woman, but she's not invincible, and she can't cast. You want to send that up against a nest of probable sorcerers?"

"All right, so what about Wylan? He's tough, and he could get in and out—"

Ganti laughed incredulously. "Yes, let's send the *Hunter* on a reconnaissance mission. If nothing else, he's a representative—he's known."

"And the same would go for the rest of the Hunt," Diriem added. "Most of them don't stray far from the lodge without orders."

A thought occurred to me. "Annie sneaked into the lodge once, didn't she? Wylan mentioned that…he was telling me about her scars," I said, racking my brain for the details. "She had something that made her invisible—"

"A ring," said Diriem, coming in with the save, "plus a scent-neutralizing potion. I remember it well. The combination almost killed her."

"But that was just because of the other crap in her system, right? That's what Wylan said—there was a weird cross-reaction. What if I tried? If y'all could get jewelry to hide me and a potion in case of, like, trolls, I could sneak in. Maybe even grab Lonvi's note."

"You just said Yacovi has a security system," Ganti pointed out, cutting short Connor's protest.

"Sure, but *I know about it*. I can't get into his greenhouse if he's locked it, but I should be able to skulk around the place. Come on, I grew up there," I said, grabbing a chip. "Don't tell me you never sneaked out of your parents' house."

Diriem rubbed his chin. "Getting an invisibility ring for you shouldn't be difficult if I explain the situation. They're rare, but I can probably borrow the one Annie used. Scent neutralizer we have on hand at the office—"

"I'll go in," Connor interrupted. "You get the stuff, I'll sneak around Yacovi's house."

"*Connor*," I said, staring him in the eye. "Let's not be stupid. *I* know the place. You don't. And if need be, I can always start a fire." Before he could renew his objections, I turned to the agents. "I like this plan. If I can get into the storage room, I'll grab Mom's things. If not, at least we'll have an idea of who's in the house."

Ganti looked at the director and shrugged. "Logically, it seems as sound as anything we can do in a hurry. Do you see a problem?"

"I'm too close to see anything clearly," Diriem muttered, "but I don't have a feeling of doom about this, if that helps. So." With a nod to me, he said, "I'll call in the favors, and we should get some rest. We have a long drive ahead of us. Do you know if there are any vacancies in this…establishment?"

"Hold on," said Connor, raising a finger. "Why do we have to drive back to Georgia?"

"Because taking the two of you through the portals right now would be risky—I don't know if Gerem has paid off attendants, but I wouldn't be surprised. Plus, if Gerem *does* have spies at the portal building, he'll take note if I go through Central. I have no official business in that part of the world right now—"

"No, that's not what I meant. Why don't we call Annie

for a pickup?"

Diriem suddenly seemed uneasy. "I, uh…well, that might be possible," he reluctantly allowed, "but I've never traveled with the Hunt, I don't understand the magic behind what they can do, and frankly, it worries me."

Folding his arms, Connor said, "Been there, done that, survived it. She and Wylan teleported us to Richmond, SUV and all. Little freaky, but it didn't hurt."

"Yes, I know," he replied testily. "And as the alternative is a cross-country drive…"

"Through the Rockies. With *snow* in the forecast. Y'all ever driven in a snowstorm? *I* have, and I'd really rather not be anywhere near the damn ski resorts in those conditions."

Diriem gave him a long look. "I'm no stranger to snow, boy. I've been driving longer than you've walked this world, and I grew up in what is currently Norway, so trust me, I'm familiar with difficult winters. But yes, a blizzard at elevation would complicate the trip." He thought about it for a moment longer, then sighed. "Very well. I'll ask Annie—"

"*You* worry about the goods," I said, pushing back from the table with my phone in hand. "I'll talk to Annie."

"Going somewhere?" he asked when I was halfway to the bathroom.

I glanced back at the other three. "No offense, guys, but it's been one *hell* of a day, and I need a minute." And with that, I locked myself in the bathroom and turned on the exhaust fan for privacy.

The bathroom light wasn't flattering, but even with great illumination, I'd have looked like shit. My hair needed brushing, and after two days without a wash, the blonde roots were darkening. My eyes were still red and had puffed impressively, reminding me of the time my freshman roommate broke up with her high school boyfriend and stayed awake all night sobbing. She'd looked like the victim of a bad bee sting in the morning, and I wasn't far behind her. My chin had started breaking out three days ago from travel and stress, and the cold, dry air had left my lips and the tip of my nose chapped.

I wanted a hot shower and a bottle of tequila and a long, cleansing scream.

Instead, I sat on the toilet lid and dialed.

CHAPTER 10

I didn't know what time it was in the Hunt's hideout, but fortunately, Annie was awake.

"Hey!" she said when she picked up. "Can you talk? Are you really okay? You hung up so quickly earlier…"

I groaned and stared at the stained linoleum. "Do you want the long version or the highlights?"

"Hit me. The boys are outside for a little impromptu evening wrestling, so I'm holed up in my office with a glass of Riesling and a movie. What's up?"

"So, um…Connor and I left your parents' house and hung out with a grower in western Virginia for a few days—Rose's great-aunt?"

"Lily? Oh, sure. What were you doing there?"

"She made a tracker for me. I wanted to finally find my mom. Anyway, Connor's a saint, and he drove me all the way out here to northern California."

"I could have given y'all a lift!" she protested. "Jeez, that's a lot of miles to put on the car all at once."

"Believe me, an oil change is the least of what I owe him. But, uh…we found her."

Annie perked. "Yeah? Was she willing to talk? What's she like?"

"Dead."

She sucked in a quick breath. "Aw, Jane. *Shit.* I'm so sorry, hon…"

I squeezed my eyes closed against the warning pricking. "Thanks. We found her grave earlier today. Weird to see her listed as Jane Doe, you know?"

"That…would be strange. But how are you holding up?" she asked gently. "Look, this wine's not bad, and I'm willing to come to y'all—"

"Oh, I'm not done. So, we get a motel, take a nap, go out to grab food, and who should wander in on us but a couple of dudes from DOI?"

"Ooh. Who?"

"Ganti ti'Van—he helped Liogh on Sage's case," I explained—"and the director. Turns out Rose has been remotely stalking us, too. *God*, now I'm glad I've been too preoccupied to jump on Connor—"

"Diriem's there?"

She sounded more curious than alarmed, which I took as a good sign. "Ti'Dana. Redhead, gray eyes, says he's Norwegian…"

"Yup, that's him. Damn."

"You know him decently well?"

"I mean, I've spent some time at the ti'Dana manse. As far as allies go, you could do a hell of a lot worse. What're they doing there? Rose hasn't said a peep to me," she added with a hint of annoyance.

I rubbed one temple with my free hand. "Long story short, my bio-dad wasn't human. He was Gerem Aniap's son."

"*What?*"

"Yeah, basically. And Gerem's been killing his family for years with Oleum Vitae."

"The fuck is *that?*"

"Super-illegal potion. Apparently, Diriem got a vibe or whatever, and Ganti's been poking around in the past, and the plan now is to confront Gerem at Dad's upcoming hearing. And it goes without saying, but this is top-secret, yeah?"

"Naturally, but…shit, Jane. That's a ton to throw at you at once…"

"Tell me about it," I muttered. "So, all of that said, the four of us are out in Cali, and we'd prefer to avoid a long drive home, especially with snow moving into the mountains—"

"Say no more," Annie interrupted. "I can get y'all to Ragged Gap...I mean, I'm *pretty* sure I can do it on my own steam, but is Diriem going to blow a gasket if I loop in Wylan?"

"Can Wylan keep his mouth shut?"

"He will. Now, where am I dropping y'all?"

A good question. "Not Dad's house, since that's still occupied, and my house is probably under surveillance. You don't know where Tabitha lives, do you?"

"Your witchy friend? Sorry, no."

"How about Connor?"

"No dice. I could get you to Mystic Mountains, but that's a commercial area, and I don't know who around there would have a security camera."

Not Mystic Mountains, but Stephanie's neighbors were probably wiser. "Which means the Mercantile is out, too."

"True, but...thought. What about that cabin you torched?"

"The one in Whitford?"

She paused. "Have you torched *multiple* cabins?"

"Not to that point. Uh...yeah, that should work. I don't know if they've rebuilt anything, but—"

"I'll check. It's about nine-thirty their time. Just a second..." The line went staticky but cleared an instant later. "Okay, I'm here, and *Jesus*, a coat would have been a good idea. Oof. All right...debris has been cleared, but there's nothing here but dirt. No new construction. Are you in vehicles that can handle the road up here?"

"Yeah, we should be able to manage. Do you know if it's chained off?"

"Can't see that far. I've got great night vision now, but not all the way to the bottom of the hill. No moon yet."

"That's fine, we'll make it. Get out of there before you freeze, huh?"

"Don't have to tell me twice." The blip of static

heralded her departure. "*Oh*, that's better. Brr. Okay, when do you want to leave? I've got the night free."

I thought about sleepy Leighfield and wondered how much of a stir it would make if the motel's cameras caught our vehicles vanishing. "Would you be willing to wait a few hours? Say ten our time? That's about one in Beukal."

"Yeah, sure," said Annie. "I'm going to need a reference photo or two."

"You'll have them just as soon as I figure out where we're meeting you. And I owe you one—"

A sharp knock at the bathroom door interrupted me, and I unlatched the knob with a scowl. "Yes?" I asked.

Diriem gestured for the phone. "Let me speak with her, please."

I flipped it to speaker mode. "Annie, I've got Diriem here."

"Hi," she said, switching to Pactish. "Sounds like you're up to no good."

"Always," he replied, faintly smirking at the phone in my hand. "Are you coming after us tonight?"

"Shouldn't you know the answer to that?"

"I'm not actually omniscient, child."

"Then yes, I'm coming. Around ten, Jane said."

"That works. Before you come, would you please visit Rose? She'll have a package for you to bring along."

Annie agreed, and after reminding me to send pictures, she hung up. I put the phone in my pocket and shrugged. "There, no problem. You've told Rose what we need?"

"Not yet, but I have a good feeling about this. Go finish your dinner before Ganti steals it."

"I heard that!" he called from the far side of the room.

"Hey, I'm still here," said Connor, who sounded miffed to have been cut from the conversation.

"You didn't miss much, Con," I replied, slipping back into English as I returned to the table. "Annie's picking us up in a few hours. She's going to take us to the cabin I burned down...and since my house is being watched, any chance that I could camp with you tonight?"

"I'll have to think about it...*ow*," he complained as I punched his arm. "Damn, woman."

"You're going to make me sleep in the *car*?"

"Of course not. If I did that, I'd probably come out in the morning to a melted scrap heap." He dodged when I started to punch him again, then grinned impishly at me. "So, for the sake of my insurance, mi casa es su casa."

I wanted to kiss him. It'd been a long day, and as boyfriends went, Connor had been turning in a top-tier performance in the last week. But whatever I might have been, *he* was definitely human from a Pactlands legal standpoint, and I didn't want a lecture or worse from the DOI crew.

Diriem shook his head as he sat on the bed and took out what seemed to be an ordinary smartphone. He scrolled briefly, then dialed...and what followed was incomprehensible to me. Catching my consternation, Ganti murmured, "He's speaking with Teolm ti'Cren. Teolm's father made incredible jewelry, and since he's incarcerated for the next few centuries, Teolm is overseeing the family business and minding the loaner stock."

"What'd he do?" I whispered.

"Long story. Hold on..." He listened in to half the conversation, then said, "Teolm is willing to loan him an invisibility ring again. Good."

I frowned as a thought occurred to me. "Ti'Cren..."

"You met his younger sister Liliol a few days ago."

"*Ah.*"

"Liliol and her eldest brother are probably the best of that brood still living. I never had much contact with Fradin, but he's remembered well in agency circles. As for the rest..." He grunted. "Criminals or useless. The youngest actually eloped with a ti'Gata guy until she realized Daddy would cut off her allowance."

Not knowing the Halls well, I suspected I was missing

something, but Ganti's disdain was unmistakable. "Why would he have done that?"

Ganti looked at me like I was crazy, but his expression shifted as he remembered his audience. "Ti'Gata, like ti'Van, is at the bottom of the heap. We're two of the 'new' Halls," he said, rolling his eyes. "Ti'Cren is the highest of the old southern Halls remaining, so...you see how that complicates matters?"

"Still?"

"Yacovi didn't teach you much about our politics, did he?"

Before he could launch into a lecture, Diriem hung up, then quickly dialed again. That time, he spoke in English. "Hello, Rosie. I need a favor tonight...thank you. Call the overnight assistants and have a bottle of scent neutralizer pulled from our stash. If you could please collect that, then meet Teolm at the store and pick up a ring. He says he'll have it within the hour, and he's expecting you." He paused, staring at the wall while he listened. "Appreciated, but it's best for you to remain in the dark for now. Once you have the potion and the ring, call Annie, and she'll take them from you. Yes?"

Apparently, Rose was amenable to his request, and Diriem stood and stretched once he'd finalized matters with her. "Have you decided to poach her from DPP yet?" Ganti asked with a little chuckle.

He winced as he unkinked his back. "She's where she needs to be, and as long as Pateme does right by her, I'm not going to apply pressure."

"DPP could always *borrow* her," he suggested. "Laws certainly borrows me."

"True. But she's upended her life of late, and I'd like for her to feel stable enough to think about planning her wedding."

Ganti's eyebrows rose. "She's not yet *thirty*."

"It's what she wants, and it's not my decision."

"I know lots of people who married in their twenties,"

I pointed out. "It's not like she's sixteen."

"It's a little different in the Pactlands," Diriem said before Ganti could counter that. "Thirty-five is full majority. Has Yacovi not mentioned this?"

"Oh, I've been told," I muttered. "Repeatedly. By people who seem shocked that I can handle my own shit."

He smiled, a flash of sharp teeth. "I see why you and Annie hit it off. Speaking of whom, where is she meeting us?"

"Not here—there are cameras on the property. We need somewhere that's not going to see much traffic late tonight."

"Cemetery?" said Connor. "Maybe it's not ideal, but I didn't see so much as a traffic camera around there today."

Little as I wanted to return to *that* part of town, he had a point. "Want to do a drive-by and double-check?"

Leaving the other two to decompress from their own drive that day, Connor and I climbed into his SUV and set off to scope out the cemetery. We hadn't gone two blocks when he started laughing to himself. "What?" I asked.

"You know, I've never been to California," he said. "I was actually looking forward to those redwoods—don't get me wrong, I'm happy to go back tonight," he hastily added, grabbing my arm, "but that would have been interesting. So, I get out here in freaking February, drive my girlfriend right up to her mother's *grave*, and now there's a couple of damn elves getting Cheeto crumbs on the floor in my hotel room."

"You've been a real trooper to do all of this for me," I said, taking his hand.

"And I'd do it again, Janie. It's just..."

"Long week?"

"Oof."

I tightened my grip. "Tell you what. Assuming we can get to a point where Gerem's *not* trying to kill me, I'll spring for a real trip."

"Huh...Myrtle Beach?"

"Doable. Or—*or*, hear me out—we make it a shorter drive, book a long weekend at the Ritz in Atlanta, and get room service."

"Yeah?"

"A *lot* of room service."

Though I couldn't see Connor too clearly in the dark, I could make out his grin. "So...you, me, and an HBO binge?"

"I mean, if that's what you want, though I imagine there are other ways we could entertain ourselves between overpriced meals."

"Mm. Tempting. Of course, if we went to Myrtle, I'd get to see you in a swimsuit."

"Not unless you want to wait a few months." I rubbed my thumb against his hand. "You are, however, forgetting a salient point."

"Oh?"

"Uh-huh. You saw how the elves can mask, right?"

"Yes..."

"I can do it, too," I murmured. "Clothes and all. So...send me photos of some of your favorite ensembles, and I'll see what I can manage."

He mulled that over as he slowed at an empty four-way stop. "Just checking, but is there any prohibition on the use of magic for, uh...adult fun times?"

"Not as long as everything's consensual."

"In that case, I think Atlanta sounds *fantastic*. But we really don't have to hash this out tonight," he added, and pulled my hand closer to kiss my fingers. "I can't imagine where your mind is right now."

"I don't even know. It's all a fucking blur," I said, leaning back against my seat. A nagging thought crept to the fore, and with some hesitation, I said, "If...after everything that's come out...if you're not comfortable dating me, I get it."

"What would give you *that* idea?" he asked, his voice sharp with shock. "Did I say something wrong?"

"No, no, you didn't do anything," I reassured him. "What I meant was…um…well, I guess I'm not human," I blurted. "Not at all. And if that's a dealbreaker—"

"You're beautiful and smart, and you make fancy bath stuff out of weeds, and when people piss you off, you burn shit down. You're amazing."

I laughed aloud. "That may be the nicest thing anyone's ever said to me."

"And I'm *really* looking forward to Atlanta."

We drove on in silence for a moment, but as we neared the cemetery, I groaned. "Goddamn it."

"Anything in particular?" Connor joked.

"Gerem's my fucking *grandfather*. What the hell?" I griped. "I finally get grandparents, I've only got three left, and one of them is, like, a serial killer!"

"Two out of three ain't bad?"

"Not helpful, babe," I said, and tried not to look into the shadows where my mother's gravestone sat as the cemetery came into view beneath the streetlights.

My phone said it was two minutes until ten when Annie appeared by the cemetery gate, well out of the way of any cameras. She hadn't come alone—the big man beside her had to be Wylan, albeit masked to hide his rack.

I stepped out of Connor's SUV to meet them. "Thanks so much," I began. "I'm sorry about the late pickup—"

"Don't worry about that," said Wylan, and crooked a finger toward Diriem as he approached. "We need to talk."

"Of what?" Diriem asked, hurrying to join us. "I trust Annie filled you in."

"Absolutely. But what is *this*?" he demanded, pointing to the canvas tote bag slung over Annie's shoulder. "Scent neutralizer and Teolm's invisibility ring?"

"They're for me," I explained. "I'm going to use the ring, douse myself with that potion in case of trolls or whatever, and sneak into my dad's house to see what's going on in there. Grab some stuff if I can."

Even with the darkness, I was close enough to them to catch Annie's wince, and Wylan shook his head. "That's a terrible idea," he said. "When Annie did that—"

"Annie had Roulette in her system," Diriem interrupted, "and I've never heard of another person exhibiting the cross-reaction she suffered. These should be safe for Jane. *I* would use them in combination."

"Then why are you sending her?" he retorted. "No offense, but I've seen the agencies' willingness to toss undertrained humans into the line of fire."

"I know Dad's security system. He doesn't," I said. "And I'm not helpless. Or human, for that matter," I mumbled.

"You also have zero training in espionage," said Annie.

"And your training in that regard was…"

She made a face. "Also not much, but I *was* a PI. I've professionally sneaked around."

"I grew up in that house. Guarantee you I know it better than Gerem's folks do."

"I don't doubt that, but…you know, I could get in there—"

"*No*," said Diriem, even as Wylan's mouth started to open. "Not you, Annie. We can't risk word coming back to Gerem of DPP snooping."

Wylan had no objection there, and though he still seemed dissatisfied with the plan, Annie handed the bag to Diriem. "Get back in your vehicles," she said. "We'll take you one at a time."

"Since she's the only one who knows where we're going," Wylan added.

I climbed into my seat and buckled up. "Everything all right?" Connor asked, lifting a hand in greeting to our chauffeurs.

"More or less," I replied, and clung to the handle as Annie took Wylan's hand, then gripped the front bumper. "Hold on—"

An instant of disorienting, stomach-churning blackness later, I opened my eyes to find ourselves back in the mountains. When Annie and Wylan vanished, I climbed out on shaky legs and looked to the sky—stars instead of the solid bank of clouds I'd seen moments before, and the air was warmer and drier. Connor joined me, coming around the vehicle to survey the cleared spot where the cabin had been and the miraculously unburned woods. "Returning to the scene of the crime, huh?" he teased, but before I could respond, the DOI Jeep appeared about ten yards away from us.

Annie released it and dusted off her hands. "Ta-da!" she said, taking a bow. "Everyone's alive!"

"Are we sure about that?" Wylan asked.

In short order, the doors of the Jeep opened, and Ganti and Diriem staggered out. "That is *insane*," Ganti said, propping himself on the hood. "Wow. Not what I was expecting."

"I warned you," Annie protested.

"Yeah, but experiencing it is another matter entirely." He raised his head, looking over the vehicle. "Boss? Are you with us?"

A sudden retching noise made me grateful for the darkness.

Connor sighed and opened the back door. "That sounds like fun. Think we've still got a bottle of Gatorade in here."

With Whitford being three hours ahead of Leighfield, and considering the delay due to sickness, cleanup, and embarrassed apologies, my confused phone decided it was nearly two in the morning when we pulled into Connor's driveway. As nice as it was to be back in Georgia after nine days away, all I wanted was my own bed—but since that was out of the cards, I'd settle for one of Connor's.

My boyfriend owned a surprisingly nice house for a

single guy a few months shy of thirty-one, a two-story brick home with tidy if somewhat sparse landscaping. He hadn't bought it, however, but rather inherited it upon his parents' deaths, and whether due to his sentimentality or apathy toward interior design, many of his mother's turn-of-the-century touches remained in the space: wallpaper borders, floral prints, a sponge-painted powder room, and even bunches of dusty plastic purple grapes that decorated the top of the kitchen cabinets. Having learned why much of the house seemed to have been decorated with tips from mid-nineties magazines, I didn't say a peep about it, and I hoped the newcomers would have sense enough not to critique.

We got out and retrieved our bags from the back, and Connor smiled wearily. "Play your cards right, and I'll let you run a load of laundry in the morning."

"Is that your way of telling me I smell?"

"Never," he deadpanned, and I nudged him in the arm as we started up the walk toward the front door.

He flipped the lights on inside, then locked the door once the agents were standing awkwardly in the foyer with their bags, Ganti flagging and Diriem still a little green in the gills. I caught the director as he glanced at his boot, noticed a dried splotch that hadn't been there before our trip, and gestured it into oblivion.

"So," said Connor, stuffing his hands in his pockets, "bed? Or do we need to wind down for a minute?"

The milk in the fridge was well past its prime, but the beer was cold, and Diriem settled for mint tea. We flopped on Mrs. Willow's overstuffed couch and chairs in the den, and though Connor offered the remote, no one moved to turn on the TV—the one major improvement he'd made to the room, a nice flatscreen probably twenty-five years newer than the fussy furniture.

Connor took a long pull of his beer and sighed. "Question."

"Just one?" asked Ganti.

"For now. How the hell do you decide on a career in espionage? Like, I grew up here, right? Cops and firefighters were the options, paramedics if you were feeling fancy. Anyone I knew who ever talked about being a professional spy gave that up by around, oh, fourth grade."

"I was going to be a ballerina and a veterinarian," I offered.

"And I was totally going to be a fighter pilot, once I understood that those cool mecha in the cartoons weren't a viable option."

Ganti sat back and crossed his legs. "I thought about architecture when I was young, but once my talent manifested, that shifted my career path."

That took me aback. "You didn't have it as a kid?"

"No. Farsight isn't like most wild talents. You're a pyromancer, correct? You've always had that affinity for fire."

"Much to Dad's chagrin," I replied, and drank.

He snorted. "And Yacovi is a known floramancer, which shows up early. Farseers don't usually get their first flashes until they're in their twenties, and learning to control farsight takes practice. There are some who have the talent to a mild degree and live more or less normal lives, but if you have a stronger version and an iron stomach, and show control…" He cut his eyes to Diriem, who was carefully nursing his tea. "It's a matter of time before you're recruited. DOI came wooing when I was thirty-four, and once I graduated, I did an extensive apprenticeship to ensure that my talent was sufficiently useful."

"He doesn't give himself enough credit," Diriem cut in. "Ganti's the finest past-oriented farseer in the agency. Probably the best I've ever known."

"But why do you want people who can see the past?" Connor asked. "Wouldn't it be more helpful to see the future?"

"We perform various functions," said Ganti. "The future group does its thing and says as little as possible. There aren't many of us in the past-oriented group. Most farseers who can see the past tend to go into academia, since the things we're called upon to witness while doing agency work..." He grunted. "We liaise with Laws as needed, and let's just say our in-house therapist is great."

"I guess cold cases aren't as much as a problem for y'all, huh?"

He cocked his head. "Cold case?"

"One you can't solve. Can't narrow your suspects or find enough evidence to take it to trial. Yeah?"

"Hmm." He considered that as he drank. "I mean, if you throw blinding potion into the mix, we're not helpful—such as here, with Gerem—and Laws has the occasional case like that, but in general?" He shrugged. "If they tell me their suspects, I can usually clear or pin them with a few days' work."

"What about you?" Connor asked Diriem.

His brows rose as he cradled his mug. "Me? Well...I established the agency shortly after the Pact was signed. It wasn't as well defined then as it is in its current iteration, but we did recognize the utility of farsight."

Connor regarded him curiously, and I could almost see the question in his thoughts: *How old* are *you?* Instead, he joked, "So, what was your career path before then, enigmatic village oracle?"

"Something like that." He sipped, then carefully put the mug on a coaster and stood. "Sorry to trouble you, but—"

"Back that way," said Connor, pointing toward the hall. "On the left. Mauve, can't miss it."

"Thank you."

He hurried out of the room, and I soon heard the sink running. "Poor guy," I murmured. "Is he prone to motion sickness?"

"This is the first of it I've seen," said Ganti, "but since he normally drives, perhaps he's been hiding it." When the water continued to run, he scooted forward in his chair and lowered his voice as he leaned toward Connor. "You asked about the time before the Pact, yes?"

"Yeah…"

"He wasn't some random seer. He was our king."

I stiffened in surprise, and Connor's eyes opened wide. "Come again?" he said.

"We had two, Lord ti'Dana over the northern Halls and Lord ti'Ammaas over the southern," Ganti said quietly. "Or so I've been taught—I certainly wasn't around then. The boss saw that if we remained here, in this world, we'd be annihilated. So, when a group of sorcerers—including your ancestor," he added, glancing at me—"came to him for protection while they built the Pactlands, he sheltered and supported them. And when it came time to forge the Pact and the various factions decided that we needed a representative government to protect everyone's interests, he relinquished his crown and signed. The northern Halls and the associated families like mine—the little people," he muttered—"followed him, as did a few of the southern Halls. Lord ti'Ammaas had refused to help the sorcerers, and he likewise refused to give up his throne. Those within the Pactlands sent out scouts on occasion, but within five years, there was no trace left of the southern kingdom. Those Halls had been wiped out, just as he predicted," he said, cocking his head toward the bathroom.

"By *what?*" Connor asked.

"Humans," he said simply. "You're weaker individually, but we could never match your numbers. That's why we fled. Anyway," he said, sitting back, "I wouldn't give you a dog's fart for most of the so-called lords and ladies, but there's little I wouldn't do if Lord ti'Dana asked. That man saved our *species*, and possibly quite a few others, and he seldom even mentions it. And he's treated me like a colleague since I finished my apprenticeship, which is far more than I'd ever expected from a ti'Dana." The water shut off, and Ganti glanced toward the hall. "Hope he's all right…"

Diriem returned a moment later, pale and damp-faced but with his dignity intact. "I'm going to ask your pardon and retire, if possible," he said, nodding to Connor. "I'm afraid I'm poor company tonight…"

"Been there, don't worry," said Connor, going to his feet. "Y'all can follow me upstairs and decide who's taking which room."

We trooped after him, and as Connor pulled linens from the bathroom closet, they each laid claim to one of the available bedrooms, Connor's utilitarian former room and the overly floral guest room. I hung a pair of towels in the shared bath while they quickly made up the beds, and Connor stepped aside as Ganti headed back downstairs to retrieve his bag. "So, uh…I think I'll hit the hay," he said to Diriem. "If your stomach doesn't settle, I've got some anti-nausea meds."

"Appreciated, but sleep should rectify the situation." He paused, peering at the two of us in the hallway, then asked, "Speaking of sleep, where's Jane's room?"

I stepped closer and gave him a silent *look*.

He grinned. "Indeed?"

"With all due respect, mind your own business," I replied, and disappeared into the master suite to freshen it up before Ganti could be scandalized.

CHAPTER 11

I awoke disoriented, tangled in sheets that smelled like someone else's detergent, and found myself alone in Connor's bed. He'd held me until I drifted off, but somewhere between the wee hours and dawn, he'd slipped out. I tapped on my phone, which I'd barely remembered to plug in before collapsing, and saw it was nearly eight.

In fairness, that was only five in the time zone we'd just left.

Groaning, I pulled myself out of bed and threw on rumpled clothes from my bag, then peeked into the hall. The other two bedroom doors were shut, so I tiptoed downstairs, sniffing at the aroma of bacon.

To my surprise, I found Connor in uniform, albeit puffy-eyed with his brief night's sleep, frying bacon at the stove. His only apron was a heavy-duty canvas number, but with the way the grease was popping, that wasn't a bad thing. "Hey," he said, lifting his spatula in greeting. "Want some?"

"If you've got enough, sure." I kissed his cheek—he'd shaved, though given the state of his hair, I doubted he'd showered—and considered the setup. "Want me to make some eggs?"

"I'm out."

"Toast?"

"Loaf molded while I was gone."

"Hmm." I opened the freezer. "Waffles?"

It was the best of our limited options, we decided, so I wrangled his old toaster and made coffee—Connor's caffeinated tea selection was limited to a box of grocery store–brand teabags—while he finished the bacon. He was, he admitted apologetically, fresh out of anything resembling maple syrup, but bacon alone covered a multitude of sins, and we were slowly starting to wake up when the others appeared, both dressed and looking far perkier than the hour warranted.

Ganti peered at us and cocked his head. "Rough night?"

I lifted my mug in mock salute and sipped. "The magic bean water is still kicking in."

"Y'all help yourselves," said Connor, gesturing toward the food on the counter. "Pickings are slim here, but we've kind of been on the run."

They didn't complain, though Diriem, who looked far less liable to be sick that morning, opted only for coffee. "Going somewhere?" he asked Connor. "You seem to be rather formally dressed."

"Got to put in an appearance," Connor explained. "I've been gone for nine days, and since the rest of the department is two guys and a dog…"

"A dog?" Ganti echoed.

Connor nodded. "He's a good boy and great for drug sniffs, but he's shit at paperwork, so…" Shrugging, he added, "No one's called me with news of a mass murder in the last week, but little things pile up all the same."

"At least the local arsonist has been out of town," I mumbled into my coffee.

"Thank *God.*" Glancing around the table, he asked, "What's the plan?"

Ganti looked to his boss, whose thousand-yard stare into the recesses of the kitchen suggested that he, too, was awaiting chemical assistance that morning. "We need to get Jane to Yacovi's house as quickly as possible," Diriem murmured. "Our time is running. How far is it from here? Reasonable on foot?"

"Miles," I replied. "We're in Whitford right now. Dad

and I live in Ragged Gap—that's in the valley southwest of here. Well, technically, our houses are up on the mountains *around* town, but you get the gist."

Connor pointed toward the garage. "You could take my ride. I'll be in the Explorer today. Or if I need to drive—"

"*You* need to do your job," I insisted. "We'll manage. And y'all have a back seat in that Jeep, right?"

"Sure," said Ganti, "but it's an agency vehicle. Better to not have it spotted near the property—"

"It's just a black Jeep. We get tons of those around here—Jeeps, Subarus, pickup trucks…"

Diriem shook his head. "Ours is equipped with an agency tracker. Technically, no one without agency equipment should be able to pick up its signal, but certain equipment has a nasty little habit of winding up in unauthorized hands. I don't know that Gerem's team has the capability to detect us, but better to not take the risk." He sipped his coffee. "Actually, better for *us* not to be seen."

Connor's brow knit. "Couldn't y'all just change your faces?"

"It's scent I worry about. The bottle of neutralizer Annie delivered wasn't as large as I'd hoped, and we need to douse Jane to keep her undetected."

"But…if y'all are just inside a car?"

He shook his head. "Presumably, you've never dealt with a troll. They have *incredible* noses. Just in case Gerem's hired one to assist…"

I perked as the solution came to mind. "Tabitha."

"Who?" asked Ganti.

"My friend Tabitha. She's been driving by Dad's house a couple times a day to keep an eye on the place, so if there *are* trolls, they won't be surprised to smell her nearby. She could drive me to the back of Dad's property and let me out, then come pick me up once I've poked around. Simple."

But Ganti seemed unconvinced. "This Tabitha, is she…"

"Human," I replied. "Got a problem with that?"

"Uh, *yes*," he said incredulously. "How are you planning to explain invisibility jewelry to—"

"She's in on this," I said, cutting him short. "Known about the Pactlands since last fall, and she's probably the best friend I have in Ragged Gap. I trust her, but if you're worried about her learning the big secret, that ship has sailed."

"You *trust* her?" Ganti demanded.

I glared back at him. "She's never given me shit about my ancestry or, you know, *sent a death squad after me*, so…yeah, I trust her. More than I trust y'all, no offense."

He didn't blink.

"Tabitha's fine. Her reaction to seeing Sage's true condition last fall was to buy her clothes, get her a real haircut, and try to help her learn to read. Feel free to sneak a peek, if that's what it'll take," I snapped.

Diriem stepped in before the hostilities could escalate. "A trial basis," he said, looking at his agitated subordinate. "If she becomes a problem—"

"No one is fucking killing my friend," I interrupted.

He shot me an impatient glance. "Of course not. Memory potion is non-lethal."

"Not an option."

As Diriem's expression shifted toward bemusement, I wondered if he were accustomed to hearing the word *no*. "What do you mean?"

"Tabitha has been helping me with Pactlands-related problems since last September. You're not drugging her, and you're certainly not erasing five months of her life."

"Not erasing, merely modifying—"

"No." Holding his gaze, I said, "Here's the truth: I don't owe the Pactlands a *damn* thing, especially not now. Y'all are the ones who've let Gerem have free rein and kill his family. This problem sure ain't of my making. So, while

I've had to get special dispensation to even visit the Pactlands because my blood might not be *pure* enough for you assholes, Tabitha accepts me. Connor accepts me," I added as he nodded. "And you *will not* hurt the people I care about. Ragged Gap is *my* town, and I will defend it. Who the hell do you think you are?"

Ganti reddened, but Diriem continued to stare at me for another moment before barely smiling and looking away. "You're right."

"*Boss*—" Ganti began, but Diriem silenced him with a quick shake of his head.

"My late granddaughter sounded very much like you, Jane," he murmured. "That anger, that frustration…it's warranted. And it's also entirely fair that you would trust a proven friend over two strangers who've been, shall we say, stalking you."

"There's no compromise here," I said, suspecting he was just trying to soften me up. "No one screws with Tabitha."

"You have my word—we'll offer no threat to her. Give her a call."

Though Ganti seemed displeased with this pronouncement, I decided it was good enough and retrieved my phone from Connor's nightstand. I sank onto the edge of the bed and hoped she wasn't slammed at work.

Fortunately, she picked up before it could go to voicemail. "Jane, hey! What's up? No change at your dad's this morning…"

"I'm so sorry to bother you—"

"You're not bothering me. Everything okay?"

"Not exactly, but…could you give me a ride to Dad's house?"

"You're home?" she asked, taken aback. "Since when?"

"Early this morning, and I'm hiding out at Connor's. With backup from *elsewhere*," I added, just in case of eavesdroppers in her shop. Ragged Gap Apothecary wasn't large.

Her tone took on the notes of a cautiously disapproving big sister. "Jane Fortune, what are you planning?"

"We've got a way to clear Dad's name, but we need to grab some stuff from the house. I want to get in there and steal it or at least case the joint so we know what we're up against."

"Uh-huh. What's so damn important?"

I closed my eyes and rubbed my head. "Quick version, since I'm seriously under-slept: my bio-dad wasn't actually human, he was on the run from *his* dad, the guy who's trying to kill me—"

"*Excuse* me?"

"Gerem, the asshole rep with a posse at Dad's house? He's my grandfather, but he doesn't know the connection."

Tabitha was silent for a beat, then sighed. "Aw, hon. Okay…"

"The worse part—"

"There's a worse part?"

"Yeah. He's used this potion for a century or more to boost his own power, but it runs on family members' blood, and long story short, he's killed, like…"—I paused to tally them—"six of his own kids, probably his sister, and some cousins. Or so the guys with us think. My grandmother found out and killed herself, but she left a suicide note with my father, and Dad sneaked him out. I need that note."

"Holy shit." She whistled low. "Okay, so how are you getting in?"

"Freaking invisibility ring, plus this potion that'll allegedly mask my scent. But I need a lift, and since you've been driving by—"

"They won't suspect me," she finished. "Got it. When do you want to do this?"

"How soon can you be free?"

"Mm…noon? I've got a couple orders to handle this morning. Send me Connor's address, and I'll come get you."

"I owe you big time."

"My renovated kitchen says otherwise," she replied. "Hey, question: these guys with you, are they going to flip out when I roll up?"

I chose my words carefully. "They are…aware of you, not entirely comfortable with this plan, but resigned to it."

"Fair enough. Do me a favor and go back to bed for a bit, eh? If you're going to sneak around, I want you firing on all cylinders."

"Yes, Mom," I muttered, and started to hang up.

"Speaking of whom, did you ever find her?" Tabitha asked before I could press the button.

I froze, freshly reminded of the previous day's discovery, then pushed down my feelings before I could start blubbering again. "Yeah. She died about a year after she ran off. Explains why she never called, right?"

"Oh, *Jane*—"

"I'm fine," I quickly said. "See you at noon, okay? I'll send that address."

"All right," she replied with reluctance, "but when this is all said and done, we're going to have a long talk. With wine."

"You're my therapist now, too?" I joked.

"I say this with love, but you *need* one. Get some rest," she said, and ended the call.

Before I could forget, I texted her my location, then shuffled downstairs only long enough to share the plan before sending Connor out the door and retreating to his room to pass out for a few more precious hours.

Surely, I mused, slipping under, the elves could entertain themselves without burning the house down.

Every bit of Ganti's body language told me how much he

hated the plan as he watched from behind the den curtains while Tabitha's black Camry slowed to make the turn into Connor's driveway. The tension in his shoulders and back, the way he stared out the window as if tracking a wolf from the underbrush, the repetitive finger twitches more suggestive of quick casting than of a tic…suffice it to say he was far from a happy camper.

"Be nice," I muttered, and swept past him through the house, following Diriem out to the open garage. I'd told Tabitha to park inside, and as she eased into the open spot between Connor's storage boxes and an ancient treadmill, Diriem tapped the button on the wall to close the door behind her.

She climbed out of her car, sporting her usual business attire of a loose-fitting blouse, dress trousers, and sensible flats; her white coat lived on a hook at the pharmacy. She'd pulled her box braids back into a thick ponytail, the hints of gray in her dark hair the only real indication that forty had come and gone. Tabitha's skincare routine was practically magical. The most important part of her ensemble was kept hidden beneath her blouse: at the end of the silver necklace chain she frequently wore was a pentacle. Cognizant of her customers' overwhelmingly Evangelical leanings, Tabitha kept her beliefs to herself in public, but she'd been a practicing Wiccan since her college days.

She gave Diriem a long look, though in fairness, as he'd masked, there was little about him to suggest he was anything but a guy my age with longer than usual hair and a strange lilt to his accent. "Hey, there," she said, squeezing between the hood of her car and a disassembled Christmas tree in a plastic storage bag. "Feeling better, Jane?"

"Slightly closer to human," I replied without thinking.

"And how would *you* know?" she retorted, teasing, then pulled me into a tight hug. "Good to see you, girl. Glad you're home."

"Or somewhere close enough," I mumbled into her shoulder.

"At least I know where you are. Where'd you end up, anyway?"

"Northern California."

"*California?* Sheesh." Releasing me, she eyed Diriem again, then stepped closer and extended her hand. "Tabitha Bradley, amateur heist getaway driver."

He retreated but quickly explained, "Best not to get my scent on you, just in case. Diriem ti'Dana, professional snoop."

If she took offense, she hid it well. "Y'all realize that I'm going to come back here and whoop your asses if something happens to Jane, right?"

"Understood, so let's avoid that." He glanced over his shoulder as Ganti appeared in the doorway, then said, "This is Tabitha. You can stop skulking now."

"Hey." She held up her hands, adding, "Guess you don't want me to smell like you, either?"

"That would be safest for all of us, yes." He sidled into the garage. "Ganti."

"Tabitha. Welcome to…Earth, I guess?" Turning back to me, she asked, "How are we playing this? I was debating where to drop you this morning, and I think the best option would be the curve on Satterley, but what are your thoughts?"

"That's…probably smartest," I concurred. "Going to be a hike, but I can manage."

She looked at the agents. "What's y'all's take?"

"Not knowing the terrain, I can't exactly offer an opinion," Diriem replied, "but if you have an atlas…"

A few minutes later, the four of us clustered around Tabitha's iPad, which she'd put on the kitchen table with her map app running. "It's hard to see in this view, but Coby's property is about halfway up this mountain. Now, the thing is, the mountain itself undulates—you go up to his place, then down for a bit where the stream cuts through, and then climb again to the actual peak. See?"

"I'm following," Diriem murmured, peering over her shoulder.

"Okay. So, once you start down toward the stream, you've got woods, but then you hit some rental cabins. Satterley Lane follows the water—it makes a long loop and connects at both ends to Maple Ridge, which runs on the front side of the mountain. Coby's driveway comes off of Maple."

"It's more like a private road than a driveway," I explained. "Dad bought a chunk of land to avoid neighbors."

"The only way on or off that property by road is that driveway to Maple," Tabitha continued, zooming in on the map. "But if I take Jane to Satterley instead, she can go up the back side. I don't know if there's a trail or anything…"

"There's not," I told her, "but I used to go down to the creek as a kid, and I had a few spectacular wipeouts on my bike in those woods. I know the mountain."

"Then we have a plan. Yeah?" she asked, looking up at Ganti.

He scowled at the screen for a moment longer, then nodded. "It's reasonable, I'll grant you that. My concern comes back to scents, however."

"I told you Tabitha's been driving by," I said. "If anyone in that house can smell her, they'll recognize her."

"Yes, but *how* does she go by the house? On Maple or on Satterley?"

Tabitha's nose wrinkled. "Maple. But come on, who the hell could smell me in a *car?*"

The agents traded glances, and Diriem said, "A troll."

She looked at him, taken aback. "Say what, now?"

"Trolls have incredible noses. *Trained* trolls can smell traces of potions in blood, so it's certainly not outside the realm of possibility for a troll on that hill to pick up your scent. A vehicle isn't a perfectly sealed container, right?"

"Well, no, but…you think there's a troll up there? I

haven't been able to get a good look..."

"If there is one, he or she would be masked by necessity. You wouldn't be able to tell," he said gently. "Not from the road, anyway. Now, I suspect we're being overly cautious—Gerem strikes me as the sort of person who insists that no one can do anything better than a sorcerer can, and he's unlikely to hire outside that pool. But we can't be certain, we don't have a way to see inside the house, and so—"

"Better safe than sorry," Tabitha finished. "Got it. Small but non-zero chance of masked trolls." She smirked at him, then said, "Don't suppose y'all are going to tell me whether you're masked as well, huh?"

To my surprise, Diriem rapidly gestured, and his mask vanished. He cocked an eyebrow as Tabitha goggled, then just as quickly replaced his false face. "Oh, my, yes," he said. "Necessary measure out here."

"You..." She paused, pointed at him, then tapped her finger against her pursed lips. "Okay, little freaky, not going to lie, but, uh...sure. Right..."

"Let's take this to the garage so we can ready Jane," he suggested, and started off. "Tabitha, I need to spray a potion inside your car. It's green, but it vanishes as it dries. Won't hurt the interior."

She grabbed her tablet and followed him. "Uh...what kind—"

"Scent neutralizer. I don't want Jane picking up any scents from your upholstery. Cleaning agents, fries, you get the picture."

"What's in it?"

He opened the garage door and plucked a bottle of bright green liquid off Connor's workbench, then turned to show it to Tabitha. "I haven't tried to brew this myself in decades. Yacovi may have the formula memorized, but all I can give you is a guess. It's difficult to brew, and some of the ingredients are quite expensive, but if you want a partial botanical list..."

"Maybe I'll just ask Coby later."

"Probably for the best," he replied, nodding, then cocked his head and considered her. "You have an interest in brewing?"

"I'm a compounding pharmacist. Related field, yeah?"

Diriem chuckled softly. "Distant cousins, I should think. Add magic to the mix. You, um…you don't have any talent in that regard, do you?"

"What," she said, laughing, "like Jane? Hell, no. Not even like Connor. I…" Folding her arms, she cut her eyes toward a pile of moldering carboard boxes. "Look, I…I'm a Wiccan, yeah? And I do believe in the spells I know and cast. But…" She sighed. "Let's just say the effect isn't instantaneous. Nothing that's going to be particularly useful today, anyway."

"Probably not," Diriem agreed, "but your assistance is appreciated nonetheless." Turning to Ganti, he asked, "Do you have the ring?"

Ganti produced a jewelry box from his pocket, and Diriem opened it to reveal a thick gold band covered in etched characters. "Are those…runes?" Tabitha asked, squinting at it in the shaded garage.

"Not precisely. More like a physical manifestation of several spells," he explained, holding it up to show her, then passed it to me. "Try it on."

The ring was cut for a linebacker, but as I slipped it onto my right hand, it shrank to fit my finger. "Convenient. How does it work?"

"See that mark that looks like a quartered circle? Press your thumb against it and hold for two seconds."

I did as he instructed, and Tabitha gasped. While I'd felt no change, I lifted my arm and was unnerved to find that it had vanished—I could sense where my limb was, and my other, equally invisible hand could feel it, warm and solid as ever, but I could look straight through it at the floor. "Wow," I mumbled, turning my hand back and forth as if I might catch a glimpse of fingers.

"That's...weird."

"Hold still," Tabitha ordered, then stepped forward with her arms outstretched until she bumped into me. "Jane?"

I grabbed her shoulders, and she jerked at the unexpected touch. "It's me, I'm here."

"Oh, this is *creepy*. How the hell do y'all keep Peeping Toms at bay?" she asked, looking back at the agents.

Ganti frowned bemusedly, but Diriem understood the reference. "Frankly, cost. That's a loaner, and a ring like that is very expensive."

"How expensive?"

"An adjustable ring, that level of detail and craftsmanship...whatever else can be said for him, Inade has an eye for design," he muttered. "I haven't seen the asking price, but I'd be shocked if it were less than a quarter-million marks."

"Meaning?"

"Our currencies are close. As I said, a very expensive piece."

Suddenly reminded of my low-five-figure bank account, I asked, "Hypothetically, if I were to, um...scratch this?"

"It would probably be reparable," he replied. "And if not, the loan is to the agency. Now," he continued as my heart rate slowed, "turn off the ring for a minute. Let's descent you."

I was quietly relieved to see myself appear again, but as I checked myself out for missing pieces, Diriem asked, "Does anyone know where Connor keeps his bar?"

Tabitha folded her arms. "If Connor's got two bottles of decent hooch in this place, one's from Coby, and the other's probably Jim Beam. What are you looking for?"

"A shot glass, actually, but...eh, this is faster." With a gesture, a glass appeared in his hand. "There, that should suffice."

She goggled. "Sorry...*how*..."

"Practice. And since my glassware always tends to be somewhat shatter-prone, not my first choice." With that, he poured about half a shot of the green potion into the cup and handed it to me. "Tastes like lavender, but I still wouldn't sip it."

Having grown up a brewer's daughter, I knew damn well that potions were the kind of drinks best taken quickly and with a chaser, so I knocked back the potion and steeled myself for the aftertaste. Diriem was right about the flavor profile, but while I didn't mind the odd lavender note in my tea, drinking the potion felt akin to licking one of my bath bombs.

Before I could return to the kitchen in search of a Coke, Diriem ordered, "Arms out, close your eyes, and stand still."

The potion had come with a spray top, and Diriem liberally misted me from head to toe, which left me looking like I'd had a bad run-in with a bartender on dollar margarita night. "Let it dry," he said before I could gripe, then asked Tabitha to open her car doors and squirted the last of the potion all over the front seats and into the air vents. "You'll be on your way in about five minutes," he assured us. "Wait until the color fades."

And it was, to my relief, quickly disappearing as it dried. "How do we know it's working?" Tabitha asked, eyeing her car.

"Unfortunately, I don't have the nose to confirm. This bottle came from agency stock. It's got a long shelf life, and our inventory manager is diligent about removing expired potions, so…"

"You're telling me we're taking this on faith?"

"Do you sample every drug you make?" he countered.

Her mouth tightened, but she muttered, "Touché."

Within a few minutes, the car and my clothes were dry once more, and Tabitha and I loaded up and backed out as Diriem and Ganti watched from the garage. We weren't half a mile down the road before she murmured, "Did I just see what I think I saw back there?"

"Elves with shot glasses?"

"Yep. That's what I was afraid of." She shook her head. "Not to be rude, but those ears…"

"You should see nymphs. Theirs make elf ears look subtle and dainty. And did you miss the teeth?"

"I…" she began, cutting her eyes toward me, then shook her head. "Nope. Don't want to know. Got enough weirdness for the moment, thanks."

"I'm sorry to drag you in like this—"

"Don't be," she insisted, reaching over to pat my knee before she recalled my scent situation and yanked her hand back. "I'd rather know than not, it's just…a lot, and my friend is in danger, and I stood back and let an *elf* spray some unknown green stuff all over my car."

"You've seen Sage. Are Diriem and Ganti that much weirder?"

She mulled that over as she turned south toward Ragged Gap. "Guess not, but what's their deal?"

"They're farseers from the Division of Intelligence. Ganti's the one who realized what Gerem is up to because he can see the past, and Diriem's the agency director. Sees the future."

"Huh. Okay, no more weirdness until I digest this current batch."

"Roger that."

We rode in silence for a while, and we'd just passed the town limit when Tabitha asked, "Are your new buddies going to, say, erase my memory of all this? Is that a thing?"

"It's a thing," I admitted, "but they won't do it."

"You sound awfully sure about that."

"I've got a guarantee. Don't worry," I replied with forced confidence, and hoped my trust hadn't been misplaced.

CHAPTER 12

All too soon, Tabitha turned off Maple onto Satterley and followed the creek that had worn a valley into the mountainside like a serpentine wire through a layer cake. It wasn't a large creek, even at flood, but the Appalachians were ancient, and over the millennia, even the narrow waterway had left the indentation of its progress. Satterley, a two-lane road, followed the creek's path through the winter-bare trees, past a few lonely cabins and little else. I'd always found the creek-side area picturesque, but tourists tended to prefer the cabins higher up the hill, the ones that offered better views but were squeezed together to maximize every square foot of land. In February, especially, with tourism at an ebb, the area around Dad's property was dead in the middle of the day.

Tabitha slowed and pulled onto a gravel patch, a makeshift parking lot for those who wanted to fish the creek, and smiled tightly as I unbuckled. "I'll be back in an hour, and I'll park here. If you're not finished, I'll drive on after about five minutes, and then I'll rinse and repeat. If I don't have you back by sundown—"

"I won't get caught," I told her, then opened my door. "Wish me luck."

"Be careful."

"Will do. See you soon." With that, I quietly closed the door, stepped away from the car, and waved Tabitha on. I waited until she'd started to move before engaging my ring, then jogged across the road and started up the slope toward Dad's house.

The mountainside was treacherous on a good day, steep and littered with the slippery debris of rotting leaves, and there was no trail to speak of. I'd dirtied my share of jeans and skinned my knees more times than I cared to recall while navigating the hill between the creek and home. Going down, if it had rained in the last days, I'd often resigned myself to scooting on my butt. Going up, I'd learned to use the saplings and odd rocky outcroppings as handholds and objects against which I could brace my feet. One such outcropping halfway up the hill was my favorite, a proper stone ledge overhanging a shadowy spot covered in moss. If I tucked my knees close to me and wiggled back against the mountain, I could almost vanish from view, at least if sought from above. Dad had always cautioned me to avoid it for fear of snakes, but I'd liked the notion of sitting invisibly above the creek, still and quiet as the stone around me, watching cars pass whose drivers had no idea they were being observed.

True invisibility was less satisfying than I'd imagined back then. Unable to see my hands, I gripped what I could and hoped for the best as I made my slow, cautious way upward. I wedged my unseen feet into the angled gaps between the mountain and the trees to steady myself, and I paused every few seconds to allow the evidence of my passage, the sounds of footsteps and the motion of shaking branches, to fade away. A pair of squirrels ran by overhead, chittering at each other, but no one peered over the lip of the hill to look for a trespasser.

But getting to the top would only be the first hurdle.

As a grower and brewer, Dad was required by the terms of his license to take precautions to secure his facility. Humans couldn't be permitted to wander in, of course, but the premises also needed to be protected against, say, rogue sorcerers seeking to make black-market potions. Dad's greenhouse and brew room were always locked down in his absence, but he'd gone a step further and constructed ward systems around most of the property, which he engaged whenever he left for more than a few hours. Only the driveway was left unwarded, allowing him to pull off the street before disengaging the security system.

In layman's terms, a ward is like a tripwire for a spring-loaded spell. If something triggers the ward, the spell will deploy—perhaps something like a barrier wall on the basic end, or maybe jets of fire if you're not too concerned about subtlety or casualties. Dad had shown me the three wards around the property, built in concentric circles and carefully calibrated so as not to be activated by the deer roaming in the area. At the outer edge of the property was a ward that would cause a sudden sense of overwhelming anxiety in anyone who touched it, perfect for scaring off the odd hiker and even the occasional bear. A few yards in was a ward that caused fatigue and nausea. These two had been chosen for plausible deniability, as it was far easier to sympathize with a trespasser puking in the bushes than it was to explain away anvils falling from a clear sky. The third ward, which encircled the house, barn, and greenhouse, was a different matter, but I'd never seen it triggered.

Just as Dad had taught me where the wards were, he'd also shown me how to get through them. I wouldn't have trusted myself to build a functional ward system yet, but I'd practiced my lock-picking skills under Dad's watchful eye, and I was confident that I could make it to the house without setting off the traps.

You can't see a good ward. You *feel* it, a faint pulse of energy like moving water. It's not painful on its own, but once that flow is broken—say, by the body of an unsuspecting person—you get to experience the booby prize of the associated deterrence spell. To get through a ward, you need to create an outflow channel, so to speak, like digging a ditch beside a river.

I knew where the first ward ran through experience, but I crawled upward with my fingers extended until I felt the warning tingle of proximity. Once I was right on the edge, I knelt and began building the channel behind me, curving it around my body until it was long enough to reach the ward. I joined both ends to the ward at the same time, and once I was sure the energy had begun flowing through its new pathway, I constructed temporary dams on the original ward and walked—well, crawled—right on over. Since Dad's wards only worked if broken from the outside, I didn't worry about making my way back down the hill later.

The second ward was at the top of the hill, just before it leveled out into the fenced pasture Dad used when customers brought multiple horses for shoeing. I squatted in the dirt, once again crafting an outflow channel, and waited until I was sure it was working before passing through the ward and hopping the fence.

There were no horses on the property that day, which was a *damn* good thing, as I saw once I crested the hill that the third ward—the big one—had been activated.

A moat perhaps six feet wide now followed the path of the third ward. It wasn't deep, not more than a foot or two, but that didn't matter, as making contact with the water would result in a nasty electric shock. The corpses of the birds and squirrels I spotted along its edge and floating in the moat were silent testament to the efficacy of Dad's work, and while a jolt probably wouldn't be lethal to an adult without a pacemaker, it would hurt like hell.

Unfortunately, while the electric moat might stop a human, it didn't present an insurmountable barrier for someone with sufficient magical ability. Thus, while the trespassing assholes had left their rides on the far side of the moat, the noise of the television from inside the house told me they'd found their way across.

I made a note of their vehicles: two black SUVs, nothing flashy, maybe Grand Cherokees, though their angularity suggested they weren't newer models. Assuming everyone was home, that would mean no more than ten people…unless these were souped-up Pactlands models with impossible storage areas. I'd seen agency vehicles with whole labs hidden beneath the trunk, so the number of seats alone wasn't a guarantee of the maximum number of goons on the premises.

I crossed the pasture to the moat and levitated across with a bit of air manipulation—not my best trick, and I'd earn no points for style, but it worked—then crept up to the house, grateful for the loud TV inside. While the walls muffled the sound, I suspected by the cheering and the voice of an announcer that someone had found a sporting event. Stepping carefully to avoid crunching any of last fall's leaves, I moved from window to window, peering in and looking for life on the ground floor. The kitchen was empty—messy but unoccupied—as was the downstairs bathroom. The mudroom at the rear was dark and quiet. I doubled back to the front to look through the big windows into the curtained dining room, but aside from the dirty dishes on the table, it was likewise empty. Assuming everyone was home, then, they were all either clustered in the den or napping upstairs.

Slipping around the house, I peered through the den window and smiled to myself.

Bingo.

Five men lounged by the TV, all staring intently at a cage fight. The coffee table and end tables were covered with chip bags and half-empty longnecks and cans, and someone had turned a salad plate into an ashtray. I considered the group, looking for details, but everyone seemed to be human and no more than about forty.

Surely they would unmask if they were alone like this, wouldn't they? The DOI agents had been eager to get their masks off, so wouldn't this bunch do likewise? Assuming, then, that they *weren't* masked, I was dealing with five sorcerers, possibly ranging in age from forty to a hundred forty—honestly, it was difficult for me to judge.

Five *trained* sorcerers, I amended. This wouldn't be like

the Golden Children in September, a few self-taught sorcerers and kids. If Gerem had sent these guys after me, then presumably they had a full Pactlands education. Surely he could afford decent hitmen.

And there might be more of them. I wouldn't know for sure unless I could get inside.

With the sorcerers distracted by the fight on TV, I sneaked back to the front of the house and considered my options. No one had left a window open on the ground floor—not altogether surprising, considering the weather—and I didn't want to try the door. But one of the dining room windows had a broken latch, and Dad never bothered locking it. With the screens off for the winter, I could ease the window up from the outside, let myself in, and run upstairs to check for more goons.

A good plan, I mused, except for the creaking. Dad lived in an old farmhouse, and while he had renovated enough to add his brew room, he hadn't bothered to shore up the floors. The downstairs floor sagged in places, while the upstairs squealed and groaned unless you knew *exactly* where to step. And the staircase, old as it was, with open storage space underneath—that thing creaked like a haunted house.

But the TV *was* loud, and the men were engrossed in their fight, so maybe, if I moved slowly and levitated a bit, they'd think it was just the house settling.

Maybe.

The wise thing to do would be to go back down the hill and wait for Tabitha, then report what I'd seen to the agents...but my temper was rising, and even though I couldn't see the flames dancing above my skin, I could sense them there.

These assholes were squatting in my dad's house, eating his food, drinking his beer, watching his TV, fucking *smoking* inside, because they were waiting for me to be stupid enough to come home and try to go on with my life. I couldn't say what they would do if they found me, but I suspected that the death draught would be the least of my worries. Gerem hated Dad—was he a sick enough bastard to have me murdered outright instead of jabbed with the potion that would kill me before I could draw Social Security, just to mess with him?

I didn't want to find out, but I wasn't getting any answers to the questions I needed to resolve by hanging around on the porch.

Okay, I told myself, just get inside. One step at a time. Open the window, climb into the dining room, close the window, and wait for your opportunity to move. Maybe the sorcerers would go out for pizza or something.

I could do this.

After a few deep, cleansing breaths to psych myself up, I gripped the wood on the unlocked window and began to slide it upward…

…and a klaxon blared all over the house.

It was then that I noticed the subtle tingle of energy in the window frame. The sumbitches had *warded*.

Fuck.

As the TV snapped off and heavy footsteps ran toward the front of the house, I jumped off the porch and spun around, trying to strategize on the fly. I could run down the driveway, but what if they had some way to see through my ring's protection? Could they track me? Maybe one of them *was* a masked troll, and the cold sweat beading on my skin would drip off and leave a handy trail.

I needed a distraction, and I needed one *now*.

"Sorry, Daddy," I whispered, and shot a string of fireballs at the big oak tree in the yard, the one on which Dad had hung a tire swing I'd loved until it rotted. The burning tree crashed through the porch roof, and with a little assistance from me, tongues of flame began licking at the windows and doors.

I didn't stick around to watch the conflagration. A burst of air carried me back over the moat, and I ran like hell toward the slope down to the creek.

As I sprinted across the pasture, I risked a look back and found the five squatters hurrying around from the back door. While three started toward the fire on the porch, one set off down the driveway, but the last, a blond who looked like he could have held his own in the fight I'd interrupted, jumped the moat and headed for me.

Sure, he couldn't see me—I wasn't even casting a shadow—and he probably couldn't smell me, but I was sorcerer enough to know that my disguise wasn't impenetrable. I glanced at my hand, and while the illusion was excellent, I picked up a telltale wavering in the sunlight. How savvy *were* these guys?

I climbed over the fence, then paused at the second ward, which had repaired itself in the short time I'd been away. It wouldn't affect me when I crossed from inside...

A quick glance over my shoulder told me I might have sufficient time.

I stepped outside the ward, went to my knees to keep from sliding down the mountain, and hastily reconfigured the settings. Though I couldn't change the effect of the boobytrap spell, I'd learned just enough to reverse the trigger direction. My override wouldn't last long...but since my pursuer was halfway to the fence, it'd be long enough.

There is no quiet, dignified way to run down a mountain in a hurry, and I'd ventured to the creek enough times to know that rushing this would be an easy way to faceplant and tumble all the way to Satterley. Putting my dignity aside, I flipped onto my butt and slid down in little bursts, navigating around rocks and trees. I made it through the last of the wards without incident—I had no time to fool with that one—and just as the sorcerer behind me reached the fence, I scrambled beneath the stony overhang and tucked up my knees like I was a little kid once more, trying to still my breathing and hoping he hadn't followed the rustling to my hiding place.

If he had, he soon had much more pressing problems,

as he hit the reconfigured ward. Before he could take two steps down the mountain, he was retching violently, and I risked a peek back up the hill to find him holding on to a young maple and puking his guts out. As soon as the initial wave of nausea passed, he slumped to the ground and sat there, dazed, with vomit drying on his chin and shoes. When he leaned over and threw up again, I almost felt bad for him, but the feeling soon passed.

A few minutes later, when the sick sorcerer had yet to budge from the spot where he'd landed, one of his buddies ran up to check on him. "What's wrong with you?" he called in Pactish. "Find anything?"

"No," he croaked. "I thought I...no...aw, damn it..."

I curled up in the shadows while his stomach convulsed once more, wondering how it could possibly still have anything left in it to vomit.

"Idiot," the newcomer groaned. "Went the wrong way across the puke ward, huh?"

He coughed and spat. "I didn't know it wrapped back here, too!"

"Well, guess you do now. Come on, let's get you cleaned up," his partner said with a sigh. "On your feet, that's—oh, *gross*, you're a mess. Damn, what did you *eat*?"

"Please don't mention food."

Just then, the alarm finally fell silent, and I took care not to move a muscle for fear of revealing myself.

"What happened?" my pursuer asked. "How'd that tree fall?"

"Probably some dumb kid," the other muttered.

"You think a *youngling* did that?"

"Humans are bizarre, man. You've seen the 'flaming bag of dog shit on the porch' trick, yeah?"

"Yeah, but that's a whole damn *tree*. And it was on fire. Unless they're prone to getting lightning from cloudless skies..."

"Power lines," said his fellow. The two men's voices began to fade as they walked away from me. "I bet the tree hit one on the way down. Kid's probably shitting himself."

"But aren't the power lines those things running from the pole on the other side of the house?"

"It's a big tree," he replied with unwarranted sagacity. "Don't worry, we put out the fire."

"Dumb bastard's going to wonder what happened," said my pursuer.

His companion laughed. "You think that little peon is ever leaving the Pactlands again?"

Soon, I could no longer hear their conversation, but I didn't risk abandoning my hiding place for another twenty minutes—not until the world around me was still once more but for a passing squirrel and the low rush of water in the creek. Only then did I crawl out from beneath the overhang and carefully start back up the slope, hoping for another shot at the house. I reached the modified ward, which was already beginning to revert, and diverted the flow once more to give myself passage, then topped the hill and climbed over the fence, listening.

A hawk screeched in the distance, and I could hear the occasional sound of tires as a car passed, but otherwise, the place was quiet.

The squatters had put out the fire, but they hadn't repaired the porch, the roof of which was smashed where the tree had landed. The charred tree itself had been moved aside, and while I hated to see it lying there, I couldn't touch it. I crept to the back of the house once more and peeked in the den window to find the five men, including their unfortunately nauseated comrade, back in front of the TV with fresh beers.

Some crack hit squad *they* were.

I still only counted five, which gave me hope that I was seeing the full crew—wouldn't anyone else in the house have woken and come downstairs when the fire started? But I couldn't be sure, and so, taking care not to touch the window, I staked out the place and waited.

By the time the fight ended, I felt more confident in my

initial estimation. No one else had joined the men in the den, and no other cars had driven up. There had been no phone calls to inform absent associates of the fire and downed tree. As they began to bicker about the next show to watch, I backed away from the window and started to leave, then paused as another black SUV rumbled up the driveway.

Taking no chances, I ducked around the side of the house and watched as a dark-haired man climbed out, carrying Dad's ancient bag of seldom-used golf clubs over his shoulder. He frowned at the damage, then muttered at the front door and let himself in. "Hey!" I heard him yell before the door closed behind him. "What *happened?*"

Slipping back to the window, I watched as the golfer confronted the other five in the den. "What do you mean, a kid did that?" he demanded after a brief explanation. "How would a kid chop down a tree and set it on fire without you idiots knowing?"

"It hit the power lines," one started, but the golfer was apparently the brains of the operation.

"There are no power lines in that tree's path! Seriously, what happened?"

And that was my cue to split.

I made it back across the pasture without spotting a pursuer, but I took the hill cautiously, moving in short bursts and sliding down on my rear because I didn't dare risk standing. By the time I reached the bottom, I was shaking from adrenaline, and my jeans were soaked from the wet dirt. I staggered across the street to the creek, willed my clothing dry and cleaner, and plopped onto a rock to wait for my ride.

I didn't have a watch on, but it couldn't have been more than ten minutes before I spotted Tabitha's car coming around the curve. She slowed and pulled over onto the gravel, and I turned off my ring and waved at her as she unlocked the doors.

"*There* are you. Are you okay?" she asked as I climbed

inside. "See anything?"

The clock said it was nearly three-thirty. "Yeah."

She was moving again before I'd buckled my seatbelt. "Were you able to get that note?"

I leaned back against the seat and closed my eyes. "I wasn't even able to get into the house. They warded the windows."

"Come again?"

"Alarm went off when I tried to sneak inside. I ended up setting the porch on fire to make my getaway."

"*Jane...*"

"Best distraction in a pinch."

"I'm not complaining," said Tabitha, "I'm just concerned that you were in a situation in which starting a fire was the best option available. Arson's usually not the answer, you know?"

"So y'all keep telling me," I mumbled, drained. "Shit. Okay, there's at least six men in the house. Might be more, but I couldn't check upstairs. I think they're all sorcerers, which is good and bad."

"How so?"

"They can't smell me coming, so all this de-scenting may have been overkill. On the other hand, they're definitely better trained than I am, and I'm not going to be able to get in there as long as their ward's in place." Sighing, I said, "That was almost a complete bust, and I'd have missed the last guy if I'd left five minutes sooner. Asshole went golfing with Dad's clubs. No guaranteed headcount, no note, no names or anything..."

"Are *you* okay?" she asked again.

"Kind of shaky," I admitted, "but I'm not hurt."

"You didn't answer my question."

I looked at Tabitha, whose no-nonsense expression demanded the truth. "Nothing is okay right now, but if I focus on what I can do, I'm less likely to spiral into a breakdown."

"That's what I thought."

When we turned toward downtown Ragged Gap instead of Whitford, I asked, "Where are we going?"

"First," said Tabitha, "we're going to my place, because I think you could use a stiff drink and maybe a shower."

That *did* sound nice.

"And after that," she continued, "we're going to pick up dinner and head back to Connor's house. All right?"

"Thanks, Tabitha," I murmured, and reached across to take her hand.

She squeezed mine and smiled grimly. "Sure thing, hon. Now, I do have a question."

"Only one? I'm shocked."

"For the moment. Do you suppose those elves of yours eat barbeque?"

CHAPTER 13

For Diriem and Ganti, at least, the answer to that was a resounding *yes*.

"This is amazing," said Ganti through a mouthful of pulled pork. "What's in the red sauce?"

"Big John's skews Carolina-style," said Tabitha, who was helping herself to the baked beans. "Vinegar base, hot sauce, red pepper, and spices. There's probably molasses in there, too—something sweet."

"Brown sugar?" Connor suggested.

"Not sure, and I sincerely doubt that John would tell me if I asked."

"They've got that white sauce, too…"

The look Tabitha shot Connor across the loaded dinner table at the suggestion was withering. "White barbeque sauce is an abomination, and that's final."

Connor raised his tea glass and loaded fork in surrender, then took another bite. "Thanks again for grabbing dinner. I was going to pick up Mexican or something, but this is quality."

"Hits the spot on occasion," Tabitha concurred, and glanced at Ganti, whose expression was reminiscent of a kid tasting chocolate for the first time. "Y'all don't have this, huh?"

Mouth stuffed, Ganti shook his head.

"There have been…attempts," said Diriem, who had approached his plate with far more restraint than his colleague demonstrated, "but nothing great, and they've never lasted. Those of us who have reason to come out here usually learn of barbeque and spread the word, but I've yet to sample anything in the Pactlands that measures up to the offerings here." Tearing off a piece of white bread—Big John wasn't fancy with his mopping carbs—he said, "The other consideration is that many of us lean vegetarian."

Frowning, I said, "I thought it was tough to grow more than grass."

"Oh, certainly, but once you factor that in, it's even more difficult to raise livestock. They have to eat, too. But some certainly acquire a taste for meat," he said, smirking at Ganti as he groaned in pleasure, "and those of us who grew up outside generally haven't lost it."

Tabitha considered that as she stabbed a chunk of potato salad. "So...you're in the same boat as Jane, then?"

"Come again?"

"Like, you lived out here, then got citizenship somewhere along the way?"

"*Ah.*" He smiled briefly, revealing a flash of teeth that, at least to my eye, seemed well-suited to a carnivorous diet. "Not precisely. The Pactlands wasn't finished until 1538, so I spent my first couple of centuries out here. I'm sure the landmarks have changed, and I would have a difficult time trying to pin my home to a map, but I grew up in a remote corner of Scandinavia, if that helps."

Slowly, Tabitha lowered her fork. "I'm sorry, *how* old—"

"Old enough. Ganti's only about two hundred or so..."

"Two hundred eleven," he managed, though with as much sauce-drenched bread as he'd crammed in, I wasn't quite sure how he formed the words.

"Anyway, to answer your question," Diriem continued, "technically, no, I haven't always had citizenship, but that's because I predate the Pactlands. I *did* sign the Pact, so I've had it from the beginning, but..." He shrugged. "What's the term, 'old fart'?"

I could understand Tabitha's skepticism, as masked or not, Diriem looked barely older than thirty.

"O...kay," said Tabitha. "And *why*, now, are y'all stalking Jane?"

The agents shared a look, and Ganti deferred to his director with a wave of his fork.

"Multiple reasons," said Diriem, pushing his largely cleaned plate aside. "I don't know what, exactly, Jane has told you, so forgive me if I seem condescending. Do you know what it means to be farsighted?"

"Um...around these parts, it's when your near vision ain't great, but I'm guessing that's not what you're after."

He grinned. "Hyperopia, and no. It's a wild talent—an inborn ability beyond the norm. Jane is a pyromancer," he explained, "which means she has a natural affinity for fire magic. As wild talents go, that's one of the more common ones, particularly in sorcerers, though no wild talent is *common*. Ganti and I are farseers. In basic terms, he can see a person's past, and I can see their future."

"Which is why they're spooks," said Connor, digging into the container of pulled pork.

Ganti's brow knit. "*Spooks?*"

"Spies," I offered.

"Oh? Huh." Satisfied, he returned to his meal.

"The Division of Intelligence is more than a spy agency, but that is part of the mission," Diriem allowed. "Anyway, farseers often get flashes of information, even if we're not actively seeking it. Call it intuition, premonition, whatever you like—it can be a useful guide. And for several months, mine has been gravitating toward Jane."

"Because of this mess?" Tabitha asked.

"In part. I don't yet see the full picture, and you must realize that much of what I ever see is potentials. But this present matter is certainly notable. I asked Ganti to search, and the result was staggering. A representative is a killer, Yacovi's only crime would be excused by necessity, and now there's an unknown Aniap in the line who's been raised in exile."

"Fortune," I muttered into my baked beans.

He didn't argue with me. "Our task here is twofold," he told Tabitha. "Vindicate Yacovi and bring down Gerem."

She nodded, swirling the ice in her glass. "So, y'all've worked with Coby or something?"

"Not directly," said Diriem, and Ganti shook his head. "But I certainly knew *of* him from his agency days, and he had a stellar career. The only blot was at the end, when he gave a trainee the draught...or didn't, as the case may be," he added with a half-smile. "What we know now is that he saved Jane's father's life, helped her parents run away together, raised Jane, and has kept up a cover story that could end with him incarcerated. He's owed exoneration." He paused to drain his beer. "Beyond that, Gerem's a murderous ass, and if I can do my part to put him on a penal farm, so much the better."

"Hmm." She rose from the table and pulled the tea jug from the fridge. "Do I detect the faintest hint of bad blood?"

Ganti laughed, though Diriem maintained his poker face. "One might say that."

She turned, glass in hand. "Oh? Might one? Do tell."

He sipped his beer. "Gerem's grandfather was a friend of mine. His father was a good man. Gerem, putting aside the fact that he's been killing his family, has been an obnoxious blowhard on the Forum for the last one hundred twenty years. Good at speeches, a savant when it comes to expressing outrage at the most opportune moments, and jealous of anyone he perceives as a threat to his position. You're either beholden to him or an enemy. As he has nothing I want, we've never been more than cordial."

"Would we go that far?" Ganti quipped.

Diriem grunted. "He's only worsened with age. Now that he's entrenched as a representative, he refuses to negotiate, and he tries to lord what power he has over the agencies. It's true that the Forum superintends us," he allowed, "but some of the stunts Gerem has attempted over his career..." He shook his head. "There comes a point at which I begin to take matters personally. And as I've had the misfortune of serving on the Tribunal Committee with that man, I can tell you from experience that he's no better behind closed doors than he is in front of a camera. Oh, and then there's the 'seniority' issue," he added, rolling his eyes. "Sorcerers vote for their representatives, and for unknown reasons, they've been sending Gerem back to the Forum all this time. *We* rotate among Hall leadership, so I only sit on the Forum every few terms. Gerem insists that he has seniority for things like committee assignments because his tenure has been unbroken, and then I'm forced to remind him that I've been on and off the Forum since the damn founding, and—"

"It gets petty?" I suggested.

"Very much so," Diriem grumbled. "He's long been an annoyance, but he finally went too far last summer. Have you met Annie Humphries?" he asked Tabitha.

"Yeah, briefly," she said, nodding. "With that Oil of Life business."

"Ah. Did Annie mention her background?"

"Not really. Jane's told me a little..."

He finished his beer with a final sip and set the can aside. "Annie was born in Richmond. Perfectly ordinary human. She and several friends were dosed with a novel and rather insidious potion against their knowledge—most were unaffected, several died, and Annie grew antlers. While DPP worked on an antidote, she and another victim were kept in the Pactlands for their protection and our continued security."

"So...abducted by aliens," said Tabitha.

He winced. "Close. To keep this brief, despite the fact that she had no actual talent, she rescued a woman kidnapped by the Wild Hunt as prey—"

"Wait, *wait*," Connor interrupted, turning to me, "that guy who showed up with you and Annie—"

"That's Wylan," said Diriem. "The *current* leader of the Hunt. His father was the one responsible for the kidnapping. The former Hunter tried to kill Wylan, and Annie saved him. Then the Hunter snatched a group of DOL agents, and once again, Annie jumped in to help. The Hunter would have killed her that time if Wylan hadn't stabbed him first."

By that point, Tabitha's dinner had been forgotten. "*Shit*," she muttered.

"Exactly, but back to Gerem. Once DPP found an antidote, Annie wanted to remain because she and Wylan were quietly a couple, and part of sending her home involved a memory potion. My counterparts at DPP and Laws and I went to the Forum and asked for an exception to be made for her. That was rejected, and Gerem not only took pleasure in it, but he alone of the representatives insisted on being at DPP when her memory was altered. The healer that day was your cousin," he said, glancing at me, "and she slow-walked the final preparations, but had Wylan arrived a minute later than he did…"

"He'd have lost her," I murmured.

The corner of Diriem's mouth twitched. "Possibly. I may or may not be aware that our other guest's memory wipe was…imperfect, shall we say?"

I kept my expression still, but he didn't need confirmation.

"In any case, Gerem was furious at being thwarted. He never liked the fact that agency funds were going to house and feed a couple of humans, never mind that both did more for us than we ever did for them. And now that Rosie's existence is no longer a secret," he added, glancing my way again, "he takes every opportunity to insult me for my son. I've tolerated it to this point, but wouldn't it be a pity if Gerem's own family were his undoing?"

"Sorry, not following," said Tabitha. "What's wrong with your son?"

He smiled grimly. "Speaking as his father, only the fact that he's dead."

Her eyes widened, and she sucked a quick breath through her teeth. "Oh, gosh, I'm sorry—"

"It's fine," he insisted. "He's been gone for fifty years—this isn't exactly fresh. But we kept it quiet when he left the Pactlands to be with Rosie's grandmother, and I had no choice but to give him the draught on his way out. He was farsighted, too—we knew the time would come," he murmured, then lifted his beer, realized it was empty, and set it aside once more.

Aghast, Tabitha demanded, "You killed you own *kid?*"

"I didn't force it down his throat, but I put the potion in front of him. Connor, do you mind if I—"

"Go for it," he replied.

Diriem gestured at the fridge until a fresh beer floated into his hand. "Thanks," he muttered, and popped the top before continuing. "It's our law," he told Tabitha. "Has been almost since the founding. It's not intended as a punitive measure, but rather for everyone else's protection. If you want to be with a human, that's your business, but you do so without any…quirks, let's say, that could lead to the neighbors asking questions. The draught dampens all magical abilities, and we can apply permanent masks as needed. That's what I did for my boy," he said softly. "His daughter looked human and had no talent of her own, and her descendants might never have known there was anything odd in the family line had she not married a man who was *also* the half-elven product of a parent who'd taken the draught. The potion is effective, but it's unstable and poorly studied over multiple generations, so no one without the benefit of farsight anticipated that the effect would be canceled in their daughter. Rosie may have human features, but she's *very* talented." He drank again. "Those few who knew where my son had gone covered it up, and it wasn't safe to reveal the truth about Rosie until two years ago. But as it's considered a demerit against the family if a member takes the draught, Gerem seems to find ways to bring up her ancestry whenever possible."

"And that's shitty, I'm sure," said Tabitha, "but I'm still stuck on the fact that you gave your own kid that potion."

"Believe me, if there'd been another option—"

"There was! What about everything Coby did for Jane's parents, huh?"

Diriem remained calm in the face of her indignation. "I loved him dearly," he said after a moment. "He and I ran through every possible alternative, as far into the future as we could see them play out. We brought in other farseers we trusted for second opinions. And in the end, what we saw was that if he didn't take the draught, he would eventually be discovered and forced, and then he would be watched for the rest of his life. His daughter would have met with an unfortunate accident before her wedding day because her father-in-law's father is a monster in his own right. For the same reason, I never visited her again after collecting my son's remains. Couldn't even explain. While we chose the path of least harm, that doesn't mean it wasn't a harmful path all the same."

Tabitha's expression had softened as he spoke. "So…guess we can agree that the draught is an awful idea, yeah? Why not do something about it?"

"Because these things take time," he replied, "and to be blunt, we didn't build a pocket world and hide away for centuries because humans make great neighbors. Any action that could risk exposing ourselves to the *seven billion* of you would be extensively debated. In the meantime, though, I'm here to keep Jane safe, because even if she had been half human, there's no need to punish her with the draught for merely having been born."

I locked eyes with Connor across the table, thinking of the community at East Branch. If they had a sorcerer or two in their gene pool, I certainly wasn't going to bring it up—not without solid assurances that a hit squad with vials of the draught wouldn't descend upon them.

Of course, given how Diriem hadn't even blinked when Connor's "touch" had flared back in California, I suspected he knew plenty already.

Trying to steer the conversation away from that direction, I said, "What now? We've got a headcount, kind of. Do we storm Dad's house? Fight them? I realize I'm not fully trained," I added before the agents could object, "but I do know how to throw my weight around. I mean, hell, I set the porch on fire this afternoon."

Connor rubbed his forehead and groaned.

"What? It *worked.*"

"I'd expect nothing less from you, Firebug."

But Diriem didn't seem eager to stage an invasion, and Ganti, who was finishing the potato salad straight from the container, wasn't jumping at the idea. "Assume we have six sorcerers in that house," said Diriem. "They're in a defensible location, which isn't great, but we can work around that in theory. The problem is that we don't want to stage a full-on, spell-slinging, fire-throwing, magic-fueled fight in the middle of a human town. Far too great a potential for collateral damage and casualties, not to mention the problems inherent in merely being *witnessed.* Even Gerem's crew should understand the risks, and we don't want a situation in which they conclude that the easiest way to clean up the mess is by killing civilians. Making corpses is seldom the best plan."

"I've got an idea."

The table turned to Connor as he mopped up the last of his sauce. "*Oh?*" said Ganti.

"Yep. Look, everyone in the freaking county knows that Yacovi's a moonshiner. It's hardly a secret. I mean, most of the Ragged Gap PD and the Sheriff's Office *buy* from him, for heaven's sake."

"True," I said.

"Which is why no one around here knows *nothin'* about

any illegal activities on good Mr. Hewt's property," he said with all the faux sincerity of a choirboy caught playing cards during the sermon. "No one's ever going to raid the place, and if the state folks were to come sniffing, I'd bet good money that our local law enforcement would develop a sudden case of amnesia." He smiled and leaned forward. "But you know who doesn't know that? Those bastards up at the house right now. So, what if we staged a raid? If y'all could change your faces, put on the right gear, and let me do the talking, we might be able to make this look convincing…*if* you're confident that they're going to try to avoid killing anyone."

"Killing police would be a difficult matter to cover up," Diriem mused. "I'm not positive that they wouldn't, but if Ganti and I were on hand to shield…"

"Uh, problem," Tabitha cut in. "Coby lives outside your jurisdiction, Connor. How do you plan to convince Ragged Gap's cops to go along with this?"

"I don't," he replied, "hence the *staged* raid. Here's what I'm thinking: we pull together enough gear to look passably like Ragged Gap PD, at least in the dark. Y'all two," he continued, pointing to the agents, "Jane, and I can fake our way in. We either run off the squatters or we arrest them, and if they start with the magic shit, I have every confidence in Jane's fireballs. She's got an impressive track record around here."

Diriem looked at Ganti, who finally put the empty potato salad container aside. "As plans go, I don't hate it," Diriem said slowly, "but fire's a definite concern. We don't want to alert firefighters, but more importantly, Yacovi's a brewer, and I've yet to see a brew room that wasn't a good spark away from blowing up. I don't suppose you have a list of what he keeps on hand," he said to me.

I shook my head. "No. Dad's only recently begun teaching me to brew, and he doesn't let me touch anything for export."

"So, we have to assume the worst and minimize fire,"

said Ganti.

Well, at least I'd kept the afternoon's conflagration confined to the porch.

"And there's the matter of the actual police," Diriem added. "Suppose magic proves necessary, or suppose we end up in a shootout. How do we guarantee that the true Ragged Gap officers stay away?"

Connor deflated in his chair, and Tabitha scowled into the middle distance as she tried to work out the kinks...but as I mulled over the variables, a possible solution occurred to me.

"I think I've got it," I said, hastily pushing back from the table, "but I need to make a call, pronto. If I can get this to work, are we up for raiding Dad's house tomorrow night?"

"Certainly," Diriem replied, puzzled, "but what are you—"

"No time. Tell you later," I said, and ran from the room with my phone.

To my relief, Stephanie wasn't giving a lecture or doing yoga that evening—and judging by the muffled sound of a laugh track in the background, she was engaged in far more mundane pursuits of the rerun persuasion. "Hi, Jane," she said cautiously. "No recent sightings in the shop."

"Great. Listen, I need a favor."

She hesitated. "What sort?"

"You want to make things right after that whole business last fall? You do this, and we're square." Before she could object, I added, "This isn't for me. The guys who are stalking me are hiding out at my dad's place, and he can't get them out by himself."

Not entirely true, but close enough.

"I've got some help, and I think I can run them out of town, but I need your assistance."

Stephanie sucked a breath. "I…I'm not a violent person. I don't even own a gun…"

"Oh, no, I'm not asking for anything like that," I reassured her. "Nothing violent. What I want is for you to get a crowd together tomorrow night and throw the biggest, most insane party you've ever thrown in Ragged Gap. Do it somewhere in our police jurisdiction. Maybe Yancey Park?"

Named for an early mayor, Yancey Park was more like a wilderness preserve on the edge of town, offering trees and trails instead of fountains and playsets. Local birders who didn't feel up to venturing into the mountains haunted the place during the spring and fall migrations, and at least one or two adventurous kids got lost in there every summer without fail.

"Uh…I don't think you can get permits for Yancey," said Stephanie. "The point is to keep it natural."

"Exactly. I need you to do something so notable that the cops get called."

"*Why?*"

"Distraction, and that's all I can safely tell you."

"But…" She huffed on the other end of the line. "What sort of party? We're still a few weeks out from Ostara, so I don't have a real reason to get people together like that, particularly if you're looking for a big event. And if I get arrested, it'll be bad for business. I've got a pristine record, Jane," she protested.

"And I appreciate that," I replied. "But I've told you those guys are bad news. This whole town is in danger until they're gone. My dad is in trouble, and they're part of it."

"Who *are* they?"

I closed my eyes and rubbed my forehead. "You believe in magic, right?"

"Yes…"

"Remember Warner Cavanaugh? He used to come around—"

"*Oh*, yeah. The creep in the black duster? The 'warlock'?" she said with disdain. "I finally had to ban him after he got handsy with some of the younger staff. Whatever happened to him? I heard he skipped town last year."

"I ran him off. He's not a warlock, but he's worse than you know."

"You…"

"We're playing the plausible deniability game, Stephanie."

She sighed. "Fine. What about Warner?"

Dad had taught me that for sorcerers, magic wasn't classified into good and bad. Spells and potions were considered tools, more or less complicated and possibly requiring questionable components, but technically neutral in their alignment. What you did with them was another matter—fire, for instance, could cleanse or destroy, depending on the hands of the wielder. Personally, I wouldn't have minded slapping a label on Oleum Vitae, but in general, we didn't speak of "working for the Light" or "practicing black magic."

But Stephanie didn't know that.

"The men at my dad's house are the real deal," I told her. "Warlocks. Maybe stronger than I am. And if you and I don't put our grievances aside and make them leave…"

"You think they're—"

"Practicing death magic. I *know* they have plans to kill," I said, omitting the part about how I was the target. "Stephanie, we've had our differences, and I ordinarily wouldn't think of dragging you into this, but I'm desperate. So, for the good of this community, I'm asking you to help me. You've got the clout to pull this off."

She was silent for a few seconds, and I held my breath.

A long sigh heralded her decision. "I…might have an idea."

"Yeah? What's that?"

I could almost hear the smirk in her voice. "Plausible

deniability, right? Just be ready. You'll get your distraction."

CHAPTER 14

Dawn Friday morning found Connor in the kitchen in his sweatpants, arranging a cannister of instant oats, a bag of raisins, and a box of brown sugar on the counter beside some bowls and spoons. "I'm not being a good host," he muttered when I came downstairs in his bathrobe and asked what the hell he was doing. "Haven't shopped, food situation is bordering on dire, and this is the best I can do today. Don't even have OJ…"

"Con," I murmured, hugging him from behind, "we can manage. Go get ready for work."

He turned to hug me properly. "I could stay. Let the guys handle it. What are the odds of a major felony being committed in Whitford today, huh?"

"Probably slim, but you have a job to do. Go keep up appearances, Chief. I'll handle the rest."

We'd talked this over the night before, but he wasn't keen on the day's itinerary, possibly because he still didn't fully trust his other houseguests. Personally, I thought it made sense: Connor and Tabitha would go to work as usual, and I'd stay in with the agents, throwing together our fake police gear. During the day, Connor would drive to the pharmacy and deliver a scanner to Tabitha, who would monitor the Ragged Gap cop chatter that night and let us know when it was safe to head for Dad's house.

By the time Connor was dressed for the day, Diriem was sitting at the kitchen table with a laptop—one with Pactish characters on the keyboard, I noted—and a cup of coffee. "We have the matter well in hand," he told

Connor, minimizing a document. "No one will hurt Jane while you're away."

Though Connor seemed unsure, he let it go. "What're you working on?"

Diriem made a face. "Quarterly report to the Forum. Trade you."

He patted the pistol at his hip. "Ever handled one of these?"

"Dear boy," Diriem replied with a look of incredulity, "the first firearm on which I qualified was a *musket*. A semiautomatic is child's play next to a flintlock model."

Once Connor had slunk sheepishly out to his Explorer, I muttered in Pactish, "You didn't have to embarrass him."

"We're testing each other," he replied, cradling his mug. "This happens. Both of us are accustomed to being in charge, neither is fully confident of the other's capabilities or trustworthiness, and so we're each feeling the other out." One shoulder barely rose in a mild shrug. "Not my first time to play this game. He's nipping, and so I bite back."

I rolled my eyes and waved the stove on to heat the kettle. "*Men.*"

"It's not as bad as it seems," he protested. "I'd be concerned if Connor weren't behaving like this. He's confident, asserting command...*quite* worried about you, I should add...but now he has two new potential teammates, and so he's testing us. It's nothing personal."

"What, you're doing the same?" I asked with a smirk.

He grinned. "No need. I've seen something of him by now, and I'm satisfied for the moment."

Ganti shuffled into the room before I could press Diriem for details, and despite his feast the night before, he spotted the oatmeal and brightened.

I left the matter and made my tea, and once Ganti had put down a second bowl, Diriem closed his computer and absently massaged his shoulder. "Well, shall we get to it?"

My thought had been to pile in one of our vehicles and

visit a military surplus store in Tennessee that also catered to law enforcement. While my bank account had taken a hit that month with our travel, I calculated that I had enough to spring for gear sufficient to make us look passably like police in the dark. Ganti, however, had other plans.

"Do we have reference pictures?" he asked me. "What would one wear to a raid around here?"

I grabbed my own computer and pulled up screengrabs of various police raids, and Ganti studied them quietly. "Helmets, yes," he said after a moment, scrolling through, "probably black clothing, that top layer with the patches…"

"Bulletproof vests," I offered.

"Ah, got it. Ours are a bit slimmer."

"What are *you* doing with bulletproof vests?"

"Protecting the squishy bits," he replied. "I've been fortunate to this point, but I know plenty of people in Laws who've been shot at."

"If you're not magically adept and trying to commit a crime," Diriem explained, "a gun is a useful thing. Even if you *are* adept, it's a decent backup option. Laws' armory is testament to that." Turning to Ganti, he asked, "Seen enough?"

He cracked his knuckles. "Let's find out…"

Ganti closed his eyes, took a deep breath, then slowly exhaled. On his next inhalation, his fingers began *flying*, twisting and dancing like he'd discovered the only other speaker of a rare sign language at long last and was desperate to be understood. Though I couldn't see the logic to his movements, they did the trick for him, as a passable copy of a bulletproof vest, down to the POLICE patches, suddenly appeared in the middle of the table.

Even as a moderately trained sorcerer, I was taken aback by this development, and I reached for the vest, which I found to be solid and heavy. "How…what did you…" Rapping my knuckles against it, I heard the thud from the hard plates within. "You didn't mask anything…"

"No," said Ganti, shaking out his hands. "And it's a technique you would learn in your thirties, were you still interested in school," he added with a teasing smirk.

"Dad has *never* created anything like that—"

"Oh, he probably has. Common trick with brewers. Glassware breaks *all* the time."

In fairness, I'd never seen Dad go out to buy so much as a replacement flask. "Well, he's never mentioned it to me."

"Because you're young," said Diriem, "and that's complicated. Making something that will last more than a few minutes takes concentration and skill…and some of us never quite master it."

Ganti cut his eyes to the director. "Yours aren't *bad*."

"Eh." He waved it off. "Yours are far better."

"And then there's the boy…"

Diriem chuckled and shook his head. "Honestly, I don't think he realizes how talented he is in that regard."

"Who?" I asked.

"Yven, Rosie's fiancé. No wild talent, absolutely horrible with defensive magic, but he can almost pull small objects from midair, and they *last*. I seldom attempt more than the odd handkerchief, and he casually produces notebooks." Diriem sipped his coffee, then added, "I won't say he's *wasted* in his position—he's fastidious enough to work in Regulatory, and that man loves his plants—but he's more talented than he gives himself credit for."

"But since he's not available," said Ganti, "we'll make do." Standing, he tried on the vest, which fit him well and, at least to my layman's eye, passed muster. "Feels solid," he said, patting it all over, "but I'm not sure I'd risk a bullet with this."

"Hopefully, we won't need to," Diriem replied. "Think you can manage the rest?"

"With sufficient caffeine, all things are possible. Jane, is there more tea?"

"Yeah, sure," I said, heading to the cabinet. "What, you can't just make that, too?"

"I can give you a cup of something hot, brown, and liquid, with no guarantees as to palatability or potability." When I glanced back at him, he shrugged. "We all have our limits, right?"

"Fair," I said, "but should we have to skip town again, you are *not* in charge of snacks."

With Ganti producing and fine-tuning our gear, I was left to my own devices for much of the morning. I attended to my backlog of emails, apologizing to my customers for the delay and blaming it on a vague family emergency. I was itching to drive to my house and at least make the belated delivery run to my B&B and rental cabin customers. While spring tourism had yet to surge, I hated to leave anyone scrambling for toiletries. But I knew that wasn't an option: I always made those deliveries in person, and until Gerem's people were out of Dad's house, I couldn't be seen around town.

Gerem fucking Aniap.

My grandfather.

Had I only found my mother's grave two days before? Had it only been two short days since Diriem and Ganti interrupted our dinner with the news that would upend my life and everything I thought I knew about myself?

Superficially, I was coping. We had things to do, bigger problems to solve, Dad to rescue, and I could deal with whatever the agents threw at me. But if I peeled back a layer or two, I found a chaotic maelstrom of emotions swirling at my core, and I had no idea how to calm them.

My bio-dad was a sorcerer. My mother was dead. My grandfather was trying to kill me. And I wasn't even slightly human.

Part of me wanted to call Rose and ask for pointers on how to process the discovery that you've been mistaken about your own species, but I suspected her to-do list was already full. So, I lay back on Connor's bed beside my laptop that afternoon and stared at the ceiling, trying to poke at my complicated mess of feelings without triggering a breakdown.

Strangely, of all my emotions about the last two days, the strongest of them was loss. Since I was old enough to understand that my mother was a sorcerer, I'd come to terms with my identity as a product of two worlds, part of but not quite fitting into either. So what if I wasn't good enough for the Pactlands? I was the best damn witch in Ragged Gap, the person desperate folks sought out when they had nowhere else to go. Maybe I was a little different, sure, but I had a role in the community I called home—I was, at least in part, one of them.

But now I knew I no more belonged in Ragged Gap than Dad did. I was an interloper, a stranger not to be trusted...the granddaughter of a man who fed on his own children. I could smile and pretend and keep selling my candles and lotions under the name my father had used to hide himself, but I would never really belong. As for that awkward teenager who'd desperately sought friendship at Mystic Mountains, the community was right to have shunned her...

My ringing phone pulled me from my spiral, and I tapped it open without looking at the caller. "Hello?"

"Jane? Please don't hang up."

The voice was familiar, but it was one I hadn't heard in months. "*Bitsy?*" I said, sitting up on the bed. "Is that you?"

Bitsy Prescott hadn't spoken to me since the Oil of Life fiasco. She'd booted me from her circle as soon as she found that her fingertips would no longer glow at her command, and with our friendship had gone our business relationship as well. Finding my wares behind the

Mercantile in cartons labeled BITCH had made it clear that Bitsy wanted nothing further to do with me.

She sighed on the other end of the line. "So…I got a call from Stephanie Love late last night. There's going to be a gathering at Yancey Park tonight around seven, and she said I need to come."

I wasn't sure how to respond to that, so I settled with a lame, "Oh?"

"Yeah. And…and Stephanie told me the truth about what happened last fall. About, you know…"

"Katarina?" I offered.

"Yeah. *Her.*"

Bitsy paused, but I didn't rush to fill the silence.

"After Katarina disappeared, Stephanie didn't tell us what actually happened," she said slowly. "She said we should decide our own truth about why Katarina left. But when she called yesterday, she…she said she didn't want this on her conscience anymore. Bad karma, I guess," she added, weakly chuckling.

"What did she tell you?"

"That Katarina had lied to us. That Oil of Life was all a hoax, and worse, that the people who got sucked in and used the top-level stuff ended up as zombies at a cabin in Whitford, doing…something for her. Working. I've heard that from a few people, but I didn't believe them, and Stephanie certainly didn't back them up, but…but now she says they're absolutely right. She told me that some of the details are fuzzy, but she remembers that Katarina was awful out there, and she barely fed them or let them sleep. And then *you* showed up and set the cabin on fire and saved everyone."

I let that hang between us for a moment, then murmured, "Yeah. More or less."

"You ran Katarina out of town?"

"She and her people were taken away, and they won't bother y'all again." I hesitated, then asked, "Do you believe Stephanie?"

"Yeah." Bitsy's voice began to tremble. "That would have been me, wouldn't it? Stuck at that cabin? If you hadn't…"

"What Katarina gave you in those first two bottles was a pretty harmless potion," I said softly. "It makes your fingers light up—that's it. Well, and your toes, but that's the only effect. It's not a sign of great power to come. The first dose was weak, diluted with alcohol and some essentials oils. The second was more concentrated. And the third was a different potion entirely."

"When you say 'potion'…"

"I mean exactly what I say. You were playing with magic—you just didn't know *what* you were playing with, and Katarina was pulling the strings. That third potion…to put it simply, it bound the drinker's will to Katarina. You had to take it willingly for it to work, but since she was so lovely and warm and believable…" I paused, but when Bitsy didn't interrupt, I pressed on. "Most folks ended up at the cabin. *You* had a bad reaction—like an allergy. You had a seizure in the middle of the Mercantile, and we gave you a potion that neutralized the effects of the others in your system."

"You and that pharmacist?"

"Yeah," I replied, omitting any mention of Annie, who'd actually dosed Bitsy with neutralizer while Tabitha held her down.

The line fell quiet again, but just before I was about to speak, I heard Bitsy sniffle. "You told me what was going on, and I…I didn't want to believe you."

"I know," I said as gently as I could. Having caught the man she had thought was her loving husband with his girlfriend bent over his desk, Bitsy surely couldn't bear the thought of being made a fool once more—not Bitsy, the successful businesswoman who'd fled Atlanta for the mountains and rebuilt her life. "Maybe it was easier to blame me than to blame Katarina, eh? I mean, she had a *damn* good pitch. Born saleswoman."

"That's generous to say," Bitsy muttered, "but how would you know? You never came to her seminars. I invited you once—"

"I was there."

"I didn't see you!" she protested. "Where—"

"I can't tell you, but trust me that I saw the whole spiel." Choosing my words carefully, I said, "Katarina is the real deal. That power she showed you, levitating objects and stuff? That wasn't a trick. But that's not the sort of talent you get from essential oils or a potion or anything else. It's inborn, like having perfect pitch or a photographic memory."

"You have it, too, don't you?" Bitsy softly asked.

"I do."

"And you really can't teach me?"

I exhaled slowly. "Bitsy, we were friends. If I'd been able to teach you, I would have. It's just not possible—like trying to teach you to breathe water. And, uh…we *were* friends, right?"

"Yeah," she whispered.

"Then do you really believe I'd have done something to hurt you? All I wanted was to keep you safe. I *care* about you. And…I know it was hard, okay? I know how much you wanted to do real magic, and I'm so sorry that I can't give that to you. Katarina was selling a beautiful dream, but that's all it was…I mean, aside from the eventual zombification and kidnapping, but you know what I'm saying," I mumbled.

"I…yeah. I think so." She paused, then asked, "You're selling at The Robin's Nest now, aren't you?"

"Yup. Juanita took me on. And the Apothecary."

"Any chance that you'd be interested in selling at the Mercantile again?"

That was, I suspected, an apology.

"Yeah, I'll think about it," I replied. "Let me talk to Juanita first, but…thanks."

"Sure. It, um…it'd be nice to have you back. My

customers love Fortune's Fancies." She cleared her throat, then said, "Listen, whatever's going on...you be careful, okay? Will I see you at the gathering tonight?"

"Probably not, and it's best if I don't give you any more details."

"Okay," said Bitsy, though she sounded uncertain. "Um...is this about magic again? *Actual* magic?" she asked, picking up speed. "Like, is someone in trouble? Stephanie sent out a message a few days ago about people asking where to find you—"

"I'm taking care of it," I told her with undue confidence. "Got to run some folks off again, that's all."

"If there's something I can do..."

"You just go hang out at the park. Have fun, and whatever Stephanie says, go with it." I couldn't believe those words were coming out of my mouth, but we *were* living in strange times. "And...thanks for calling, Bitsy. I appreciate it."

"Can I ask you one question?" she blurted before I could start to hang up.

"I might not be able to answer it, but you can ask."

"Are you a witch?"

"Not exactly," I said, which was true. "See you around."

I'd just put the phone aside when Diriem appeared in the open doorway and rapped his knuckles against the frame. "Oh—sorry," I said, "need something?"

"Just came upstairs for a minute, and I overheard part of that."

I snorted. "Not even going to pretend you didn't eavesdrop?"

"Seeing as I've made a career of it?" Leaning against the door with his arms folded, he asked, "What's going on?"

"That was...well, a former friend of mine, who might be trying to patch things up? I think we're going to have to take this slowly."

"You quarreled?"

"I caught her in the middle of a seizure after she dosed herself with Velvet Leash last fall, and Annie gave her a neutralizer, and when she woke up and couldn't make her fingers glow anymore, she decided I'd stolen her powers and blew up at me." Shrugging, I said, "I've been something of a pariah around here since the Oil of Life incident, but now that the leader of the woo-woo brigade is at least now telling people that I wasn't the bad guy, maybe there's a place for me here after all. Hell, as long as I don't tell them I'm not even a little bit human…"

He nodded slowly, then said, "It's okay to have mixed feelings about the truth, Jane. There's no right or wrong way to react to this mess."

"Shouldn't I be happy?" I replied, smirking, and dropped into the most sarcastic register I could muster. "I'm no longer tainted by those *foul* creatures, after all."

An eye roll was his answer to my theatrics. "Intrinsically, there's nothing *wrong* with humans," he murmured. "They are what they are, and I've seen good and bad among them, just like anyone else. Now, is there general antagonism toward them in the Pactlands? Absolutely. One doesn't abandon one's homeland without some bitterness about the situation. But trying to look at it objectively…I do understand their hostility. If you don't know how to work with magic, if you've been taught that it's evil and your very soul is in peril simply from proximity, if you immediately consider a sentient being with horns or hooves to be monstrous, then yes, I can see why we were such a perceived threat. And had we not fled, they would have eradicated us to protect themselves." Spreading his hands, he said, "I can't change history, and it's not fair that we had to leave. That we needed the Pactlands at all is a massive injustice. But I do wish we could have continued to coexist here, because as I said, I've known good people of the human persuasion."

"Why do I suspect that yours is a minority viewpoint?"

Diriem grinned. "Perhaps not such a small minority as you would imagine, given your introduction to the Pactlands. But as for you, now…the important thing is *who* you are, not *what*."

I chuckled. "Been talking to my dad, huh? He used to give me that same spiel."

"Because it's true. Genetically, you're an Aniap, a Nerin, and that's all well and good, but that doesn't explain Jane Fortune, Yacovi Hewt's daughter, the vigilante pyromancer of Ragged Gap."

"Nature, nurture."

"Precisely. This place, these people in your life—*these* are the forces that have shaped you, and wherever you go, you'll carry their impressions. And that's not a bad thing," he said. "Consider how many people have been born in the Pactlands and never stuck a toe outside. For some, humans are as frightening a prospect as we ever were to them. For you…they're people. That's a strength, youngling, not a cause for shame."

"A nice thought," I replied, "but tell that to Gerem."

"His attitude isn't unique," Diriem admitted, "but then he's never been outside. Practically provincial," he added, pointedly considering his fingernails. "And too stupid to realize it."

"You really hate his guts, don't you?" I asked, grinning.

"Why limit it to his guts?"

Leaving his post by the door, Diriem sat on the bed beside me, his expression difficult for me to decipher—inquisitive, perhaps, with a touch of melancholy. "Gerem is useless, but he came from far better stock. His father and grandfather would have been proud of you."

"For *what*?" I muttered. "Cornering the market on small-town witchcraft?"

"Hardly. You're undertrained, but you're a damn fine sorcerer already. And that worrisome little vigilante streak of yours…" He smiled then and gripped my shoulder. "I've seen it before."

"What do you mean?"

"Kereb Aniap." Releasing me, he sat back and laughed to himself. "Hall ti'Dana—the original, that is—was located within about an hour's walk of a settlement of sorcerers. That's where Kereb was born. Only pyromancer in the community, perhaps the first they'd ever had. He was driven out when he was about fifteen, and he settled in a human village. Strong back, good aim—he found a place for himself. And when others came raiding or seeking gold or food, he unleashed everything he had in defense of the people who'd taken him in."

That did sound slightly familiar.

"All was well until the village received a new priest, who learned of Kereb's abilities and condemned him. He had a choice: stand his ground and kill his friends and neighbors, or run for his life. He could have burned that village to ashes, but he ran to me instead. And he was such an *angry* young man," said Diriem, a distant look in his eyes. "Exiled twice for his ability—he couldn't trust other sorcerers, couldn't trust humans, and it was only once he realized there were pyromancers in my court that he began to lower his guard. He lived with me for about forty or fifty years, maturing in his talent, and visitors took note of him. When the first sorcerers began to make plans for a world of our own, they sent an emissary to him, recognizing his power. He was the one who arranged for them to come to me," he added with a little grin. "I had space, a considerable library, resources to take them in, and protection. He broached the idea with me, and that was that."

"Huh. Kind of figured you'd have foreseen that many houseguests coming," I replied.

"Oh, I *absolutely* did, but it was Kereb who put the plan into action. He grew into a skilled statesman. Learned to navigate among various groups and find commonalities. I'm sorry you never met him," he said, holding my gaze, "but take it from someone who knew him well and watched him grow into himself that Kereb would have recognized so much in you."

With that, Diriem pushed himself off the bed and headed for the door. "Free advice?"

"Sure."

"Take a nap. This could be a long night."

I huffed and followed him out of the room. "That's the best I get? I am in *crisis*, here."

"I know." He glanced back at me over his shoulder before stepping into his own bedroom. "But even large crises are often solved bit by bit, so rest, Jane," he said, and waved the door closed.

Connor came home after a long shift with pizza, for which I covertly kissed him in the garage, out of view of prying eyes. "Did you get the radio to Tabitha?" I asked as he pulled the boxes from his SUV.

"At lunchtime. She said she'd tune in at six and keep it on."

Half an hour, then. "Great. I think the festivities kick off around seven, so at least we'll have time to eat."

He shut the vehicle door with his elbow and leaned closer to kiss me again before going inside. "Everything okay today?" he murmured.

"Yep. Under control."

"That's not the same as okay."

"Good enough for now, yeah?"

He gave me a look but dropped it as I opened the kitchen door.

Since there was no point in Connor changing out of his uniform, our foursome quickly tucked in, particularly once Ganti discovered the joy of garlic knots. I'd just reached into the pepperoni box for seconds when my phone rang, but when I grabbed it, the caller wasn't Tabitha.

Frowning, I opened the line and switched to Pactish. "Liogh? Hi."

Diriem's eyebrows rose, and he tapped his ear. I turned on the speaker and put the phone down, catching the end of the detective's greeting. "Sorry to use the speaker, but my hands are busy at the moment. Is everything all right?" I asked.

"Not ideal," they replied, "but more importantly, are you safe? If you need help, I'll find a reason to slip out."

"I'm just fine," I fibbed. "What's up?"

"Unfortunately, I've got some bad news. Yacovi's hearing will be Monday."

That gave me two days to get organized. "What time?"

"Eight that morning, but Jane…I can't bring you in for it."

"Why not?" I demanded.

"It's not my decision," they insisted. "The director says no—it's not safe for you. But I promise you that Laws will be there, as will DPP. We'll do everything we can for your father."

I huffed a sigh, absently wiping my greasy fingers on a paper towel. "Okay, but if the director changes her mind—"

"You'll be the first call I make. But listen, I feel good about this hearing," they said. "Believe it or not, there *are* sane representatives, and I know there have been backroom talks in the last days. Don't despair." They paused, then asked, "Are you sure you're safe, Jane? Seen anything suspicious of late?"

Plenty, but I wasn't going to tell Liogh that, and Diriem's head shake reinforced my gut decision. "Nah. Things are relatively peachy."

"Huh?"

Apparently, I could add another idiom to the "does not translate" list. "I'm fine. Just keep me posted, will you?"

As I hung up, Connor, the one of us not fluent in Pactish, asked, "What was that all about?"

"Dad's hearing is Monday, and Laws won't bring me in for the occasion," I replied, again reaching for the pizza.

"After last time, I can't say that I entirely blame them…"

"Kabno is no fool," said Diriem, and Ganti, having resumed his attack on the garlic knots, nodded vigorously. "Neither is Pateme…most of the time," he muttered. "And they're wise to be cautious. The Forum's gallery will probably be packed, and that would present an ideal opportunity for Gerem to send a minion with a syringe through the crowd to dose you."

I eyed him as I folded up my slice and took a bite. "But?"

The corner of his mouth twitched. "I think you should be there, don't you?"

Ganti hastily swallowed. "What's the plan, boss? Sneak her back in the hold, hide her at the office?"

"No…I don't think so," he replied, squinting into the distance as if he were trying to read a convoluted eye chart. "But it'll come to me. One problem at a time," he said, and raised a slice in salute.

CHAPTER 15

The anticipated call from Tabitha came a few minutes after eight. "She's throwing a *rager*," she announced as soon as I said hello. "The two guys on duty are inbound, and the chief and everyone else have just been called in. Sheriff's waiting to see whether they need backup."

"Dare I ask?" I replied, nodding to the others, who started grabbing gear.

"There was a report of a massive bonfire in Yancey Park—no permit, of course—and then someone else called in to report naked people in the woods. Our anonymous narc says there's booze and drugs."

"*Drugs?*"

"Pot and shrooms, from the sound of it, but don't hold me to that—some of the chatter on this radio is tough to make out. Anyway, this is almost fun, so be a dear and tell Connor that he's lost a radio, will you?"

"Hell, I'll buy her a spare for her birthday," Connor told me once I'd conveyed the message. "That woman's earned it. Let's roll—"

"Not yet." Slipping into the powder room, I double-checked the ersatz uniform Ganti had made for me, then worked out a quick mask in the mirror. My blonde shoulder-length hair darkened to black and rose to a bob, my eyes shifted to icy blue, my complexion evened out—once again, stress had brought a fresh crop of pimples—and I added fuller lips and a daintier nose for fun. When I emerged, Connor gave me a once-over, then quietly asked, "Preview of Atlanta?"

Dropping my voice about half an octave, I replied in a husky whisper, "Maybe," and waggled my newly shaped brows. "But for now, down, boy."

"Yes, ma'am." He stepped back as Diriem and Ganti— or rather, as two people I assumed to be the agents— appeared from the hall. The elves were slender in build and about six feet tall. *These* men were a few inches taller and looked like they might bench-press loaded refrigerators for fun. One had put on a deep tan, and both had traded their ponytails for dark crewcuts.

Hands on his hips, Connor looked them up and down. "Been hitting the gym, have we?"

"Not frequently enough," one replied—Diriem, I guessed, meaning Ganti was the one who'd opted for a sun-kissed glow in February. "Passable?"

"Until you open your mouth."

"Which is why you're on the bullhorn tonight, yes?"

He nodded. "Load up. Y'all have guns?"

"In the Jeep. We'll follow you," he said, and the pair headed out.

I took shotgun in Connor's official Explorer, and with lights on and siren blaring, he sped off toward Dad's house. As we crossed the Ragged Gap town line, he said, "Tell me again how to avoid the wards."

"Stick to the driveway. Dad left that open on purpose. The third ward has been triggered, and I'll need to either float you across or make a bridge."

His eyes didn't leave the road, but his voice rose with uncertainty. "*Float?*"

"Basic levitation spell. I learned it as a teenager. Not going to drop you in the electrified moat."

He grunted.

"You could have dated a nice girl from Ragged Gap Baptist."

"Unlikely. And then I'd have missed out on this fun."

"I'm sorry, Con."

"Don't be." With the speed he was traveling, he didn't

remove his hands from the wheel, but I heard the warmth in his voice. "Just do me a favor and let me take point tonight, okay? Let's try to get them out of the house without resorting to fireballs."

"You've got it, Chief. Besides," I said, shifting so that my borrowed pistol wasn't digging into my waist, "I've already set Dad's house on fire once this week."

Connor knew the way, so all I had to do was sit back and cling to the door until he barreled up Dad's driveway, blocking in the hit squad's three SUVs. By the time Diriem and Ganti squealed to a stop behind us, Connor was out, standing behind his open door with a bullhorn in hand. "Police!" he bellowed. "Coby Hewt, come out with your hands up! You're under arrest for illegal distillation!" When that garnered no immediate response, he added, "We have a warrant for your arrest. Come out, or we're coming in!"

A few seconds after that warning, the front door cracked open, and one of the sorcerers peeked into the night. "He's not here!" he called. "We're just house-sitting for him!"

"Get out here, *now*!" Connor yelled back. "Hands where I can see them!"

In response, the door slammed shut, and a burst of light flashed within the house.

"The hell is that?" Connor asked.

"Probably a block on the door," I said from the other side of the Explorer. "Good luck with a battering ram."

"Backup?" asked the burly guy I suspected was Diriem.

Connor nodded curtly. "Whatcha got?"

He made a complex gesture, and when I looked behind us, I saw a shadowy army of several dozen people in raid gear spread out across the hill. Connor turned, spotted the new arrivals, and said, "Huh. Can you send some around the back?"

Another wave of Diriem's hand caused half the group to sprint toward the far side of the house. Connor watched until they were in position, then took up the bullhorn again. "We've got you surrounded! There's nowhere to go, so come out." He paused, waiting in vain for their surrender, then said, "This is *not* going to end well for you if we have to come in. Think about it."

An upstairs window barely opened, and another sorcerer called, "He's not here! Hewt's not here!"

"I'll be the fucking judge of that. Get your goddamn asses out of that house, and do it now!"

"We've done nothing wrong!" the sorcerer protested.

At that, Connor held up the fake warrant we'd printed at the house after dinner. "I've got a piece of paper here saying there's probable cause to believe that residence contains evidence of a crime. So, you can leave of your own accord, or you can leave in handcuffs."

"Whatever Hewt has done has nothing to do with us—"

"And we can sort that out!" Connor told him. "But if I have to come in there, I will make your night *very* unpleasant, got it?"

The window closed, and the sorcerer disappeared from view.

Connor sighed and turned to the agents. "All right, guys. Now what?"

"Let's make this simpler," I said, spotting the tree I'd felled the day before. With a muttered command, it rose and landed across the moat, a natural bridge.

I was fairly proud of myself until Diriem said, "Allow me." A flick of his fingers split the tree in half lengthwise, and the trunk fell apart into two bridges with flat walking surfaces.

"Showoff," I muttered.

"Running across unsecured logs is never ideal," he replied, and nodded to Ganti. "After you."

Ganti led the charge, holding his arm in front of him like he was carrying a shield. In the darkness, I could just make out the edge of the energetic field protecting him as he ran across the moat. Diriem followed, but before

Connor could do likewise, I pulled him back and let some of Diriem's puppets go first. "If they get shot, no harm done," I said. "I can't cover us both."

"I'll cover *you*—"

"No, shielding. What Ganti's doing. He's got a barrier up against attacks. I can shield myself, but I don't know that I can protect you."

"Then I'll just try to duck," he replied, and hurried after the pack.

By the time I crossed the moat, shield in one hand and a fireball in the other, Ganti had blown the front door off its hinges, and the sorcerers' new ward was wailing its alarm. But as he started into the house, a blast from the foyer sent him flying head over heels off the porch, and he groaned as he picked himself up and staggered back to his feet. Though I was no strategist, I could see the problem: the front door was a chokepoint, and the sorcerers could cluster up inside and shoot whatever came through. Even with the puppets trying to break down the back door, the bulk of the firepower was situated directly in front of us.

Lucky for me, I knew the layout cold.

"This way," I told Connor as Diriem covered Ganti and the puppets swarmed the door. He ran along behind me around the side of the house, and I paused in front of the window to the powder room. "Stand back."

"What are you doing?"

"Making another entrance," I muttered, then dropped my shield and threw all of my focus into the five-foot ball of flame coalescing between my hands. Once I could feel the power simmering, I quickly compressed it into a white-hot sphere the size of a tennis ball and lobbed it at the siding.

I pulled my shield back together just in time to block the worst of the shrapnel as my shot blew a hole through the wall, the toilet, and the vanity.

"Holy *shit*," said Connor, but the explosion stayed him only for a second while he swiped the dust out of his hair.

"Remind me not to piss you off, Firebug—"

"Ladies first," I said, catching his arm, then led the way through the hole, pushing everything I had into the shield.

A good shield is selectively permeable, rigid on the far side but flexible enough for the wielder to shoot through it, and Dad had taught me well. The two sorcerers who'd come running at the blast shot at me constantly, unable to break through. Meanwhile, as I gritted my teeth and braced myself against their onslaught, Connor reached over my shoulder and started firing through the shield—which in turn put the sorcerers on the defensive, it being surprisingly difficult to throw energetic blasts while also shielding against a semiautomatic. They blocked most of his shots until he fired lower, catching one in the knee and the other in the thigh. The two cried out, and one went down, but the other tried to limp off in retreat.

"Grab him," Connor said, nudging me toward the fallen sorcerer, then turned to go after the runaway.

Whatever training Gerem's boys had undergone, it wasn't up to agency standards. As I pinned my guy and knocked him out with a quick blow to the head, I saw the other sorcerers begin withdrawing from the foyer as Ganti and Diriem fought their way inside. I started to get up to help Connor, but as I turned, the limping sorcerer hurled a blast at his face.

"Con, *duck*!" I cried.

He had no time. Instead, as the missile flew toward him, Connor threw up his left hand, palm out and fingers splayed, as if he were planning to catch a ball. To my surprise, a shield manifested in front of him, only about the size of a dinner plate but respectably solid. The sorcerer's blast dissipated, and Connor, perhaps too focused in the moment to recognize what he'd just accomplished, tackled the man and wrestled cuffs onto his wrists.

"Stay down!" Connor barked, planting his knee on the twisting sorcerer's back. "I don't want to hurt you—"

I sent a short blast at the sorcerer's head, and he groaned and passed out.

Connor looked up in alarm. "Did you—"

"He's just unconscious."

"Yeah...that's still not good," he muttered, but rose and headed toward the front to help the rest of our team.

For two and a bunch of ephemeral puppets against four, the agents were holding their own, but neither complained when Connor came up the hallway and started shooting. He aimed for the knees, incapacitating without inflicting life-threatening injuries, and three of the sorcerers went down quickly between the agents and the ambush. The fourth made a valiant stand on his one good leg, holding a shield and shooting through it, but he was tiring, and Connor still had plenty of ammo...and when I walked up with a basketball-sized fireball in my hands, he finally dropped in surrender.

We didn't have enough cuffs, so Connor resorted to zip ties and had all six bound at the wrists and ankles by the time Diriem returned from their vehicle. Dropping his mask with a careless gesture, he unzipped a black nylon kit on the dining room table and began removing small vials of peach-colored potion.

"Uh...Diriem?" I said, glancing around at the encroaching crowd of phantom police.

"Hmm? Oh." With another gesture, they disappeared. "Sorry, distracted."

"That's a pretty sweet trick."

He grinned, a flash of sharp teeth that wasn't altogether friendly. "Ganti, help me with this."

There were only four syringes in the kit, but cross-contamination didn't seem to be high on DOI's list of concerns that night as they quickly crouched by each sorcerer and injected a dose of an evident sedative. The last to have been subdued craned his neck to look up at Diriem and scowled. "Wait...I know who you are!"

"I should hope so," he replied, and jabbed a needle into

the man's shoulder. "Don't worry, you'll be dealing with Laws instead soon enough."

Within minutes, all six sorcerers were unconscious, and the agents floated them into the foyer. "So...those two are going to have nasty headaches in the morning," said Ganti, pointing to the pair I'd knocked out. "Has Yacovi ever mentioned that head trauma is a bad thing?"

"I blew a hole in the house. Do you think I really care tonight?" I countered.

"No, but that's a little consideration for later. Just...leaving it there." Turning to Diriem, he asked, "Storage?"

"If you'll unlock it, I'll transport," he replied.

Connor and I stood back while the sorcerers were levitated out the door, one by one, and around to the rear of the agents' Jeep. The carpet in the back had been removed, revealing a hatch that should have gone nowhere but instead opened into a hidden hold about eight feet tall and substantially wider and longer than the vehicle. As Diriem guided the bodies through the hole, Ganti met them down below and secured them to gurneys for transport.

Peeking into the impossible storage compartment, Connor goggled in silence for a few seconds, then pulled his head out and stared at me, wide-eyed. "*How* is that possible?"

I shrugged. "Magic."

"Unbelievable. That...*where* does it go? Is it like a wormhole or something, or—"

"It's a pocket tethered to the Jeep," Diriem interrupted. "Same principle as the Pactlands but in miniature. I could walk you through the theory, but honestly, tonight..."

"Yeah, no, that's okay." He peered through the hatch once more and muttered, "*Damn.*"

As Connor tried to come to terms with the elves' blatant disregard for the laws of physics, I returned to the house and took a good look at the damage. Aside from the burns on the porch, the foyer was scuffed, with chunks either gouged or shot from the walls and ceiling. The floor bore holes from at least two of Connor's bullets that had missed their mark. I walked down the hall to the powder room, which was a shattered disaster, and sighed as I removed my mask.

This was going to be a *long* night.

So preoccupied was I with the destruction that I didn't notice Diriem come up behind me. "Where might your mother's belongings be?" he asked quietly.

Jumping at his voice, I recalled the other purpose of our raid and mumbled an apology as I led him to a storage closet under the staircase. "In the back," I said, making a gap in the rack of coats to reveal the piles of boxes in the rear. "Hang on, I'll dig it out."

There was only one box marked ESSA, and though I'd never opened it, I had kept tabs on it over the years, just in case my mom ever returned. Since that day would never come, it was now up to me to sort through the detritus of her life.

I backed out of the closet with the dusty carton in my arms, then dropped it on the floor and knelt beside it. "Cross your fingers," I said, and ripped open the disintegrating strip of tape over the top.

A denim jacket, cheap and unadorned. A thin afghan, neatly folded. A pair of dirt-grayed Keds. A men's windbreaker, decorated in the garish colors of the early nineties, which rustled as I removed it from the box.

And below that, a black leather satchel.

I pulled it free and unbuckled the clasps. The leather was smooth and thick beneath my fingers, a quality hide, and still smelled faintly of cleaner and polish. Whoever had owned it had taken pains to keep it nice...

On the inside of the flap, stitched in Pactish characters in bright red thread, was the answer to that question: NORANN ANIAP.

"It was his," I murmured to myself.

"Do you need a moment?" Diriem asked.

I needed more than a moment—this was the first piece of my bio-dad's life that I'd ever held—but I said, "No, I'm okay. Let's see…"

The main portion of the bag was divided in two, and a pair of small pockets were sewn onto the inside front and snapped closed. Both of those were empty but for an old ballpoint pen, but in the main pouch I found a sheaf of papers, which I pulled free to examine. A rental agreement. A falsified birth certificate and school records. A marriage license for Aaron Fortune and Essa Nerin…and behind that, a stack of three-by-five photos. Essa on a park bench in the denim jacket I'd just found, beaming at the world, her blonde hair permed and teased. Another of Essa in a pale blue broom skirt and sweater, a mischievous grin on her lips. The photo behind that was Essa again, but standing with a man who appeared to be about her age—a blond with dark brown eyes and a dimpled smile, just as Dad had told me.

Norann.

She was wearing a knee-length white dress, while he was sporting a suit, and I realized I was holding my parents' wedding picture. They looked so damn *happy* together.

I'd always assumed I favored my mother, but seeing them together, I found aspects of my face in each of theirs.

My eyes started to blur, but I blinked back the tears and flipped to the next photo: Essa, visibly pregnant and almost glowing. After that was a shot of newborn me, red and wrinkled, lying on her bare chest as she regarded me with an expression of relief mixed with joy. Last of the photos was a family portrait, Essa sitting up in bed, holding me in a blanket, while Norann leaned in with his arm around her.

They seemed excited, I thought. Perhaps kind. Very much in love.

Diriem's hand landed on my shoulder as I sniffled.

"I'm sorry, dear girl," he murmured.

I swiped at my watering eyes and weakly laughed. "Why am I such a damn *mess*? I don't remember either of them! Why am I mourning people I don't even know?"

"Could you be mourning the idea of them? The childhood you didn't have?"

"Dad's been wonderful to me, and I couldn't have asked—"

"Yacovi could have given you the world, and you still wouldn't be faulted for mourning what might have been."

"Yeah, well, I can deal with that later," I said, and put the photos aside.

Beneath them was a manila envelope, clasped, sealed, and taped shut, and I carefully opened the flap. When a piece of lined paper scrawled over in Pactish slid out, I held it up and quickly scanned the text:

My dear son...

It only took me a moment to read my grandmother's suicide note, the account of her horrifying discovery and her guilt and despair over the fate of her children. "Here," I said, passing it to Diriem. "I think this is what we came for."

He read it and nodded. "Poor woman. Give me the envelope, would you? Let's keep this safe."

As he repacked it, I put my parents' clothes back into the box, but I slung the satchel over my chest and replaced the papers and pictures within. "So," I said, sliding the box into the closet, "I guess I should clean up around here. Are you heading home?"

"I think a stop by Laws is in order, but yes." He glanced around at the damage. "Do you need help?"

"Eh, I can manage...though could you wait until I get the moat ward disabled? I think I can do it, but just to be sure..."

"Of course."

He followed me outside, where Ganti and Connor were waiting, and watched for the next few minutes as I reset the inner ward. The moat finally vanished, leaving the halved tree lying in the grass, and Diriem grunted his approval. "Not bad. A little sloppy in the execution, but all things considered…"

"She *is* twenty-eight," Ganti pointed out.

"True. Well, the night's not getting any younger," he said, unbuckling his reinforced vest. "Shall we?"

"Did y'all leave anything at my place?" Connor asked.

"We packed this afternoon," replied Ganti, removing his vest as well. "And *these* can go in the storage room…"

"I'll secure them," Diriem offered, and raised the hatch.

Once he'd climbed down into the hold, Ganti stepped closer to Connor and murmured, "I saw what happened in there."

"What do you mean?"

"You shielded. I was at the other end of the hall, but I'm not blind. Thought he was going to smash your face to pieces, but…you're surprising. Not to be crass, but what the hell *are* you?"

Connor shrugged. "Just a guy doing what he can for his town…and the next one over, technically."

"Come on, be frank with me."

"I don't know. Honest truth."

The agent seemed unsatisfied, but when Diriem emerged, he let it go for the night. The two loaded up, and Diriem rolled down his window after turning the Jeep around. "I'll have the other three vehicles removed," he said. "Please don't incinerate them, Jane."

I flashed a thumbs-up, about all I could muster with the weight of the long night ahead pressing down on me.

"See, this is why I recommended a nap," said Diriem, and nodded to us both. "I'll be in touch. Rest well."

And with that, they drove away, taking the immediate threat with them.

Once they'd rumbled off into the night, I turned to consider Dad's house and groaned. "Shit."

"Yeah?" Connor asked.

"I've got work to do."

"Mm. Can I help?"

He couldn't fix the damage, but he could make coffee, which was aid enough. By midnight, I'd repaired the powder room, patched the hole in the wall, and scoured the foyer and hall for bullets and missing plaster. The porch took some doing to rebuild, and I dismantled the sorcerers' ward around the windows and doors, but there was nothing I could do for the tree I'd downed but to render it firewood and stack it by the repaired porch to cure for winter. I did a careful sweep of the house, picking up after the squatters, tidying the rooms, and cursing at the state of the bathrooms, then came downstairs to find that Connor had manually cleaned the kitchen. "Come on, Janie," he coaxed, ushering me out the front. "It doesn't have to be a showpiece tonight."

I hoisted myself into Connor's Explorer, trying not to melt into the seat as he headed down the driveway. "You want to go home?" I mumbled.

"*God*, yes."

"How about my place? It's closer."

"Huh...you know, that's a point," he said, and started in that direction.

I unlocked the door and stepped inside to find the house as I'd left it, albeit dusty and with deflated balloons and dead flowers in the kitchen. A few quick spells took care of those problems, and while I tidied, Connor changed the sheets. I realized as I slipped off my shoes that my toothbrush was at his house, but I didn't give a damn that night.

Connor didn't have any pajamas at my place, and I wasn't in the mood to root for something cute, so we fell into bed in our underwear and migrated toward the middle of the mattress. He spooned behind me, warming me against the chill of the heating cabin, and I murmured, "I still owe you for Valentine's Day, remember?"

"Not tonight," he mumbled back. "I love you, Janie, but I'll take a rain check."

Though Connor was soon asleep, I lay there in his embrace for several minutes longer, listening to him breathe and replaying in my mind what he'd said. Maybe he was just tired, and yes, our relationship was still young, but...

I love you, Janie.

Smiling to myself, I finally slipped away.

CHAPTER 16

Saturday morning dawned cool and foggy, perfect weather for staying in bed and ignoring one's responsibilities. While I was on board with that game plan, Connor dragged himself into the shower, made tea, and raided my granola bar stash, then woke me enough to explain that he needed to keep playing catch-up at the office. I grunted acknowledgement and pulled the blankets more tightly around me, only to be awakened again an hour later when Connor returned to drop off my luggage. He kissed me and promised to let me sleep, then slipped out once more.

God, I was *exhausted.*

Using magic is like working out: the more you do it, the stronger you get, but it's entirely possible to overexert yourself and need a recovery period. Between the emotional rollercoaster of the last few days and the extensive home repairs I'd made the previous night, I felt as boneless as a slug and allowed myself to become one with the sheets.

The ringing of my phone finally jerked me from sleep, and I caught the time on the bedside clock as I rolled over. Nearly ten. "Hello?" I mumbled, having ignored the ID.

"Um…Jane?"

Distantly, my brain recognized Canna's voice and woke me enough to switch into Pactish. "Hey, sorry. Groggy."

"Did I wake you?"

I wasn't sure whether I detected incredulity alone or mixed with jealousy in that question. "Long night. Did Pars let you sleep?"

"Pars did. The *twins* did not, so all four of the little miscreants are at the park with Daddy. Anyway, I'm sitting here with Annie—"

"Oh, hey."

"Hey, there!" Annie chirped. "*You* sound like a ray of sunshine today."

I groaned. "What's up?"

"Well, Annie just popped by," said Canna, "and she tells me that, uh…a request has been made to have your bloodwork done."

"A request from whom?"

"Tell you in person," Annie cut in. "So, can you put on some clothes and let us come by?"

I sat up, recognized my bag sitting by the wall, and vaguely recalled Connor's delivery. "Uh…ten minutes?"

"Let's say fifteen. See you soon."

Aching deep in my bones, I shuffled into the bathroom to splash water on my face and brush my teeth, then threw on leggings and an oversized hoodie. I was still wearing the remains of yesterday's makeup, and dust from my impromptu bathroom demolition fell out of my hair as I ran a brush through it, but the notion of masking to make myself presentable never crossed my fuzzy mind.

Right on schedule, I heard Annie call from the kitchen, "We're here! Are you decent?"

I emerged from my room like a half-baked butterfly to find her and my cousin standing at the counter by a piece of black machinery the size of a toaster oven. Canna—who, I suddenly remembered, had never left the Pactlands—was studying the room as if trying to commit its details to memory, but Annie took one look at me and winced. "*Yikes*, girl. You weren't kidding, huh?"

Canna's eyes snapped to me, and she made a similar face. "Jane, dear, what *happened?*"

"Gerem had a hit squad camping in Dad's house. We ran them out of town last night, but I had to blow a hole in the house to make that happen, and then I had to *fix* it, and some wards, and—"

"*Sit*," Canna ordered, pulling out a chair. "Where do you keep your tea?"

"You draw blood, I'll make drinks," Annie offered, and filled the kettle.

I sank into my seat, and Canna opened her kit on the table. "Sorry for the intrusion," she said, snapping on gloves, "but apparently, *someone* at DOI thinks it would be beneficial to have your bloodwork done before Monday."

Annie pointedly looked away and whistled tunelessly.

"Diriem?" I asked, smirking. "It's okay, he's been here. Surprised he's up already, to be honest."

"I wouldn't presume to know *his* schedule," Canna replied, "but Annie said he called and asked for me to do this, so here I am, sneaking out," she said with a nervous chuckle. "If Pars knew what I was doing…"

"He'd understand," said Annie. "Jane, one sugar or two?"

"Two, please." I pushed back my sleeve as Canna readied the syringe. "And hey, fasting conditions! You've got great timing."

"I'm just looking at your genetics, not your levels," said Canna, "unless you're feeling poorly—"

"No, just hungry and tired. Pretty sure I overdid it."

Annie grinned as she fixed up my mug. "Diriem said you'd probably be useless this morning."

"*Harsh*, man."

"Eh, he also mentioned that you and your boyfriend held your own against a couple of sorcerers, so I don't think that was meant as criticism. Milk?"

"It's probably chunky by now, so no, thanks."

"Ew. Where is the boyfriend, anyway?"

"Serving and protecting, or some such. I think he mentioned paperwork, but I'm not firing on all cylinders yet."

Annie got the reference, but Canna, briefly bemused, let it pass and began inspecting my bared arm for a vein.

"Do either of you have any clue why DOI would want Jane's genetics? We already know her makeup."

I froze, realizing I hadn't spoken to Canna since delivering the bad news about my mother. "Uh...*well...*"

She stopped prodding my elbow. "Well, what?"

"So...my bio-dad? That human guy Essa ran off with? He, um...turns out he wasn't human after all."

Canna's eyes widened. "What are you saying?"

"I'm not half—I'm a full sorcerer."

"Then..." Her brow knit as she processed that information. "Then why would Essa have faked taking the draught and run away? I don't understand."

I glanced at Annie, then back at my cousin. "This *does not* leave the house yet, got it?" Canna nodded, and I blew out a quick breath. "Long story short, Gerem Aniap's my grandfather. Dad helped my bio-dad run off so Gerem wouldn't kill him, and Essa faked everything to keep up the cover story. Once...Norann died"—saying his name still felt strange—"Essa couldn't come clean and go home with me because Gerem would have killed me, too."

Canna stared, her mouth flapping as she tried to speak, then managed, "I...I don't..."

"Gerem's been using Oleum Vitae for, like, a century or more. Killed most of his kids and some other family members. I'd have been an easy target, so Essa protected me here." As she fumbled for words, I said, "One of the past-oriented farseers told me everything."

"Ganti ti'Van?" Annie asked.

I nodded. "You know him?"

"We've met. He's *good.*"

"And he eats like a garbage disposal, but whatever." Turning back to my stunned cousin, I said, "Technically, I don't need the Forum to sign off on my citizenship, but since Gerem's little buddies have been trying to stick me with the draught for the last ten days or so, I've got to be smart about this. Diriem's got a plan."

The gears clicked. "Yacovi's hearing."

"You got the memo?"

"Liogh let me know it had been scheduled. The whole family's coming...oh, *Jane*..."

I stuck out my arm again and cocked my head. "Want to see if Ganti's right?"

By the time Annie brought over my tea, Canna had pulled a blood sample and affixed a bandage, and she busied herself with the machine on the counter. "Portable analyzer," she explained as she worked. "I pulled this out of storage—we seldom have a need, but I thought it would be wiser to come to you instead of sneak you into the office."

"That one does genetic screening?"

"*And* it's connected to the sample database, but it's a longer cycle. This will take about fifteen minutes," she said, tapping a button. "Drink your tea, dear. Do you want something to eat?" She looked around the kitchen, which wasn't nearly as nice as hers, and settled on the stove. "Eggs, perhaps? Do you have any?"

"I've been gone all this time, and I just got back in last night," I replied, "so anything in the fridge is suspicious. Don't worry, I'll grab something in a bit. Tea's great," I added with an appreciative smile for Annie.

While the machine worked and I tried to wake up, Canna explored the house, peeking into the other rooms and out the windows. She gasped when she caught the view. "The *trees*!" she cried. "Heavens, Jane, they're enormous!"

"Mountain town," I said. "The tourists come for the view."

"But...they grow like this? On their own?"

I thought of the time Pars had driven Sage and me to the nature preserve outside of Beukal and proudly shown off the rather ordinary woods. "Yep. If you don't cut them down or lightning doesn't strike, or the bugs don't get them...or I don't set them on fire...they just keep growing."

"These woods must be ancient…"

"Not so old as you'd think," said Annie, who'd joined me with tea. "The Appalachians were pretty heavily logged, so most of what you're seeing is only about a hundred years old."

"Remarkable." She returned to the kitchen and stepped out the back, where the land sloped down to the creek. "You have a *garden*?"

"Not a great one," I said, "but I grow some of the plants I use in my products. Foraging is fun, but this helps supplement. It's about time to start the spring planting, so I've got to get out there and dig up the mess. Tell you what: if Annie can sneak you back here in a few months, I'll take you into the hills with me. Tons of wildflowers, you know?"

"I'd love that," said Canna, "but I'm already breaking the law just being here—"

"You're here at the request of DOI," Annie interrupted, "and if anyone asks, I kidnapped you. Done. The Hunt's got a bad habit of that, right?"

She chuckled. "Would it be embarrassing if I took some pictures?"

I gave her my blessing, and as Canna circled the cabin with her phone, marveling at the winter-bare trees, I shook my head and sipped my tea. "Different world," I murmured, slipping back into English.

"I've got to bring her and Pars up to the lodge sometime," Annie mused. "We've got woods, too, and I know the older girls would love the horses."

"Thanks again to all y'all for getting me out of Beukal."

She waved it off. "Anytime. You're one of us now, yeah? Ex-pats, I mean, not Hunt," she quickly clarified, "but we've got ourselves a little sorority of sorts."

"I did mention that I'm not actually human, didn't I?"

"Pff. Close enough. And you think I give a damn?" she added, reaching down the table to take my hand. "Look, I adore Wylan. He got English from a potion, and to be fair,

I was the linguistic source. He understands me just fine, but he doesn't always *get* what I'm saying."

I grinned. "Bless his heart."

"Just bless it. He tried deploying a 'y'all' once, and it did *not* fly."

"Ooh. *No.*"

"Right? So, what I'm saying—and I know Rose is with me on this—is that it's nice to hang out on occasion with someone who gets the nuances." She sat back and picked up her mug, then considered me again. "Aniap is really your *grandfather*?"

"So I'm told."

"Not that I'd hold it against you or anything, but he's a dick."

"Worse than that…" The beep of the machine cut me short, and I looked around out back until I spotted Canna at the creek, taking pictures of the scenery. Deciding not to mention that she was standing in the spot where I'd found Daniot Frim's body several months before, I called, "It's finished baking! Want to see?"

She hurried up the hill and reviewed the report as the machine printed it. "I told it not to do your health stats, so…sorcerer markers all over the place. No human markers detected," she said, and shook her head. "I can't believe your dad lied to you all this time…"

"He was protecting me. Any database matches?"

"Still printing…and yes," she said, squinting at the paper. "Gerem Aniap at twenty-three percent. That's a grandparent." She folded up the report and tucked it into her bag for safekeeping as the machine ran its cleaning cycle. "This is *huge*, Jane. You know that, right?"

"I've got an idea of it," I muttered.

"I mean, forget the accusations about Oleum Vitae for a moment. You're an *Aniap*."

I raised an eyebrow. "Getting kicked out of the Nerin clan before I even make my debut?"

"Oh—of course not, dear," she hastily reassured me,

"but the Aniaps are an esteemed family...they go back to a signatory—"

"Old money," Annie offered. "Gerem's an asshole, but he's loaded."

"I knew about the signatory," I told Canna. "Diriem said he was fond of...Kereb, was it? Gerem's grandfather?"

"And your great-great-grandfather," she replied. "He had other descendants—there are several Aniap branches remaining, and they're not all like Gerem."

"Wealthy but not necessarily evil," Annie offered.

Canna nodded. "What I'm getting at is that once you make your debut, you'll have connections that our side of the family can't touch. We're a pretty ordinary bunch."

"I still get to meet you, though, right?" I asked.

She hugged me tightly. "Your grandparents are determined to bring you into the Pactlands. I'd say you'll have a tough time getting rid of us. Now," she said, releasing me, "I'll keep this quiet as long as I need to. Not even Pars will know. And I'll be there for the hearing Monday morning—will you come?"

I spread my hands. "Allegedly, Diriem has a plan for that, too—"

"Hi," Annie interrupted, waving. "We're the plan. Taxi service!"

"*Sweet.*"

She grinned. "And since Diriem did tell me that I should share the results of your scan with Wylan...oh, he's going to *love* this."

"He and Gerem are so fond of each other," I deadpanned.

"Total besties, so if there's anything he can do to further this particular cause, I'm sure he'll be at your service."

"Of all the people I'd want plotting my demise, the freaking Hunter would be low on my list," said Canna, and glanced at the machine as it beeped again. "All right, we're clean. Let me toss the pod, and we can be on our way."

As she started to pack up, I said, "I know this is impromptu, but it's brunchtime, and I could do serious damage to a plate of hashbrowns, so…Waffle House, anyone?"

Annie laughed. "Your brunch establishment of choice is a *Waffle House*?"

"I mean, we've got better options, but no one's going to ask questions if I roll up looking like this and Canna doesn't speak a word of English."

"Point." She turned to Canna, who'd paused in her packing. "How about it? Hungry?"

"What is, uh…Waffle House?" she asked, carefully parroting back the name.

"It's the sort of greasy diner when you can wander in at two in the morning, and no one bats an eye."

"Ah. Hmm." Glancing at her phone, she said, "No message from Pars begging me to help out, so…are you sure it's safe?"

"Oh, totally," I told her, rising from the table. "And brunch is on me, folks—least I can do. Wait right there, I'm going to pull my hair back. Get all gussied up for the occasion."

"Get all *what*?" Canna asked.

Annie laughed as I left the room. "Let me translate…"

Thus it was that five minutes later, we'd piled into my truck and started off for Blue Ridge, where no one was likely to recognize me. Canna rode shotgun, staring raptly out the windows and commenting on everything that caught her eye, while Annie sat behind me, grinning at Canna's absolute delight. We found a quiet booth and explained the options to the newbie, and soon enough, I was inhaling an alarmingly large portion of eggs and potatoes while Canna worked on a waffle and people-watched.

I could have thrown together a week's itinerary for my cousin: drives in the mountains to look at the scenery, a few hours each in the tourist towns to buy handicrafts and jewelry and fudge, a day hopping among the wineries and the apple orchards. She seemed enthralled by her surroundings, from the jukebox across the restaurant to the diesel-belching dually in the parking lot that disgorged a foursome of hungover twenty-something guys, and I wondered what was more exciting for her, being somewhere new or the naughty thrill of her unauthorized outing.

After the waitress refilled our coffee mugs, I leaned across the table and murmured, "We can make this happen more often, okay? As long as Annie's willing…"

"I'm always down for brunch," Annie replied.

"How do you feel about mountain vineyards with tasting rooms?"

"*Could do.* We just have to get a language potion in you," she said to Canna.

My cousin smiled sadly. "It's not as simple as taking one from the closet…"

"We have them in our kits."

"And I can't raid Pars's."

Annie and I traded looks. "You don't suppose we could ask a favor from someone at DOI, do you?" I said.

She grinned and sipped her coffee. "Leave that to Rose and me. She likes brunch, too."

That afternoon, once I was alone and had slept off my brunch coma, I drove back to Dad's house to do a deep cleaning.

I'd tidied the night before, but between the need to rebuild a wall and the lateness of the hour, I was sure I'd missed a few spots. A small, somewhat irrational part of me insisted that if I removed all traces of the intruders, Dad would come home, and while I wasn't completely sold on that logic, I figured it couldn't hurt. In case he did get to walk out of the Forum a free man, I didn't want him to return to Ragged Gap and find hints of strangers in the house. For all I knew, Dad had no idea his home had even been invaded.

I started at the top and magically dusted, then ran the old Dyson and sprayed deodorizer in all of the bedrooms. Fortunately for my sanity, I didn't stumble across any unwelcome surprises—a stray condom, perhaps, or whatever else a lonely sorcerer used when he needed a little attention—and as I'd removed the plates and emptied the garbage on my first pass, I found the upstairs to be in relatively good shape. Moving down, I ran furniture polish over the wooden banister, vacuumed and mopped the ground floor, and emptied the fridge. To his credit, Connor had done a fine job on the kitchen, but I could tell what food was Dad's and what had belonged to the other men, and I canned every bit of their belongings.

Once the house was clean, I turned my attention to the outside, checking my work on the porch and the side wall and adjusting the paint to better match. I found no traces of wards other than Dad's, the outer two of which were still very much activated. By the time I was finished, the only sign that he'd been gone for eleven days was the pile of junk mail on the kitchen table, which the sorcerers had been collecting. I couldn't get into the greenhouse, but it was self-watering, and I wasn't overly concerned about Dad's plants. Likewise, the brew room was securely locked, and having seen no sign of tampering during my repairs and cleaning, I trusted that it was safe.

That left only one item on my agenda.

I pulled the carton of Essa's belongings from the closet again and brought it into the den. Now that Diriem wasn't breathing down my neck, I had time to go through everything properly—a task best accomplished alone.

I carefully put the jackets, the afghan, and the shoes on the coffee table, then dug down to see what remained. A blue plastic hairbrush—Essa's, presumably, judging by the length of the blonde hairs still snagged in its bristles. A cheap black comb that faintly smelled of something musky, maybe cologne. A tube of cherry Chapstick. A dogeared copy of a pregnancy guide. And then, down at the bottom, a baby book.

Aside from the vintage design, it looked almost new, but the first few pages had been filled out, the Pactish notes a jarring contrast to the printed English prompts and labels. Someone had glued in photos of my parents, and though Essa's side of the family tree drawing had been filled out three generations back, Norann's listed only his mother. There were notes about Essa's pregnancy and an ultrasound photo, then a picture taken just before leaving for the hospital, Essa standing by the door of their apartment with her hand on her swollen belly and a nervous grin on her face. On the next pages were more of my newborn pictures, a record of my length and weight, and handprints and footprints in black ink. My tiny hospital bracelet had been taped in, along with a paper sign reading WELCOME, BABY FORTUNE! There was Essa nursing me, a wrinkle between her eyebrows as she worked out the kinks. Norann holding me in his arms and gazing at my sleeping face as if he'd never seen anything so beautiful. Another version of the photo of the three of us—taken by one of the nurses, I assumed—only this one showed my parents kissing.

Then the photos switched back to the apartment. I found shots of a nursery with a white crib and matching changing table, the sort of furniture I suspected had been purchased secondhand and magically tweaked. A mobile of teddy bears hung over the top. Another picture of Essa in a rocking chair, weary but smiling for the camera. One of Norann sprawled on the couch, fast asleep, with me dozing on his chest—maybe not safe, but sweet. I could just make out the logo of his work shirt and wondered if it was the one he'd been wearing when he was shot. A picture of me followed that, swaddled like a burrito and staring up with dark, unfocused eyes.

The next pages were blank.

I chided myself for my disappointment. Of course there was nothing more—Norann died when I was two weeks old, and Essa had gathered what she could carry to run to Dad for help. My mother's world had been falling down around her, so I couldn't fault her for the empty pages. Still, I flipped through them, seeing all the spots for monthly pictures and baby's firsts, untouched lines for notes about nicknames and favorite toys and other details so easily forgotten in the chaos of the first year. Dad had filled those out in my *other* baby book, the one he'd dutifully kept for me, and I loved him for it...but here, now, I held proof that these strangers had loved me, too. For a few short months, they'd anticipated my arrival and decorated a nursery, and then they'd held me and smiled before vanishing from my life.

But they *had* held me. They'd wanted me. That couple in the pictures who'd beamed at the camera without the faintest sense of impending doom...

I reached the back of the book, expecting to find nothing, but to my surprise, there was a note scribbled on a blank page:

> *My sweet Jane,*
> *I'm so sorry.*
> *Mommy loves you.*

My eyes blurred, and I set the book aside so that I wouldn't get it wet. Alone with the remaining fragments of my parents' lives, I allowed myself to mourn them and what might have been.

I'd lost my old anger at Essa, the deep hurt for the long-awaited reunion I'd been denied. Though she'd tried, my mother was never coming back for me, but at least now I knew why. I *had* been loved, and even in Essa's despair, she'd left me with someone who'd treated me as his own. I couldn't have asked for a better father than Dad had been...but when I saw those smiling new parents in my mind's eye, my heart broke for the family I'd lost.

The family Gerem had taken from me.

If Norann had never left the Pactlands and his father weren't a murderer, maybe he'd never have crossed paths with Essa. They ran in different circles, I gathered. But suppose they had met and fallen in love. Suppose they'd had me at a hospital in Beukal and raised me there with my cousins in a place where I didn't have to hide my true self. Maybe Essa would have stayed with DPP. I had no idea what Norann did professionally—for all I knew, he was a trust fund baby—but surely he wouldn't have died in a convenience store robbery. They'd have lived, maybe given me a sibling or two. I'd still be in school, figuring myself out as I grew in my talent. Sure, I'd never have met Connor, but maybe there would have been a sorcerer for me, someone who saw my pyromancy as a gift to be celebrated.

That would be a different life, certainly. Jane Fortune would never have existed. That other Jane—Aniap or Nerin or whatever they called her—might never have seen the world beyond the Pactlands, but she'd have grown up with parents and grandparents and more, and the assurance that there was nothing wrong with her just because fire bloomed at her fingertips.

I sat there and mourned them all—Essa, Norann, the Jane who might have been, my little brothers and sisters never to be born—and as my thoughts turned to Gerem, the choking vine wrapped around my family tree, flames licked down my arms.

That monster had killed his own children. He'd ruined my parents' lives. His wife had taken her own, unable to live with the horror. He'd killed his sister, and while Ganti hadn't given me a firm tally of the Aniap cousins who'd died of Gerem's doing, the blood on my grandfather's hands was almost unimaginable.

Because of him, my dad was in a cell somewhere, while

I'd been forced to flee my hometown to avoid death by potion.

While I wasn't thrilled that Dad had kept the truth from me for so long, I had to admit that he'd succeeded in his mission: I wanted to watch Gerem *burn*.

When my tears dried, I repacked everything and returned the box to the safety of the closet, thinking of my parents. Essa deserved better than a Jane Doe burial in Leighfield, and I wondered if I could find a way to have her disinterred and returned to her family. And Norann— for all I knew, he was buried in a pauper's grave somewhere in South Carolina. Maybe he'd been cremated. Could I get another tracker and find him? Maybe, with a little luck and a bit of magic, I could bring the two of them back together.

Someday.

But for now, there was the matter of Dad's freedom to consider.

Come Monday, I would be ready.

CHAPTER 17

By seven-fifteen Monday morning, I was dressed in my lone black pantsuit, relic of my college days, had eaten what little breakfast I could stomach, and was ready to go. I'd kept my makeup natural, but I'd left all three pairs of earrings in, even emphasizing the lowest hole with the diamond-studded silver hoops Dad had bought me for my twenty-fifth birthday. So what if earrings generally weren't worn in the Pactlands? Let them stare, I decided. Let them see me. I didn't have Pactlands formalwear anyway, so why not make a statement?

Connor sat with me at my kitchen table in his uniform, bouncing one knee and trying to keep me calm. By then, my anxiety about the plan had morphed into general jitteriness, but I was holding myself together.

"Show no fear," Diriem had told me on his last call Sunday evening. "You will not walk alone."

I'd just finished my second cup of tea when Wylan appeared by the stove, unmasked and dressed for the office in a sleeveless black robe over a black lace-up shirt, leather leggings, and matching boots. The only color on him was the silver embroidery around his collar and down the lapels, which matched the heavy silver chain around his neck. "Good morning," he said in his accented English, slipping around the counter to join us. "Are you ready?"

I took a deep breath and stood. "Ready as I'm going to be."

Connor pushed back from the table as well, looking uncertainly between Wylan and me. "I know this is your show, Janie, but if you want me there…"

He and I both knew the answer to that: of course I wanted him at my side, but that was an additional complication we simply couldn't afford, not to mention a risk to the East Branch community.

"I'll be fine," I told him, and forced a nervous smile. "Really."

"Are you *sure*?"

"Connor," said Wylan in a tone that was both placating and firm, "you're worried for Jane's safety, yes? *I get it*, believe me. But I swear to you that he won't lay a hand on her."

"Not to be rude, but you can't make that guarantee," Connor replied.

The smile Wylan flashed was nothing short of predatory, and something deep and primal in the back of my brain warned me that standing too close to the big guy with the trophy rack would be a terrible mistake. "She's going under my protection, and my brothers and I will remain with her. If anyone tries to hurt her, I'll kill them," he said simply. "Not difficult."

He arched a brow. "You think you can take on a full-grown sorcerer?"

"You don't really know *what* I am, do you?"

Connor shrugged. "Big?"

"Oh, that's the least of it. But I doubt I'll have to lift a finger today. Gerem's crack squad is still enjoying DOL's hospitality, and the Forum has its own security—if someone tried to rush our desks, they wouldn't get far."

"Unless Gerem's paid them off," I muttered.

"Which is why I have it on good authority that DOL is sending reinforcements this morning," Wylan replied, and squeezed my shoulder. "Shall we?"

I looked at Connor, who remained unhappy with the situation, and nodded. "I'll be back, okay? Don't worry."

"That's not an option," he said, and pulled me into his arms for a quick hug.

"Love you," I whispered in his ear, but before Connor had time to process that, Wylan and I were gone.

When the floor rose up beneath me again, I found myself in the vestibule of a suite of offices: institutionally bland couches, a wooden coffee table, a coatrack in the corner, and overseeing it all from an unadorned desk, a Huntsman in a white homespun shirt and leather trousers much like Wylan's. He nodded to us, unfazed by our sudden appearance, and glanced at his computer screen. "Ten minutes."

"Thank you," Wylan told him, and waited as two other Huntsmen in matching black robes appeared from adjoining offices. "Are we ready?"

"Almost," said one—Derat, I recalled, recognizing his dark ponytail and the tone of his voice. He slipped back into his office, then returned with a familiar manila envelope. "For you, Jane," he said, passing it to me. "Hand-delivered this morning."

I checked inside and found my grandmother's note waiting. "Thanks," I said, and slipped it into Norann's satchel. I'd considered a variety of purses for the occasion, but the satchel matched my suit, and frankly, I thought it fitting to bring some part of Norann back to Beukal with me.

Before we set off, three more Huntsmen in brown formal robes joined us, carrying sheaves of paper and pens. One had tucked a computer under his arm, and I understood that these were assistants to the representatives. Having never witnessed a Forum meeting, I had no idea whether the representatives regularly attended with their staff, but I saw the wisdom of Wylan's entourage when I found myself in the middle of a knot of tall, burly, antlered men—a group that everyone we passed took pains to avoid. As we neared the ornamented double doors into the meeting hall, Wylan looked back at me and murmured, "Head up. You've got this."

I smiled, as the only alternative my body could suggest right then was puking, and followed him in past the pair of cautious guards.

The Forum's main meeting hall was the Pactlands' seat of government, and its architects had spared no expense. While the ceiling in the high lobby was painted to look like a sky, the equally extravagant ceiling within the hall was instead set with stained glass in the colors of a sunrise, backlit to glow as if the noon sun were streaming through. The limestone walls were hung with tapestries, while the floor was decorated with thick green carpets. On the ground level, three aisles led into the hall and sloped downward, terminating in a dais that rose about ten feet, high enough for anyone in the back to see. Atop it sat a long wooden table and matching chairs, while behind it, covering the wall, was a massive projection screen flanked by green curtains. Radiating outward from the dais were discrete sections for each group of representatives and their guests, with tables, chairs, and mats in the appropriate sizes and configurations.

Two levels of balconies ringed the room, both outfitted with rows of padded wooden benches, and I glanced up as I settled in behind Derat's chair. The railing of the lower balcony was lined with camera crews and people in formal attire, though whether they were reporters or merely curious Forum aides, I couldn't tell. As I scanned the filling benches, I spotted Pars's hulking form sitting on an aisle, dressed in a robe for a change. The brunette beside him had to be Canna—I couldn't see her features clearly with the distance—and I trusted that at least some of the people near them were Nerin kin, though who they might be or how they were related to Essa was beyond my knowledge.

I leaned forward and tapped Wylan's shoulder. "Are there normally so many cameras here?" I whispered.

"No, I've never seen the balcony like this," he replied,

scooting his chair closer to me so as to keep his voice low. "But a proceeding like today's is rare. The Forum hasn't initiated a prosecution in decades, and news of the charges has spread." Smirking, he pointed toward the area where Pars and Canna sat. "Reserved seating for the Nerins. They've been *very* vocal in the last days."

"Oh?"

"Absolutely. They've spoken to any reporter willing to listen about how Yacovi Hewt saved their daughter's life and raised their granddaughter, and doesn't deserve this."

"And what's the media's take on it?"

"Fairly positive, from what I've read. It's a compelling story: a well-respected agent ended his career prematurely to protect a young woman foolish enough to fall in love with a human boy, then stepped up to raise their child by himself in exile. Word has now circulated that Essa Nerin died outside, and the family is adamant that their little lost youngling be allowed in." He chuckled once, softly. "Looks like Canna can keep a secret, hmm?"

As much as I wanted to wave at my cousin, I tried not to look at the balcony and stayed firmly within the Hunt's camp, flanked by aides who didn't so much as look at their papers as they kept watch over the crowd. The group immediately to our left, a troll and a pair of aides, regarded me curiously but didn't try to chat as they took their seats. Wylan might have been a friendlier version of the Hunter, but that day, he and his brothers were giving off a vibe that unequivocally discouraged small talk.

Five minutes before the hour, a door opened on the far side of the hall near the dais, and a pair of guards walked in with Dad between them. He wasn't handcuffed, to my surprise, but with the dampening potion in his system, I supposed his guards didn't need to worry about him trying to fight his way out of their custody. His jailers had allowed him to wear civilian attire to the hearing—the same old robe he'd worn to my hearing nearly two weeks before, if I wasn't mistaken—but no one seemed to have provided him with a chair, as he remained standing and scanned the room. Only one of the sorcerers, Elm Carinar, was present on the floor, and though she sat with five aides, she spoke to no one. Dad's gaze lingered on that section for a moment, and then he looked my way.

I could tell from the way his back stiffened when he noticed me sitting with the Hunt. His head cocked in query, but all I could do from that distance was nod, and Dad quickly glanced away before his guards could spot me. Following his lead, I peered up at the balcony and noticed another reserved block opposite the Nerins': Pateme, Kabno, Diriem, and Ganti sat together on a bench in the front row, their view unobscured by cameras. Given the number of people in black shirts and pants sitting around them, I suspected that Kabno was keeping her team close as backup.

Diriem hadn't given me the play by play of the plan, but *that*, I mused, should be interesting.

The room filled, but I still saw no sign of Gerem and quietly asked the Huntsman beside me where he might be. He pointed to the empty table on the dais. "The Tribunal Committee is presiding over this proceeding," he explained. "They'll enter last."

I made a face. "He's still on the *Tribunal* Committee?"

"He's a loud voice, but he's merely one voice," he replied. "Remember that."

The Huntsman was right. Just before the hour, a door opened beneath the screen at the back of the dais, and seven people in a variety of formal robes proceeded to the table. On the far left, a male centaur took up a position on a green mat, while a troll—I wasn't sufficiently familiar with them to guess a gender—sat in an oversized chair on the far right. The others filled in, alternating sides: Mirrik Voln, a male elf, a female elf, and then Gerem, who smiled smugly as he took his seat.

Last to enter was a naga who wore a purple robe that nicely matched the green and purple of their long tail. As with the troll, I couldn't discern the naga's gender, but then they spoke in a decidedly female voice. "On this twenty-eighth day of February in the four hundred eighty-fifth year of the Pact, I call this meeting of the Pact Forum to order," she began. The screen behind her came alive, projecting a larger view of her face and torso to the room.

She didn't look altogether thrilled to be there.

"As head of the Tribunal Committee, it is my privilege and responsibility to oversee this proceeding," she continued, folding her hands on the desk. "Is our secretary prepared?"

A nymph sitting at a desk directly in front of the dais nodded. "Yes, Representative."

"Kug venDar," the Huntsman beside me whispered. "She's reasonable."

"Very good," Kug replied, smiling briefly at the secretary, then turned to her left, where Gerem sat. "Representative Aniap, you wish to initiate prosecution of Yacovi Hewt...and without the support of the Division of Laws," she said, glancing toward the cluster of directors in the first balcony. "You may make your case."

Gerem stood and smoothed his robe. "Thank you," he said, and proceeded to walk around the table to address the other representatives and the eager media. "This place—this world of ours—is our only refuge," he began, his tone measured and his pauses just long enough. Obviously, this wasn't his first time in front of a crowd. "Those still among us who were born outside remember the fear. Fear of attack. Of starvation. Of *persecution*," he said, slowly looking around the room as he warmed up. "How many families were eradicated by those savages beyond our borders? Whole clans?" he said, gesturing to the group of trolls on the floor. "Nearly half the Halls?" he added, nodding to the lone elven representative below before looking behind him at his colleagues. "And I need not even speak of the devastation to our siren sisters and brothers."

I'd never met a siren, but Dad had told me that their invitation to the Pactlands had been hotly debated, as they were indiscriminatory predators. The three representatives sat without aides on the other side of the trolls, gray-skinned figures with white hair and pastel robes, and showed no emotion as Gerem addressed them.

"All of us—as families, as peoples—have suffered and lost at the hands of our common enemy. Here, and *only* here, are we safe from the brutality of the humans lurking outside—creatures who would seek to eradicate us if they knew of our existence."

Though he was laying it on thick, he wasn't entirely off base. Then again, it had to be terrifying for the average human to stumble across someone who could, say, shoot jets of fire from their hands. How do you get into a fair fight with an opponent constantly wielding a flamethrower?

"They drove us from our homelands," Gerem continued, his voice rising with his indignation. "Murdered our peoples. And yet—*and yet*—there are still those among us who not only tolerate humans, but bed them. *Bed* them!" he repeated, spreading his hands in a gesture of disbelief. "Can you imagine willingly lying with the monsters who sought to destroy us? Can *any* loyal citizen imagine such a betrayal?"

I cut my eyes to Diriem, who looked on with a stony expression.

Gerem let that hang for a beat, then slowly shook his head. "As impossible as such would be for any right-thinking person, traitors do arise in our midst. Those who, given the choice, choose our enemies. But *we* are not monsters, and so we allow them to leave with their lives, to pursue whatever twisted happiness they seek among those savages…but not without the death draught. If they wish to live with humans, then let them live human lives, stripped of any talents and locked into human guise. Is this harsh?" he asked, looking around the hall. "Perhaps some might deem it so. As for me, I see this law for what it is: a way to protect ourselves and all that we hold dearest."

To his credit, Gerem had the pregnant pause down pat.

"It is this body that has made our laws since the Pact," said Gerem, staring down at the other representatives. "For what are we without laws? If there is anarchy within the Pactlands, then how will our world ever survive? If we fall apart, what horrors await us outside? So many of us have been fortunate enough to be born and live in the safety of this place. Perhaps some of our youngest cannot imagine that the outside would be any different, but I call upon our elders to *remind* us of the dangers of the world they left." He paused for a beat, then said, "Law and order keep us safe. Keep us *alive*. Now, laws can change," he admitted, slowly pacing the dais. "Minds can be swayed. Different times may call for different regulations. But that is a matter for *this body* to decide. If a citizen does not agree with a law and chooses to disregard it, he hasn't altered the law—he's committed a crime. Perhaps one might decide that theft is justifiable because all property should be held in common. Do we give that person a pass because of his beliefs, or do we bring him before a tribunal for his actions?"

When no one answered his rhetorical question, Gerem turned his attention to Dad. "Yacovi Hewt accepted a position of trust within the Division of Plants and Potions. He swore to uphold our laws. And in time, he was promoted to what must be a floramancer's dream position, head of the DPP greenhouse. Because of the nature of that position, Hewt was obligated to spend much of his time beyond the Pactlands, but he knew—and it was his responsibility to see that his agents knew—of the dangers outside. If he believed that one of his underlings was not mature enough to live on the edge of a human town, then he had a duty to transfer that person elsewhere within the agency."

Looking back at the room, he said, "In this, Hewt

failed. One of his trainees, a young woman only forty-two—*forty-two*—years old was not ready for the temptations of her position. Hewt failed to adequately supervise her, so perhaps it came as a shock to him when he found her in a compromising position with a male human." Gerem waited while that visual sank in, then said, "Until recently, DPP believed that Hewt had done his duty. He stated in an official report that he gave the trainee—and that was young Essa Nerin, incidentally, whose family I understand is here this morning—he gave her the choice of a return to the Pactlands, to safety and her loving family, or the draught. And poor Essa, only a few years out of school, chose to betray everyone she'd ever known." Gerem shrugged and sighed. "A terrible tragedy, and it was hardly surprising when Hewt resigned his post the following year. For a career like his to end with such a blotch was unfortunate, but at least Hewt did his duty. Or so he led us to believe.

"Recently," said Gerem, ignoring Dad in favor of the cameras, "it came to my attention that another young woman was seeking citizenship. 'Who could this possibly be?' I asked myself. I knew, of course, of the scandal in Hall ti'Dana"—he looked toward the directors and smirked—"and of my colleague's affair child," he continued, turning back to Mirrik, "but what sort of sorcerer would need to petition for citizenship? And then I read her file and learned the extent of Hewt's lies. You see," he said, addressing the media once more, "Hewt never gave young Essa the draught. He allowed her to leave. Did he make her promise not to use magic? To mask herself adequately to prevent questions? Or did he simply turn her loose with her human paramour and wish them luck?"

He waited until a few mutterings subsided. "Essa and that human had a child. A child untouched by the draught, a child with *talent*—out there. Where anyone could see it."

Her, I mentally amended.

"But it seems that the human died," he continued, "as they are so wont to do, and Essa decided she wanted no part of her mistake. So, she gave the baby to *Hewt* and walked away. Where is Essa?" he asked, spreading his hands. "Hewt doesn't know. She's out there somewhere, perhaps passing as human, perhaps revealing our existence, perhaps dead herself. We can't say! But once again, instead of giving Essa the draught, Hewt allowed her to leave. Worse still, he raised that half-breed child but never thought to fix at least one of the problems he created by giving it the draught! Instead, what did I find on the other end of that petition but a talented half-human, raised outside and practically a savage, asking to be allowed in here. *Here*, our sanctuary."

He sighed as if the fact of my existence were weighing upon his very soul. "I tried to do the right thing when the half-breed so casually walked into this building. I had a team in place ready to administer the draught that day, to end the threat to us all. But like her mother, *she* fled. We have yet to locate her, though I've expended my personal resources to do all I can," he said with a hand to his breast. "She might be within the Pactlands still, or she may have found a way to return to the outer world. Who knows what damage she could do? And Hewt, traitor that he is, has refused to even call her to ask that she turn herself in—"

"Hey, Grandpa!" I called, stepping onto my chair to be seen over the antlers around me. "I'm right here, you asshole!"

The projectionist caught Gerem's shock beautifully, but the room erupted before he could speak, a chorus of voices and creaking furniture as people turned to stare at me. I held my position, Norann's bag strapped across my chest, and crossed my arms while I glared at the dais.

As Gerem flushed, Kug rapped a gavel on the table and called for order, lifting herself on her tail until the hall began to quiet. Once the noise had subsided to a low rumbling, he started to speak again, but she interrupted him. "A moment. Young lady, who are you?"

I glanced at Dad, who looked primed to run across the hall to protect me, then turned to face the dais and raised my voice. "I'm Jane Fortune, ma'am. Essa Nerin's daughter. Yacovi Hewt has been my only parent since I was a few weeks old."

"How the hell did you—" Gerem began, but a sharp bang of the gavel silenced him.

"*I* am asking the questions, Representative," Kug snapped, but her voice softened a degree as she looked my way again. "Ms. Fortune, do you dispute what Representative Aniap has said about your... circumstances?"

"Very much. May I?"

Gerem sputtered. "She has no right—"

"*Peace*," Kug barked. "You've made your accusations clear, Gerem. I'll hear the girl's rebuttal." Gesturing to me with one hand, she said, "Go ahead. What would you like to tell us?"

"Well," I replied, "let me begin with what he got correct. Dad didn't give Essa the draught."

"Are you aware that this was an illegal act?" she asked me.

"It might have been, had Essa wanted to marry a human guy. But my biological father was a sorcerer, too."

I glanced at Dad, and while I had no idea what he was thinking, I saw the surprise on his face.

"That's not what her petition says!" Gerem cut in, turning to Kug. "She's lying!"

"On the contrary," another voice interjected, and given its volume, I strongly suspected it had been amplified by magical means. "Will the Chair hear from the Division of Intelligence?"

I looked up at the balcony and found Diriem on his feet, arms folded and expression unreadable. The poor projectionist caught him a second after I did, then whipped the camera back to Kug.

"This is irregular," she said after a moment's consideration, "but I trust there's a reason for the interruption, Director?"

"Justice," he replied. "And evidence of far worse crimes than those attributed to Mr. Hewt."

"While I appreciate the impetus to see that justice is done, this proceeding concerns only Mr. Hewt—"

"The two are inextricably intertwined," said Diriem. "And the information in our possession both explains Mr. Hewt's actions and exonerates him."

"Kug," Gerem protested, but she silenced him with an upraised hand.

"The chair recognizes Diriem ti'Dana," she said. "You have evidence to support Ms. Fortune's claim?"

"I do," he said, and held up a piece of paper. "Ms. Fortune's genetic report, produced by a certified healer. Would the Chair like to read it?"

"I would."

With a gesture from him, the paper sailed down from the balcony, keeping well out of Gerem's reach, and landed on the table in front of Kug. An aide hurried up the dais ramp with a flat, slim apparatus that resembled a tablet, and as Kug put the report onto its surface, I saw that it was a document projector. The screen split behind her, with her face on the left and my report on the right.

The rumblings commenced again almost immediately, and it didn't take Kug more than a few seconds to spot the red flag. "Twenty-three percent shared with Representative *Aniap*?"

"That's not possible," said Gerem, darting around the table. "Let me see that—"

The troll on the committee caught him with an arm like a tree limb and held him back.

"All right, I'm intrigued," Kug said to Diriem. "What am I seeing?"

"Genetically, two individuals with that level of overlap

are often grandparent and grandchild," he replied. "As is the case here."

"None of my children have lived long enough to have children of their own!" Gerem yelled. "I've buried all but the youngest! How can you be so cruel as to—"

"Are you forgetting Norann?" Diriem asked.

Gerem's mouth snapped shut, and with the camera having slid in his direction, I caught the moment the blood began to drain from his face. "Norann is *dead*," said Gerem through gritted teeth. "Just like his brothers and sisters, just like his mother."

"Oh, not quite. With the Chair's permission, I'll cede the floor to my colleague."

"I'm not going to stand here and be mocked," Gerem began, but the troll grabbed him before he could leave the dais.

"No, I think you should sit," said Kug. "Foggy Lake, would you please—"

But Gerem was already struggling to free himself. "Let go of me, you stupid oaf!" he bellowed, twisting in the troll's firm grip. "You have no right! Release me!"

"Gerem Aniap," said Kug in a no-nonsense tone, "we've assembled today at *your* request. *You* wanted to present charges against Mr. Hewt. And it now appears to me that perhaps you did not have the full facts before rushing into this, particularly if that girl is your granddaughter. So, *sit down*," she growled.

Finding no friends on the dais and faced with the balcony cameras, Gerem slunk into his chair, affecting an expression of betrayal.

The camera barely caught Kug's eye roll. "Of course," she said, turning her attention back to Diriem. "The Chair recognizes…"

"Ganti ti'Van, ma'am," he said, going to his feet as Diriem sat. "DOI."

She nodded. "Agent ti'Van. I'm certainly familiar with your work, but for the record, what is it that you do?"

"I'm a farseer. Certified," he added with a quick grin. "Past orientation."

"And can you tell me how Ms. Fortune shares blood with Representative Aniap?"

"Certainly…" He paused, then absently rubbed the back of his neck. "Apologies, ma'am, I've not testified to the Forum before. Is someone going to cast the spell?"

She smiled. "For truthfulness? Do you believe that's necessary, Agent?"

"I think it would be a poor career choice to lie to the Forum," he replied, earning a smattering of chuckles, "but given the nature of the information I can convey, and as Mr. Hewt's freedom is at issue…"

"Then that can be arranged." She beckoned to an aide sitting by the secretary, who ran out the door and up to the balcony. Panting, he paused in front of Ganti and murmured something inaudible to me. Ganti replied in kind, and an instant later, a bright blue light burst forth around him.

"Better?" Kug asked.

"Unless I get creative, ma'am," said Ganti, and waited until the door slammed behind the departing aide to commence. "The connection between the representative and Ms. Fortune is, as the director suggested, Norann Aniap. He was Jane's biological father."

"Was?"

Ganti paused, then said, "Ordinarily, I would express my condolences to a parent before discussing the death of their child, but in this case, I have none for Representative Aniap. Norann died about twenty-eight years ago."

"Twenty-eight years tomorrow," I offered. I didn't know his birthday, but the date of his death had stuck with me somehow.

"He was fatally shot in a robbery," Ganti continued. "Norann worked at a convenience store in…sorry, I never got the precise name of the town…"

"It was in South Carolina," I said. "That's where I was

born."

"I see," Kug murmured. "And what was he doing outside?"

I glanced at Gerem, who had plastered on a scowl but was looking paler by the minute.

"He fled the Pactlands to save his life," said Ganti. "Mr. Hewt understood the threat, helped him escape, and assisted him in setting up a false identity. Some years later, he met Essa Nerin, and they had Jane shortly before he was murdered."

"And what was the threat to Norann?" Kug asked.

"Simply, his own father."

Gerem leapt to his feet so quickly that his chair fell over behind him. "I *will not* sit here and tolerate these lies—"

"The agent is ensorcelled!" Kug countered.

"He could have a tolerance for it—"

"Look," said Ganti, "if the Chair so desires, I'll take truth serum, but your cameras will want to focus on something else."

"That's unnecessary," said Mirrik, leaning over the table toward Kug. "Really, don't ask him—"

"I'm not," she said, and flashed her colleague a pained smile before turning back to the man of the hour. "Gerem, sit down, or I'll ask security to assist you."

The look he gave her reminded me of a cornered rat, but with no easy way out, he reluctantly righted his chair and perched on the edge.

"Excuse us, Agent," said Kug, looking up at Ganti. "Could you please elaborate?"

He nodded. "Yes, ma'am. First, a point to set the Forum at ease: we don't make a habit of looking through representatives' pasts. We generally *can't* because you're protected, but more than that, we try not to pry without reason. Here, the director had cause to investigate Ms. Fortune's background, and...well, one thing led to another. I treated this like any other investigation, with the complication that I can't directly see Representative Aniap."

"Understood. What did you find?"

The camera caught Ganti as his mouth moved into a tight line of distaste. "Lonvi Chulb, the representative's first wife, took her own life when she discovered that her husband had been brewing Oleum Vitae. Their children's deaths were hardly accidental…"

He fell silent and waited as Kug tried to restore order, both out in the hall and on the dais. By the time the room quieted enough for Ganti to be heard, both elves and Mirrik had closed in on Gerem, and he hunched in his chair, glowering up at them.

"My *sincere* apologies, Agent," said Kug, sinking back into her coils. "To be clear, you saw Gerem Aniap brewing Oleum Vitae?"

"No. But I saw his children's deaths, and none of them matched the reported cause. I saw Ms. Chulb's discovery of the representative's hidden brew room and watched her destroy his stock and supplies—"

I knew I wasn't imagining that wince from Gerem.

"—and I examined the deaths of several of his other close relatives, including a number of cousins and his own sister, Jaena Aniap."

Jaena?

"I can only speculate as to why he began brewing," Ganti continued, "but Jaena was his first victim, and she died just as she was being noticed for her work as a Forum aide. She was, I suppose, Ban Aniap's logical successor. A pyromancer of notable talent, I understand."

My parents had named me for my father's aunt, a woman who'd died fifty years before he was born but who'd carried the family's wild talent. Whether they'd intended that as a tribute or as a wish for me, I couldn't say, but from the way Gerem was staring at me, the message wasn't lost on him, either.

"Once Ms. Chulb discovered her husband's secret, she

gave her last surviving child a letter and asked him to open it the following day," said Ganti. "Norann did as she requested, only to learn too late that his mother had given him a suicide note explaining what she had found and why she could not live with herself. Understanding that he would be his father's next target, particularly as his mother had destroyed the remaining Oleum Vitae, he went to Mr. Hewt, a friend of his mother's, and asked for help. They knew that confronting the representative would not end well for Norann, and so he was smuggled out through the DPP greenhouse."

Ganti looked then at the Nerin family across the balcony. "Essa and Norann loved each other very much. She knew that to be with him, she would have to fake a human lover and say she'd taken the draught—it wasn't safe for Norann's father to know where he was. So, that's what she did. She sacrificed everything to be with him. Once Norann was dead, Essa spiraled, but she realized that if she told the truth and tried to come home, Representative Aniap would find a way to either take custody of her child or to take *enough* of her child to make more Oleum Vitae. That's why she didn't try to return. She...she did the best she could for her daughter with the resources she believed were available to her, and she wandered for about a year. Unfortunately, once she decided to come back for Jane, she was killed in a roadway accident. I *am* sorry for your loss," he said. "Truly. Essa did not deserve her fate. But whatever else can be said for her, she tried to protect her child. And Mr. Hewt, who raised that child," he continued, looking back at Kug, "understood as well as Essa and Norann did that Jane's grandfather could never know of her existence. *That* is why Jane's citizenship petition says she's half human—she had no idea of her father's true identity until I told her a few days ago."

Kug considered that briefly. "And it is your firm belief that Representative Aniap has been producing and consuming Oleum Vitae?"

"As firm as it can be without witnessing it," Ganti replied. "If his protection were to be removed, I believe I would find confirmation *very* easily. And considering that the representative still has an underage child in his household…"

"You *cannot* tell me you believe these lies!" Gerem cried. "This…this *calumny*—"

"Oh, shut *up*," I yelled, and reached into my bag. "Here, I've got Lonvi's suicide note. Dad kept it safe. And I've got some pictures of my parents, if that would help."

"Please," said Kug.

I muttered, and the envelope rose, followed quickly by a stack of photos—all copies, as I'd kept the originals safely at home. Following Diriem's lead, I whispered the documents across the hall and over the dais, but as Gerem started to jump for them, I sent them down the table to where the centaur sat. "Hey, would you pass those to the Chair, please?" I asked. "Sorry, I didn't want Gerem to rip them up."

With the other representatives holding Gerem in place, Kug picked up the projector and slithered down to join the centaur. A moment later, there was Lonvi's note, and the volume of the room's mutterings increased as people quickly read it. When she finished, Kug looked over the photos I'd given her, then slid one onto a blank space at the bottom of the note: Norann, Essa, and me in the hospital, both of my parents smiling for the camera.

A heard a soft cry from near Canna and wondered if that was my grandmother.

"Oh, hey, Gerem?" I yelled at the dais over the growing noise. When he looked my way, I let my arms flare. "Looks like *I* got the family talent, huh? You know, the one you didn't?"

Once more, Kug was forced to gavel for order, and then she looked up at Ganti. "Anything further, Agent?"

"Not from me, ma'am," he replied, "but I believe

Director Erenani has something she'd like to say."

"You know what? Sure," the frazzled Chair replied. "Director?"

Half the size of the elves sitting around her, Kabno stood on her bench to be seen, and Diriem made a quick gesture in her direction, evidently a spell to amplify her voice. "The Division of Laws is disinclined to bring charges against Mr. Hewt because his potentially criminal actions were done, if not out of strict necessity, then out of a well-founded fear for the lives of Norann Aniap and Jane Fortune."

"I concur," Kug replied, "though if any of my colleagues disagree, I'm happy to call for a vote…" No one asked for one, and she nodded. "Very good. Director Erenani, anything further before we adjourn?"

"Yes, thank you. Gerem Aniap, you are under arrest for the murder of Taya, Sheshar, Sundir, Panalea, Tenelit, and Kelir Aniap, Jaena Aniap, and others yet to be identified, and for the attempted murder of Jane Fortune. Remain seated—"

Apparently, Gerem had no intention of being taken into custody that day, as he threw a sudden blast of energy at his babysitters and scrambled out of his chair. The troll ran to block the rear door, leaving Gerem on his feet but searching for an exit.

And then I learned why Laws took orders from a gnome.

Kabno climbed onto the edge of the balcony railing, then jumped off, landed in a roll in one of the aisles, and righted herself in a matter of seconds. Almost faster than I could track her, she sprinted onto the dais and threw herself against Gerem's legs, sending him sprawling. Before he knew what had hit him, Kabno was sitting on his back, holding one of his arms in a stress position and shouting at him to stay down.

I watched, cameras flashing around me, as the extra DOL officers in the room took over from their boss, cuffing Gerem and injecting him with the dampening potion. He protested his innocence and decried his mistreatment, but they hauled him out the back as Kabno dusted off her hands and straightened her robe.

Kug, who'd guarded the documents during the chaos, shook her head. "I believe we've had enough for one day. Mr. Hewt, you're free to go. Could someone please give him the antidote?"

As one of the aides jogged away to fetch the necessary potion, I pushed out of the knot of Huntsmen and ran across the hall to hug Dad. He squeezed me almost to the point of pain, then stepped back and looked me in the eye. "Janie, sweetie, I hope you understand…"

"I love you, Daddy," I said, and hugged him again.

Suddenly, our reunion was interrupted when Mirrik called, "Kug, wait."

Turning, I saw him limping toward her. "Yes?" she asked.

"There's still the matter of Jane's citizenship to resolve."

"*Oh.* Um…well, I believe this speaks for itself," she said, holding up my report. "She's a full-blooded sorcerer and the daughter of two citizens, so there's no question in my mind. Does anyone disagree?" Again, none of the other representatives argued with her, and she shrugged. "Then that's settled," she said, and looked down at me. "Welcome home, youngling. Now, given your youth, you'll need to be tested for school—"

"Hold it," I said, raising both hands to stop her. "Thanks, but I'm heading out to my *real* home."

She cocked her head, taken aback. "What do you mean?"

"I'm tired, and frankly, your anti-human policies *suck*." I had no idea whether that would translate properly, but I pressed on anyway. "First, that whole 'death draught' thing you toss around? Hell, even I know how badly that shit messes you up. You don't get a human lifespan—you die in a couple decades. What a fucking *waste*. Second, can we talk about how no one in this goddamn place thought to look more closely at the rich dude who buried six kids and misplaced another? Would *anyone* here like to tell me why no one went after Gerem decades ago?"

"It's complicated—" Kabno began.

"It's a fucking *pattern*! Come on, I'm no cop, and even I can see that!" I was conscious of Dad's hand on my shoulder, but in that moment, I finally had a platform. "For whatever reason, no one dug around, so let's recap. My father had to go on the run and got shot. My mother couldn't go home or get help when she needed it the most, freaked out, and got hit by a car. And I just spent ten days running and hiding from dear old Grandpa's *hit squad* and had to blow a hole in the side of my dad's house to get them out of my damn town."

"You did *what*?" Dad murmured.

"I fixed it," I muttered, and focused on Kug again. "So, I'm going home. I wasn't good enough for you fine folks until you realized my blood was sufficiently pure, and since I'm the same woman I've always been, I'll see myself out. I want to get to know my mother's family," I said, turning to give Canna and Pars a quick wave, "and Representative Voln, if Sage wants to see me, the feeling is mutual. But I'm going back to Georgia, and…ah, there you are," I said, spotting Diriem, Pateme, and Ganti approaching. "Surely one of you can put together the paperwork, right?"

Pateme looked at Dad. "Feisty, isn't she?"

"That's my Janie," he replied, squeezing my shoulder again before he released me.

He grunted. "I'll have your credentials restored by lunchtime, Yacovi…and I suppose I could add permissions for Jane as well, should she feel like she needs them," he said as Wylan wandered up. "Though something tells me portal credentials aren't a major concern of yours, Ms. Fortune."

"You know, they might be nice," I said, and turned

back to the dais. "So, all of that is to say I don't plan to start school in Beukal *any* time soon."

Kug began to speak, then caught herself and shook her head. "We can discuss this later. This meeting is adjourned," she said, and slammed her gavel on the desk.

"Laws has kept your car safe," Pateme told Dad, "but you'll need to go through the property release procedure before they let you take it. Oh, and here's your antidote," he said as the aide returned with a zipped kit. "Jane, this could take a few hours, so get comfortable."

"Or don't," interrupted Wylan, grinning at me. "Have you said everything that needs to be said?"

I looked up at my mother's family again and waved once more, then turned to him. "Yeah, I think that'll do. Mind giving me a lift?"

"My pleasure," he said, taking hold of my wrist, and the world went black around me.

CHAPTER 18

My first call once I was home was to Connor, who breathed a massive sigh of relief when I told him I was standing in my own kitchen. "Thank God," he muttered. "Did you nail the bastard?"

"He got taken away in handcuffs after being body-slammed by a gnome."

"I'm sorry," he said, laughing, "*what?*"

"Seriously! She jumped off the freaking balcony and tackled him! But anyway, Wylan took me home, and allegedly, I'm getting permission to return, so...yay?"

"Yay," he solemnly concurred. "Are you okay, Firebug?"

I paused, quickly taking stock of myself: a little stunned, jittery, very much overdressed for Ragged Gap. "Kind of? I think...but don't leave work," I insisted. "I'm fine."

"Could I take you out tonight, then?"

"Ooh. What did we have in mind?"

"Fajitas?"

"*Yes.* Want to pick me up?"

Once we'd made the arrangements, I called Tabitha at her pharmacy. "I'm so glad you're back," she said once I gave her the update. "Any chance that you'll need to go on the run again?"

"If I do, you're on my contact list."

"Appreciate it. Now, are you all right? Big morning, huh?"

"Pretty big," I agreed, "and I think I'm good, just...

kind of overwhelmed? Like, I made a spectacle of myself in front of the Forum and saw my grandfather hauled off to jail, and there were cameras everywhere, but…yeah, I'm okay."

"Take a nap."

"It's not even nine," I protested.

"Don't care. Take a nap."

"Ugh. *Yes*, Mom," I promised, and hung up.

I wasn't tired, I thought, hanging up my suit and removing my diamond hoops. A bit on the shaky side, but that was adrenaline wearing off, nothing more. I needed to go out to my workshop and tackle my backlog…but my bed was right there, and surely a few minutes wouldn't hurt, right? I'd earned that.

"And I didn't see daylight again until four," I said between sips of my margarita.

Connor chuckled. "You're going to be up all night."

"Not so sure about that. Honestly, I could have kept sleeping," I admitted. "So, when you factor in booze and tortillas—"

"Good thing I'm driving."

We ordered our food and picked at the queso while we waited. I knew I was still a touch on the groggy side, but Connor seemed somewhat distant, and I decided I didn't want to play guessing games all night. "Are you upset about something?" I asked, putting my drink aside. "Bad day at work?"

"No, I'm just fine," he replied, and smiled.

But the smile was halfhearted, and I wasn't an idiot. "Connor Willow, don't lie to me. What's going on?"

He took his time in answering me, first stirring a chip through the queso and then quickly eating it before it could drip on the table. "I'm…well, I'm kind of surprised to see you here."

I frowned. "You're the one who suggested dinner—"

"Not *here* here. In Ragged Gap," he clarified, then lowered his voice. "I mean, you've got a pass to Neverland now, right? What the heck are you doing here?"

"This is home."

"You're slumming it."

I reached around the chip basket and gripped his hand. "Slumming it how? I'm home, I'm with you, and Dad's got his life back, and that's what matters."

Connor glanced at our entwined fingers, then met my eyes again. "Janie...you've got *so* much more of the touch than I do. Than *anyone* here does, except maybe your dad. I know you don't want to go back to school, and I don't blame you, but...you're bigger than this. You're capable of so many incredible, absolutely insane things, and you need to go and do, yeah? If you want to go back there, spend some time, learn a few new tricks...well, I'm not going anywhere."

"I want to be here," I replied. "You, me, bottom-shelf margaritas...this is *nice*, Con."

"It's nothing special."

"I'll be the judge of that, *thank you*." Dipping another chip into the cooling queso, I said, "I'm going to take things slowly with, uh, Neverland. I want to meet my mom's family, and I definitely want to check in on Sage, but I've got a pretty good life here."

"You could always sell bath bombs in Neverland," he suggested.

"But that's not the kind of place in which you can throw glitter in the mix and call it 'magical,'" I pointed out. "Besides, there's a certain cop here who takes me out to dinner and tucks me in and, like, fights sorcerers for me, and I'm pretty damn fond of him."

Connor grinned. "Yeah? You're fond of me?"

"I mean, Sam's still the best boy on the force, but personally, I think you're cuter."

Maybe it was the simple act of putting food in my stomach that woke me from my stupor. Maybe it was the long nap or the inhibition-killing margaritas or just the relief of being home and safe. Whatever it was, when Connor walked me to my front door that night, I pulled him inside the house and started ripping off our clothes long before we reached my bedroom.

The rest of the night is somewhat hazy in my memory, but as Connor spooned behind me once we were good and spent, he mumbled, "Remember when we fooled around on your birthday?"

"Uh-huh."

"We're square."

Around eight the next morning, after I'd seen Connor out the door to go home and shower before work, Dad finally called. "Hey!" I said, leaning against the kitchen counter in my sweats while my tea steeped. "Are you back?"

"Got here around one yesterday afternoon, but I assumed you might have plans last night, so I thought I'd wait until morning."

While Dad understood that I was no longer a little girl, we had an unspoken agreement not to discuss the baser points of my love life. "Good thinking. Is everything okay up there?"

"I mean, I do have questions about what happened to the tree out front..."

I groaned.

"And I had a rather interesting talk with Lord ti'Dana, of all people. He was very complimentary of your work."

"Was he, now?"

"Said something about you setting the house on fire?"

"Gee, *thanks*, Diriem," I muttered.

"You do know who he is, right?" Dad asked.

"Yeah, Ganti filled us in. We all camped at Connor's for a couple nights."

"This was before you punched a hole through the powder room wall?"

I rubbed my forehead. "How much *did* he tell you?"

"Plenty, so thank you for cleaning up so thoroughly." His tone grew more serious. "Would you mind coming over, girlie? I'd really like to talk, and there are some things best said in person."

I told him I'd be right over, then quickly threw on real clothes and brushed my teeth.

Traffic was seldom a problem in Ragged Gap, especially not on a random Tuesday morning after the school buses had run, so I made it to the house in about fifteen minutes. When I stepped out of my truck, I found the place as I'd left it a few days prior but for the downed tree, which Dad had re-chopped into more uniform logs. He came to the door as I reached the porch, and I hugged him before stepping inside.

The house smelled of lemon furniture polish and coffee, and Dad asked if I wanted something to drink. When I followed him to the kitchen, I was surprised to find that the coffee had just finished its brew cycle—this wasn't Dad's usual pot that had been kept warm and steadily drained since dawn, but rather something fresh, as he might put on for company.

Since when was I *company*?

"Sit down, I've got it," I said, shooing him toward the table, and poured and doctored two mugs. "You're the one who's been in freaking jail," I chided as I joined him. "No need to baby me."

"If you say so." He took a long sip, and then another—a stalling tactic, I surmised, and held my silence until he figured out what he wanted to tell me. "Janie," he finally said, "I'm sorry. I…I'm really sorry about your mom. I had no idea—"

"No one did," I assured him. "It's okay. I don't think she suffered or anything after the accident."

"Yeah, but I know you've been hoping…"

I reached across the table, and Dad clasped my outstretched hand. "I'm sorry I never got to know her, but that's not your fault. You've been a great dad."

When he spoke next, I could hear the strain in his voice. My dad seldom cried, but he was dancing mighty close to the edge that morning. "I should have told you the truth sooner. You had a right to know something so fundamental, and…" His face shifted briefly as he brought himself back under control. "If you never trust me again, I'll understand. But please know that I did what I did out of love. That's all."

"I know, Daddy," I said, and squeezed his hand. "Ganti explained. I'm not mad at you."

"Just disappointed?" he asked in a mockery of the tone he'd employed whenever I screwed up as a teenager.

"No. Shocked, overwhelmed, and still working through some shit…which I suspect isn't going to be an immediate process. But I know why you lied, and…" I glanced away, swallowing to ease the tightness in my throat. "You didn't have to keep me. You could have gone anywhere, found something better than here, but you *kept* me, and I'm so grateful—"

"Being your dad has been the best part of my life. I mean it. And…I know it hasn't been perfect, honey. I just—"

"You kept me alive," I interrupted. "If Gerem had known about me…"

"That's why I lied. Not to trap you here with me or ruin your prospects—"

"I *know*." Laughter bubbled up out of nowhere, but it was better than crying. "You were going to go to *prison* rather than come clean with me."

"Better me in prison than you dead."

I rose from my chair and slipped around the table to hug him, and though Dad held me a little more tightly than usual, he kept his composure.

"Question," I said as he released me.

"Anything."

I waited until we'd sat again and Dad had taken a

bracing sip of coffee. "Were you in love with Lonvi?"

Slowly, he nodded. "She was like my sister when we were young, but as we grew up, my feelings toward her changed. Hers didn't," he added with a sad smile. "I begged her not to marry Gerem. Told her he was no good, he wouldn't do right by her. But she saw an Aniap, and he was kind to her, I think. Certainly showed her a different face than he showed me."

"He knew you were a rival?"

Dad chuckled. "He knew I'd have liked to be a rival, but he also knew that Lonvi's feelings for me were closer to familial. I never stood a chance. But I didn't trust the son of a bitch, so I did what I could to stay in Lonvi's life. We saw each other on occasion, wrote letters—there were no phones for the longest time—and I got to know her children. Gerem and I never warmed up to each other, but at least Norann knew I could be trusted."

I thought of what had to have gone through Dad's head when Norann came to him: shock and sorrow at the news of Lonvi's death, righteous fury at Gerem, and fear for his old love's only remaining child.

"You saved him," I murmured.

"I didn't do nearly enough. If he and Essa had called me sooner, if they'd told me they needed money…"

"Dad…"

His dark eyes filmed, but he blinked the sheen away. "If there's a life after this one—if there's a reckoning— then I'm going to have to face Lonvi and tell her I failed her baby. That's something I live with."

"But you didn't fail *me*," I said, ignoring the quivering in his jaw. "And if Lonvi and Norann and Essa were here now, if they knew how far you went to keep me safe…"

"Never far enough."

"*Daddy*, no…"

He finally broke then, dissolving into a mess of tears that left him red-faced and snotty, and I sat with him until the fit subsided, offering tissues and rubbing his back. He managed to take a few deep breaths and pull himself together, then mumbled an apology. "You've done nothing wrong," I murmured, hugging him. "And a whole lot right. I love you."

He stepped out of the room for a moment to wash his face, then returned sounding a bit more like his old self and changed the subject. "So, your bathroom remodel went well. Plumbing still works."

I shrugged. "Desperate times. I tried to match the original paint."

"And that tree out front?"

"Set it on fire as a distraction. I didn't notice that Gerem's little buddies had made their own ward around the house."

He *tsk*ed. "Haven't I taught you to sense wards, Janie?"

"Okay, in *fairness*, when I arrived, there was an electrified moat around the property. I wasn't the only one tripping wards."

"You know better."

"If the fully trained sorcerers could hit a ward—"

"I'm not responsible for them. I'm responsible for *you*."

I rolled my eyes. "Okay. Whoops. Sorry about your tree."

"I'm not worried about that damn tree, and if I can't get it growing again, then I'm no floramancer. What *concerns* me is that you decided the best way to figure out what was going on here was to sneak onto the property alone."

"With an invisibility ring and scent neutralizer," I pointed out.

"And *six sorcerers* out to get you! Janie—"

"DOI thought it was fine."

"I don't care! They aren't your dad!"

"Well, since my dad was in jail and I wanted to get him out…"

He huffed a sigh, but then he cocked his head toward the powder room. "In any case, you did a good job in there. I can't tell the difference."

"Thank you. I've had some practice at Tabitha's," I added as he sat again.

"Does DOI know that?"

I sipped my coffee. "You'd have to ask Ganti. They know *about* Tabitha because—"

"*Oh*, yes, I heard. Jane Fortune and her two human accomplices."

"Seeing as they helped me pull this off, am I in trouble?"

Dad mulled over the question for a moment. "Well...Lord ti'Dana seemed more amused than anything, so you're probably in the clear. Just keep it quiet, girlie." He hesitated, then said, "Another thing."

"Yes, sir?"

"I know you're not too keen on the Pactlands at this moment—and honestly, I've got some thoughts as well— but I wouldn't be a good father to you if I didn't tell you to get your butt back over there and finish your education. You've got so much potential, Janie, and there's plenty I can't teach you. At the very least, you need to work with another pyromancer."

"My control's pretty damn good," I protested.

"Never said it wasn't, but it could always be better."

I shrugged.

"Will you think about it?"

"Maybe later," I muttered.

"I'm just looking toward your future, honey—"

"And I'm looking at my present," I interrupted. "I've got you back, I've got Connor, Tabitha...Bitsy actually called to apologize while you were gone. Heck, I even got cooperation from the Mystic Mountains crew, so things are looking up. Aside from the orders I've yet to touch, I'm in better shape now than I've been in months."

But was I? Even as I protested my present happiness, discontent curled in my gut. I had no reason to be dissatisfied, really—I had a home, family, friends, boyfriend, business—but no matter how unhappy I was with matters in the Pactlands of late, the Jane of a year prior who'd dreamed of exploring that world and mastering magic yet unknown reminded me of her presence. I was Jane Fortune, by God, and that was good enough...

Wasn't it?

"Uh-huh," said Dad, clearly unconvinced. "And since when do you work with Mystic Mountains?"

Pushing my unsettled thoughts aside, I grinned. "Stephanie Love reached out, and we had a talk, and I said I needed a distraction on the night we raided the house...so now she and about two dozen of the woo-woo brigade have citations for public intox and indecency."

"*What?*" he asked, laughing.

"I asked her to throw a party so big that the cops would get involved. She put on *quite* the shindig in the park, didn't get a single permit, and apparently, once the liquor was flowing, a bunch of the revelers decided that a little naked dancing around the bonfire was in order."

Dad dropped his head into his hands. "They really think that's magic, don't they?"

"You know, they were having fun until the cuffs came out. Or so I heard."

"Right, because when that was going down, you were here with your boyfriend, a DOI agent, and Diriem freaking ti'Dana, blowing holes in my house. Janie, what am I supposed to do with you?"

"Enjoy your new firewood," I replied, rising, and kissed the top of his head as I went to get a refill.

Three days later, on Friday afternoon, I walked into Mystic Mountains with a wicker gift basket the size of a laundry hamper. I'd done my best with my stock on hand, tucking bottles of lotion and scented hand soaps and candles in the nest of crinkled purple paper, tossing in half a dozen bath bombs, and finishing the production with several bottles of wine and the best chocolates I could find at the grocery store, plus a potted succulent for good measure.

The bell tinkled as I entered, and the familiar scent of patchouli wafted in my direction as I passed the incense bar. Carefully maneuvering around the tables piled high with crystals and assorted paraphernalia, I approached the sales counter in the middle of the store and found Stephanie perched atop the stool behind it.

She'd darkened her dye over the winter, trading the usual pink streaks in her blonde hair for a vibrant red, but otherwise, she was the same as ever: slouchy hand-knit sweater, dramatic eyeliner, a wire-wrapped chunk of quartz hanging from her neck. As I neared, she looked up from the box of new merchandise she was tagging, and one eyebrow rose.

I nodded in greeting, then put the basket on the counter, murmured, "Thank you," and started to go.

As I side-stepped an impressive amethyst cathedral on the floor, she called, "Jane, wait."

"Yes?" I asked, turning back.

"They're gone?"

"Long gone. Nothing to worry about."

She beckoned me closer, and as I reached the counter, she nudged the basket aside and leaned toward me, keeping her voice low. "We're good?"

I smiled. "We're good."

"Glad to hear it." She paused, nibbling her lip, then murmured, "Who *are* you?"

"I'm just Jane. Same as ever," I replied, and stepped aside as a customer approached to ask Stephanie about a shopping basket full of tumbled stones.

Being the chief came with certain perks for Connor, among them the ability to arrange his schedule to accommodate a super-casual Friday dinner at my place. By the time he let himself inside, still in uniform but carrying a duffel bag with his comfy clothes, my kitchen smelled like garlic, and he stopped in the doorway and took a deep sniff. "Ooh, what's that?"

"Shrimp skewers," I replied, tending them as they cooked over a stovetop grill. Early March was cooperating in the weather department, but I still didn't feel like cleaning the Weber out back. "Couscous is almost ready, and I've made fresh green beans with garlic and rosemary."

He joined me at the stove and kissed me. "This all smells delicious, but by any chance, is there some sort of potion that will fix garlic breath?"

I grinned. "Thinking of trying your luck, eh?"

"I'd be a fool not to."

"Well, then, to answer your question, there *is* a potion, but I don't have any on hand. The best I can offer tonight is mouthwash."

"Does Yacovi brew it?"

"Babe, we are *not* calling my dad about anything even tangentially related to sexytime."

He kissed the side of my neck as I flipped the shrimp. "Come on, we're all adults here, right?"

"That man is a hundred sixty-four years old, and I'm not giving him an ulcer."

"Fine. Mouthwash it is."

"Go change clothes," I ordered. "I've got a pinot grigio chilling, so if you don't like dinner, you can drink until it tastes better."

"Oh, *pinot grigio*," he said, putting on a snooty voice as he headed for my bedroom. "Do we not drink generic white?"

"It was on sale!" I called after him.

By the time I was fluffing the couscous—a boxed mix, as my culinary skills only went so far—Connor had changed into sweatpants and a T-shirt, and he puttered around the kitchen barefoot, pouring wine and collecting the plates. "Here, I'll dish it up," I said, reaching for the pair. "Let me make it *fancy* for you—"

The doorbell rang, interrupting me, and Connor and I traded glances.

"Expecting anyone?" he asked quietly.

"Nope." I grabbed my phone, saw no text from Tabitha or Dad, and shook my head. "Play it cool. Could be nothing."

"Jane…"

"Could always be Girl Scouts or Mormons."

He gestured toward the dark backyard. "*Now?*"

A fireball appeared in my hand and winked out just as quickly. "I've got this," I said, and headed for the door, hoping I wasn't going to end up at the hospital in my plaid pajama pants and faded UGA T-shirt. Taking a deep breath, I primed myself for defense, then opened the door.

On the porch, illuminated by the security light, stood Diriem. "Good evening," he said, looking me up and down. "Am I interrupting?"

Connor slipped past me and sneaked a peek at the newcomer, who was masked and had opted for business casual. "Oh, shit," he said. "Now what's wrong?"

A quick snort of laughter escaped Diriem. "I'm actually not a harbinger of doom."

"Uh…hi," I said, and then noticed his ride parked behind the Whitford PD Explorer. While I didn't recognize the lines of the red sports car, I knew the logo. "Is that a *Lotus?*"

"2019 Evora GT430," he replied with a grin.

"Jesus," Connor muttered, but he sounded grudgingly impressed.

"And…why would you drive a Lotus to Ragged Gap?" I asked Diriem.

"It's not icy, and she needed a little road time. Is something wrong?"

"That's an *Atlanta* car. This is a pickup truck sort of town."

Diriem nodded. "Noted. And as I'm obviously

interrupting, I apologize, but some conversations are best had face to face. May I come in?"

"Sorry, sure," I said, stepping aside to admit him. "How'd you find me?"

"Rosie gave excellent directions." He waited until I closed the door, then dropped the mask. "I'll keep this brief, but I come with an update."

I gestured toward the couch. "Have a seat. Want some wine? We just opened a bottle."

"I hate to impose…"

"It's pinot grigio," I said, heading for the kitchen. "Sit down, Con, I'll bring it."

Connor warily perched on the chair between the den and me, a sort of buffer, but Diriem thanked me as I carried in three glasses. "What's the vintage?" he asked.

"Discount shelf."

"The best kind." He took a sip, grunted appreciatively, and set the glass on a coaster. "So, the news," he said as I sank into the other chair. "Gerem is in *deep* trouble."

"Do tell."

"Well, following our little display on Monday, Laws had sufficient evidence to convince a judge to order that Gerem's blinding protection be removed. That came down on Wednesday afternoon, and Ganti has been a *very* busy boy ever since. His suspicions have been confirmed— Gerem's actions are as bad as we'd anticipated."

"So…he's still in jail?"

"He's not going anywhere," said Diriem. "Particularly since Laws raided his home and found the brew room. There was a fresh batch of Oleum Vitae hidden inside, presumably made with his youngest child's blood."

"Xila, right? Is she okay?" I asked.

"Understandably shaken and conflicted, but she seems unharmed. She's only about eighteen, I believe."

That my aunt was younger than me was strange enough without throwing a life-sucking potion into the mix.

"The potion has been destroyed, of course, but that

discovery will make Gerem's defense nearly impossible," Diriem continued. "I pity his counselors."

"If he's convicted, what's he looking at?" asked Connor.

"Life on a penal farm with his talent dulled to uselessness...though without any Oleum Vitae to sustain him, that won't be a particularly long sentence."

"I guess that'll have to be good enough," I said. "He doesn't deserve anything better."

"Agreed," said Diriem. "Now, once Gerem is convicted—and that's not farsight talking, that's common sense," he clarified—"the tribunal will likely split his assets among his children. In this case, since he only has one minor child and one minor grandchild, you'll likely receive half."

"*Half?*" I echoed.

"Your father's share. None of his other siblings lived long enough to have children, remember? That makes you and Xila Gerem's only blood heirs."

I frowned. "But wouldn't his wife inherit? Xila's mother?"

"Ordinarily, I would expect her to receive a larger share, but you're also a victim in this, so I anticipate that you'll get a more substantial chunk of the estate. But whether you end up with half or, say, a third, you're about to be a *very* wealthy woman, Jane." Picking up his wine again, Diriem said, "Gerem is many things, but poor is not one of them."

I mulled that over for a moment, then asked, "What's Xila going to think? I'm meddling in the family and swooping in to steal her fortune."

Diriem's mouth twitched. "You're stealing nothing, and once she accepts the truth—including the fact that your meddling has saved her life—I suspect she will come around. Perhaps you two can be civil someday, if not familial. She's your aunt, after all."

"And that's still weird," I said, taking a sip of wine.

Honestly, for a discounted bottle, it wasn't half bad. "But if you just came to try to lure me back into the Pactlands with money, you've wasted your trip."

"You have no interest in returning?" Diriem asked. "Exploring?"

Did I?

I drank again, stalling. "Maybe once things die down, but haven't I already made a big enough spectacle of myself? Here, I'm a businesswoman who can take care of her own shit and other people's. There...what, I'm an object of pity? Gerem's freaky little half-feral granddaughter with the weird accent? What am I supposed to do, just walk up to school in the fall and enroll myself? Thanks, *no*."

He swirled his drink and regarded me over the glass. "And there's the matter of Connor, of course. It's not fair to ask you to abandon this place and leave your boyfriend behind. Oh, I'm not here to criticize," he hastily continued as Connor and I stiffened, "and I won't speak a word of this in Beukal. This is your affair. All I'm suggesting is that it's part of the calculus."

Briefly, I locked eyes with Connor, then looked back at Diriem. "Can you tell us what Connor *is*?"

"No," he said simply. "I haven't looked, nor have I asked Ganti or anyone else to dig around. It's not my business at this moment, and you're not hurting anyone," he continued, turning to Connor. "But until the day comes that you're prepared to make your own push for citizenship, whatever happens between you and Jane needs to happen quietly. Understood?"

My hackles began to rise. "If you're going to tell me that I can't be with Connor, then you can keep your precious citizenship."

"Janie," Connor began, but I held up a hand to silence him.

"I've had the shadow of the damn draught hanging over me all my life," I said to Diriem. "And now you're going to bring it up again?"

"I don't like it," he murmured. "I have come to seriously reconsider the law concerning its use. But I'm not on the Forum right now. Perhaps someday, we can rewrite it." He barely smiled. "You know, Kug sent me a message this week—she was surprised by your performance, but she said she would expect nothing less from an Aniap. You come from a long line of representatives. Might be a path worth considering."

"Maybe, but that doesn't fix the problem with Connor," I pointed out.

"Not immediately, no, but if and when he decides he wants to explore his family's background, we can certainly make the arrangements."

Again, I looked at Connor, and I saw the answer in his eyes: *Not yet.* Not until he figured out how to protect East Branch from people like my grandfather.

"I understand," I said to Diriem. "But, uh…that's a long drive you made for a brief conversation."

He smiled. "True, because that was merely the preamble. I've come on behalf of DOI to offer you a job."

I burst into incredulous laughter. "What would you want with *me*? I'm no farseer!"

"Most of our agents aren't, and I'm absolutely serious about this," he replied. "You've got a massive talent—I spoke with Fellora ti'Mal at Laws, and she said you were a very impressive pyro for your age. Beyond that, you're smart, you're stubborn, and you care about people. Why *wouldn't* I want you on board?"

"I make bath products," I reminded him. "I don't know the first thing about intelligence agencies, magical or otherwise."

"The details can be learned—I'm looking at the raw material. And you already have an advantage we can't teach our people," he continued. "Our work regularly takes us outside the Pactlands, and you *pass* out here. Do you have any idea how difficult it can be to pull off the illusion? Just learning *one* believable accent can be nearly impossible for some, and the language potion's efficacy depends on the donor's knowledge, so good luck with expressions and other nuances. But you, now—all you have to do is open your mouth. You're *native*," he said, leaning closer to me, a new intensity in his gray eyes. "You understand this world."

"Just one corner of it."

"Jane, you've got the sort of expertise that I can't train into my agents," he insisted. "All right, perhaps you know this region well. But say you went elsewhere and made a misstep. You speak, Georgia emerges, and *there's* a plausible explanation. 'Oh, just a tourist. Nothing to see here.' But forget language for a moment: you don't fear humans."

I wasn't quite sure how to answer that. "I mean, there are some scary folks out there..."

"In general, then. You heard Gerem's speech—that sort of fearmongering is all too common, particularly among those who've never stepped outside the Pactlands. We try to minimize it with our agents, but there's always that hesitation about dealing with people who you've been taught might attack you at any moment, at the slightest hint of magic. Take Ganti," he said. "He's come out a few times, but his experience here is minimal, and he barely slept."

"He hid it well," Connor offered.

Diriem glanced at him and nodded. "Functioning on little sleep sometimes comes with the job. And you did nothing wrong," he added. "Insomnia was brought about by the combination of the task at hand and years of warnings about the horrors out here...and throw in you and Tabitha for good measure. Jane doesn't have that problem."

"There *is* the issue of my age," I reminded him.

Diriem waved that aside. "It's my damn agency, and I can hire whomever I like. We could do for you what DPP is doing for Rosie and give you remedial training while you learn the ropes. You're already so far ahead of where Rosie was when she started, but a little private tutelage in advanced techniques might serve you well."

"Brewing," I muttered.

"That, too." He paused for a drink. "Frankly, Jane, you would do well at DPP or Laws, and I realize you already know people at both agencies, but I had to take my shot. I can tell you that if you were to come aboard with us, I'd have no problem ensuring that your portal credentials remained untouched. And...perhaps you could study from home one day a week, eh?" he suggested, then looked pointedly at Connor. "Give you enough time here to make the commute worthwhile...if Annie can't shorten the trip for you."

It was a good offer, but still, I hesitated.

"You have your business here, I understand that," Diriem pressed. "Certainly admirable. But you and I both know that your true business isn't the one that pays your bills. You defend others," he said, holding my stare, "and you fight when necessary. I've seen you in action, and Ganti has given me a rather detailed account of your doings over the last few months. We could use someone like you."

"All I've done is look after Ragged Gap," I said.

"Don't sell yourself short. A suggestion: come try DOI for a year. Get that tutoring you need. If you hate agency work and want to go your own way thereafter, no hard feelings. But a year would give you a chance to see the Pactlands, meet your family, perhaps learn something about yourself...and I promise that you'd have plenty of time for the people here who matter to you."

The logical part of me shouted that *this* was what I needed, and getting my products back into the Mercantile could wait, but I looked past Diriem at Connor, silently asking for a second opinion. He rose from his chair and perched on the edge of the coffee table in front of me, then took my hands. "I've already told you I'll be waiting. I've got your back. And if this is something you want, then go show them what you're made of, Firebug."

He pulled me to my feet, and I kissed him, company be damned.

"I love you," I whispered as he held me.

"I love you, too," he replied. "Go figure this out. Ragged Gap will just have to find alternative soaps for a little while."

Laughing, I released him, then looked down at Diriem and let my arms ignite. "Here's the situation. I haven't had an actual employer in years, but I'm intrigued. You want to stick around for dinner and hash out terms?"

He sniffed the air. "Rosemary and garlic?"

"Green beans."

"Ah. And that's a good opening gambit, Jane," he said, pushing himself off the couch and grabbing his glass. "Let's see what we can do."

ACKNOWLEDGEMENTS

Once again, thank you so much for reading! If you're wondering what will become of Jane and Connor, don't worry—there's more of their story ahead in the next Pactlands series, The Lost Halls.

My sincere gratitude goes to Adam Domby, who somehow makes time to read these books and show me my mistakes. As always, I thank the Novel Chicks for their camaraderie in this weird endeavor we call writing.

And yes, here's to you, Mom and Dad.

ABOUT THE AUTHOR

When not writing fiction, Ash Fitzsimmons is an appellate attorney and an unrepentant car singer.

Find her online:
www.ashfitzsimmons.com

www.ingramcontent.com/pod-product-compliance
Lightning Source LLC
Chambersburg PA
CBHW030236200626
46816CB00002BA/392